The Lacquered Box

HELEN SHACKLADY

Published in 2003 by Onlywomen Press, Limited, London, UK.

With financial support from London Arts. **LONDON ARTS**

ISBN 0-906500-69-9

British Library Cataloguing-in-Publication Data.
A Catalogue record for this book is available from the British Library.

Typeset by Chris Fayers, Cardigan, Wales.
Printed and bound in Great Britain by Mackays of Chatham Limited.

For Lynn

1

Getting stuck up a fir tree, while trespassing in someone else's garden early on a cold November morning, had not exactly been on the list of what I most wanted to do when I came home after five weeks of touring with the band on the Continent. A mournful Friday sunrise illuminated me clutching in desperation at rough branches and trying to suppress the horrid trembling in my legs and the panic in my bowels. I was going to be scalped by this sharp twig caught in my curls, I was going to fall and break my neck, or worse still, every bone in my fingers, and I would never play the violin again. This was the most stupid thing I'd ever agreed to. I shut my eyes, as if blotting out the view of lawns and the mock-Tudor villa I was meant to be watching would miraculously transport me back to my cosy bed and my innocent dreams, and cursed the fates.

"Christ, Kate," the cause of my predicament hissed up at me from a nearby bush, "you got up there, why can't you get down?"

I opened my eyes and moaned down at her, "My hair's all tangled up."

"Well untangle it. I've got my pictures, it's time to go."

"I'll fall," I whimpered. "This is all your fault. I'm never going to do this again."

"I'm never going to ask you." The bush gave an exasperated shake, and Liz emerged, covered in leaf mould with a protective hand over her telephoto lens. For a moment, I forgot that she was my significant other, and that I loved her with every fibre of my being.

"I hate you, you cow. I'm a musician, not a paparazzi's lookout." If I got angry, maybe superhuman strength would get me down so I could deck her.

"You're a pain in the neck," she said brutally. She stiffened at the sound of a door slamming, "What's that?"

"Shit." I looked back at the house, and saw a burly figure in a tracksuit and a woolly hat standing on the front doorstep, staring at the shrubbery where we were hiding. "Looks like a bodyguard," I squeaked.

"Oh bloody hell." She put her camera down, and in a few relatively silent fluid movements was on the branch below me, her arms round my legs. "Right, I've got you. Let go and pull that crap out of your hair. Has he seen us?"

"Don't think so," I whispered, struggling to obey her, "ow, ow, ow, that's it. He's sort of making a circuit of the garden, he's at the other end of the lawn." The figure had moved out of my line of vision, and I prayed that his hat would impair his hearing.

She swore again, "Hurry up, put your foot here. . .No! Here, you bozo, not on my hand. . .come on, it would be really embarrassing to get caught."

I slid and panted in an inelegant scratchy descent, and dived after her retreating back towards the wall we'd climbed over to get in. It was within my reach, when a fast approaching whistling froze us to the spot. Liz turned to me in horror and, as one, we unfroze and ducked into a handy laurel. I covered my face with my hands as the whistler crashed into the bushes. He'd seen or heard us after all, and now we would be hauled in front of the magistrates, and be in all the local papers, as the sad, twisted no-lifes who had invaded the privacy of the world's top lesbian icon while she took a break from her punishing schedule, and tried to relax at her English friends' country home. I dared a glance at Liz, and saw her shoulders heaving and her face cracking up with laughter.

"He's having a pee," I lipread. I gave her a disbelieving shove, and clamped my hand over her nose and mouth to stifle her snorts. I should have known better than to harbour the mad illusion that she had settled down and become respectable, or to let her sweet-talk me into this ludicrous expedition.

That she had persuaded me last night, when I had only been home for a little over twenty four hours and my guard was down, was no excuse. She had come in from an honest Thursday's toil as a partner in a photography business, one thing had led to another, and we had decided to postpone the celebration dinner she had intended to cook in favour of snacking in bed.

"This is bliss," I said round a cream cracker, "what a shame you have to go to work again tomorrow." I rambled on complacently, "Still it's nice you've got Monday off and that Pat and Tom have asked us to supper tomorrow night. We can have a relaxing long weekend." The only engagement I had was moonlighting with a pub band on the Saturday night, and the invitation for Friday evening from Pat and Tom, my former landlords, was the cherry on the icing on the cake of my general satisfaction. "Have you anything special lined up at work?" I thought I would express an intelligent interest, not that I understood most of what she did nowadays on her and her partner's hi-tech equipment.

Her shoulder went ever so slightly rigid. "Er, no, not really," she mumbled. "Might have to get up a bit early tomorrow, though. Sorry."

"Why?"

"Um, no special reason." She cut up an apple rather too carefully.

"Oh God," the rest of the cracker exploded in a shower of crumbs down my front, "what's going on?"

"Nothing," she lied, and turned towards me, trying to stop the bad smile in its tracks. "Hm, that looks attractive, let me." She abandoned the apple, and lowered her head to hoover up the debris.

"Geroff," I tried to bat her away, "tell me."

She sat up again, still smirking. "Legions of women would give their eye teeth to have me do that for them," she said smugly.

"Legions of women already have," I replied, and watched her laugh immoderately. "Tell me, or I'll brush all these crumbs over to your side of the bed."

"Ok," she put her arm round me, "just don't get mad, this is nothing totally illegal."

"Oh for heaven's sake." I wished the feel of her thigh against mine didn't turn my mind into mush.

"Right, I'll give it to you straight, my little dove. Ben," that was her business partner, "is sleeping with a woman who's a housekeeper for those rich writer guys who live out on the valley road. And," she snuggled closer, "guess who's staying with them incognito for a week?"

"I can't." In spite of myself, I found I was kissing the inviting curve of her mouth.

"Kristin Dale, that's who," she announced proudly and smiled at my gawping surprise, "he told me today."

"No!" I drew back, "I don't believe it, Kristin Dale, staying here, only a few miles away, wow." Kristin Dale, the most out, most Australian, most incredibly gorgeous singer, whose picture adorned every baby dyke's bedroom wall, and whose smouldering good looks made hearts beat faster from Sydney to Sidcup.

"That's the bit you'll like." She pulled me back towards her, "This is the bit you won't approve of." She drew in a deep breath, and pushed out her next sentences in a rush to prevent me stopping her and throwing a fit, "Toni's been really good to me while you were away, and you know her birthday's coming up, and even though she's a big intellectual, she's got a massive thing about Kristin, and I thought it would be nice to get her something special, something no-one else has, so I've got this little plan to sneak out to the writers' house and see if I can take a few exclusive snaps of Kristin. Nothing distasteful," she took my silence as an encouraging sign, "according to Ben's friend, she goes out to the lawn early every morning to do her T'ai chi exercises, so I was going to nip out there tomorrow at dawn-ish, pop my camera over the wall, and there you go, she'll never know and Toni will have a unique gift. You can come if you like," she added generously, "be my lookout."

"Aaaagh!" I wrenched myself out of her arms and pounded at a pillow, "No, no, please God, let this be a bad dream. You

8

can't Liz, how can you think of doing such a thing? It's sick, it's what those scuzzy tabloid photographers do, it's. . .oh fuck." Words failed me, and I screamed again.

"So that's a yes?" Liz was unfazed, and brushed her knuckles up my spine, "Come on, sweetheart, it's not as if I'm doing this for commercial gain, it's for your friend. And anyway," her lips followed her hand, "Kristin isn't so famous because she's the most talented singer in the universe, it's because she plays the publicity game and lives off the media. It's not as if I'm going to photograph her with a lover like this. . ."

Not for the first time, my ethics and common sense were no match for the lust her charms provoked, and that was how I had landed up crouching in the greenery in a hideously compromising position.

"Right," I told myself under the leaves, "this has to stop. You're never going to give in to her again. You're going to go to assertiveness classes and stand up for yourself. If she won't change, you must."

Above the glum rustling of evergreen foliage and bare winter branches, I heard a sigh, a zip being pulled up, heavy footsteps receding and resumed jaunty whistling. When we were sure the coast was clear, and my feet were quite numb, we crept out of our bush and scuttled along the wall to the unmended gap by which we had made our illicit entrance. As soon as I hit the roadside verge, I ran like the clappers, pursued by Liz's wheezing eruptions, to the lay-by where we had left the car.

"Give me the keys." I spoke through clenched teeth and slowed to a jogging pace once she'd drawn level, "You're not fit to drive."

She wiped her eyes and fished in her jacket pocket, "Ok, don't get your knickers in a twist, Speedy. Whoops, we've got company."

The transit van certainly hadn't been tucked in the far end of the lay-by when we'd parked earlier. We both stopped running and began walking. After all, it would be obvious to even the most casual glance that with Liz's camera and my layers of clothing, not to mention the lumps of garden plastered over us, we weren't out for an early morning training session. I'll just pretend, I thought, that I fancied a stroll, and affected not to notice the man in overalls who appeared from around the back of the van and made his way to the driver's door. His business must have been as dubious as ours, however, because he took one look at us, snatched the door open, leapt into his seat and drove off, nearly as fast as I had been running. A quick click of the camera from Liz, and everyone could have been saved a lot of bother, but at the time, I instantly forgot him in the relief of slumping into the car and rolling a cigarette.

"Well, that went pretty smoothly," Liz remarked, putting her camera tenderly on the back seat, "this'll please Toni no end."

The awful thing was that she was right. Toni may have been a respected senior lecturer at the university, but I had come to realise that she possessed an irreverent, adolescent streak, which would respond with unalloyed delight if Liz's pictures of the surprisingly small woman posing on the lawn ever came out. I'd been too nervous stuck up my tree to fully appreciate the glory that was Kristin Dale in the flesh.

"You should have told me you weren't keen on heights," she continued kindly, "I would have found a better place for you to keep watch."

I kept my tone conversationally even, "One of these days you'll go too far. I'll snap, and you'll be nothing more than a troublesome memory in the minds of those whose lives you've blighted."

"That's why I'm so good for you, sweetie, I stimulate you out of bed as well."

There was no possible answer. I drove grimly on until the giggles hit me a few streets from home, and I had to pull in and shake against the steering wheel.

I got us back to the house in time for Liz to jump into the shower and then bounce off, still chortling, to work. I returned to bed, in the hope that sleep would erase the guilt which my fit of giggles hadn't entirely dispelled. When I woke up after midday, I suffered a brief disorientating flash, and thought that I was back in Germany with the band. Looking desperately at the clock, I flung myself upright, convinced that I had overslept, and that Fred, Jo, Bill and Dave had driven off to the next staid town without me. The terror of abandonment hammered at my chest before the sight of our unmatching furniture impinged on my senses, and I flopped back on to the pillows, putting an arm over to the empty space where Liz should have been. She never laughed at these moments of not knowing where I was after we'd been touring. Damn, why did she still want to pull stunts like our dawn raid on Kristin Dale, when so many other things seemed to have changed? I gnawed at the problem of how to reconcile my uneasy conscience with my unwillingness to fight with her. Over the summer, I had lost the frantic insecurity of our first months together, when the glorious sensations of being in love had invariably been accompanied by terrible rows and my belief that Liz would soon get bored. Nowadays, most of our arguments, lacking their former venom, were indulged in largely for form's sake. While my desire for her was undimmed, I no longer grasped at every moment with her as if it could be the last time, and a growing confidence in her fidelity had made the past three months of touring in Britain and then abroad, with only a week off in between, less of an endurance test than I had feared. The days when she had managed to join us for weekends in August and early September, or when I had contrived to slip home for a night in passing, almost made up for that dreary stretch of abstinence. I tucked the quilt under my chin, and tried to work out where gross intrusion on a celebrity fitted in on mine and Liz's undeniably separate moral scales. High on mine, I concluded, and not as high on Liz's personal measure as pleasing a friend and gaining an adrenalin rush from some gratuitous risk-taking. This didn't mean that she was an awful person, or that we had to fall out seriously, it just meant that I wouldn't go along with her next time she proposed anything so blatantly immoral, and maybe if I put my foot down, she would see the error of her ways. . . Soothed by my deliberations, I decided to get up and sort out some more washing from my half unpacked bags.

The delights of being a laundry maid palled after a couple of hours, and I was rescued by a timely tap on the window. I looked up from arranging damp clothes artistically on the radiators to see our next door neighbour, Mrs T., performing her tea-drinking, cake-eating mime and pointing to her house. I ran for the door. We had become better acquainted with Mrs Tweddle when, in a fit of altruism, Liz had offered to fix the overflow from her cistern, which was dripping annoyingly into her back yard. We had quickly discovered that someone whom we had dismissed as a fortunately hard of hearing old lady was a mine of scandalous anecdote and unlikely experience. Under her tight blue granny perm was a shrewd and broad mind, and when she turned on her hearing aid and got into the groove, she entertained us for hours with not only her colourful life story, but also all the gossip from the street. I sometimes had the feeling that she and her best friend, Edna Braithwaite from two streets away, inhabited an older city, which lay beneath the superficial seam of bars, shops and social gatherings where Liz and I moved. The two of them were a repository of encyclopedic information on the, to me, anonymous faces in bus queues, cafes and offices that I encountered on my everyday rounds. The casual mention of a neighbour or of the closure of yet another family-run business would unleash a torrent of detail explaining the marriages, births, affairs and divorces which seemingly bound in a seamless web anyone you could meet. I had believed that Liz and I would have no place in their mental map of the world, but as soon as they had found out that we were friendly with Tom, the son of "that old dog Alf Pearce, who chased after women half his age the minute his wife was in the ground", they had a fix on us, and were happy. I had the added advantage, with Mrs T., of being in a band.

"I like hearing you play your violin," she had announced, the first time she had asked me in for a spot of elevenses while Liz was at work. "My father was a violinist with the City Orchestra. That's how he met my mother, of course, visiting Russia before the Great War." Then she was off, rendering me entranced with her tale of how the young musician had

12

met a beautiful furred dancer from a lost world of candlelit palaces, frozen rivers and jingling sleigh rides, and had whisked her away to the stuffiness of England before the fragile edifice had tumbled.

"Frank and I always planned to go there," she had concluded, "I wanted to trace my mother's relatives who survived the siege of Leningrad, but there, I lost him just when it became easier to go. Have some more gingerbread." She went on to describe how she had accompanied her husband, Frank, who had been in the Merchant Navy, to Bombay, and how they had mistaken a notorious house of ill-repute for a suitable hotel, and I had never asked her about her mother's family again.

On this dank November afternoon, with the sky turned dull above the grey terraces, Mrs T.'s sitting room was a twinkling haven. Her house had the same lay-out as ours, the front door opening off the pavement into a hall with the stairs rising from it, and a door on the right leading to the sitting room, through which you passed to the dining room and kitchen at the back. There the resemblance ended. Our rented home was furnished with an eclectic mix of what the owners had left and my well-worn bits and pieces, and we'd never quite got around to changing the uniform magnolia of its walls. Mrs T.'s front room was a riot of richly coloured wallpaper and heavy velvet curtains, and was stuffed with a magpie hoard of inherited and collected treasures. A dark dresser showed off random china plates, a silvery samovar glowed on a mahogany side table, the polished tea tray and tiered cake stand balanced on an equally gleaming Indian brass affair, and a grandfather clock with a stationary pendulum stood silent in a corner. I let Mrs T. ply me with cake, and tried to smother the uncomfortable pang when I noticed that her movements were laboured and that a tiny trembling ran through her hands moving to lift the teapot.

"Here, let me, shall I do that?" I bent forward and hoped she wasn't insulted.

"Thanks, dear." She leant back in her chair, "Winter, it's a bugger for my rheumatics. And don't look at me like I'm a dying duck," she added caustically, "I've enough with my daughter on the phone, mithering over whether I'm coping. I'll let you all know when I'm ready for the H.O.M.E."

"All right," I said peaceably, "we'll come and visit you on Sunday afternoons. Take you for a spin in the car."

"I'm not going in that death trap again. Your friend Liz took me and Edna to the Day Centre in it last week. I thought my end had come, I was that shook up, I lost a fortune at cards." Mrs T. always asserted that she only went to the Old Folks' Club at the Day Centre to gamble with her cronies.

"Yeah," I grinned at the picture of Liz subjecting a pair of harmless elderly citizens to her city driving, "she does drive a bit fast at times."

"She's a maniac. She said she wanted to give us a bit of excitement. I said, young lady, if I want excitement, I'll find a man, not a car crash. Are you going to be locking her out again, now you're home?"

I laughed. This episode had tickled Mrs T. pink and, I suspected, had been relayed with embellishments to all her friends. I'd only locked Liz out one night in a summer rain shower to pay her back for carrying out her threat to throw out all the clothes I'd left strewn on chairs. She'd popped round and borrowed Mrs T.'s ladder, climbed quietly in through the bathroom window, sneaked down the stairs and pounced on me while I was scratching my head, giving me such a shock that I never did it again.

"Maybe," I said, "only this time, don't lend her your ladder. Let her suffer."

"She's a card. Kate, I've decided something." At the change in her voice, I glanced up from dabbing up the crumbs on my plate, and saw the odd mixture of embarrassment and determination in her face. "That box on the mantelpiece she likes so much, I want her to have it when I'm gone. I've told my daughter and she said she'd hand it over, but I want to tell you as well to make sure. Don't forget, will you?"

I swallowed quickly, "But. . ." There was nothing morbid in her tone, only a matter of fact insistence.

"No buts. It's settled." She crossed her ankles, "Now, tell me all about your tour. Did you go to Hamburg? Is it still such a naughty place?"

I gave her the highlights of our visit to Germany, my mind distracted by her extraordinary announcement. I knew the box, she kept photographs of her parents in it, and I had seen Liz holding it one day with the care she usually reserved for her cameras, while we were admiring the faded pictures of a serious man in a stiff collar and a high cheekboned woman with enormous eyes. The box, lacquered midnight black, and patterned with swirly figures in gold, silver, scarlet, emerald and blue, always made me think of enchanted forests, magical animals and tales of princes and princesses in disguise. I had assumed it had come from Russia with Mrs T.'s mother. I was still wondering why she wanted Liz in particular to have it, when it was time to leave and attend to my next load of washing.

"Are you still brooding about this morning?" Liz had come back from work, and was searching my face, her hands light on my waist.

"We-ell." I gazed into the limpid solemnity of her dark eyes, and my insides contracted irresistably, "It wasn't right, really, was it." Was this a further stage in her transformation into a law-abiding businesswoman?

"No darling." She drew me close, and I began to sink into her tall frame, "It was all wrong." Her arms tightened, her lips reached my earlobe, and her voice was sweet as molasses, "The light was awful. Let's go out there again tomorrow, and give it another go."

The trouble was, she was stronger than me, and easily escaped my clutches to run upstairs to the bathroom and lock the door.

"I'm going to have a bath before we go to Pat and Tom's" she shouted out through her guffaws, "and I'm not letting you in unless you promise not to be violent."

I rattled the handle, put on my folk singer's nasal whine, and started working through a dreary song with a hundred and fourteen verses until she relented.

2

"You should have let me cut your hair before you went up that tree," Liz said later on as we prepared to go to Pat and Tom's. She finished combing my hair and ran her fingers through her handiwork, fluffing up my damp locks, "It wouldn't have been so much of a hazard then."

I grinned at her eyes narrowed in concentration on my coiffure, "I'm not letting you near me with the scissors again. I don't want to have to wear a hat for the next fortnight. And no plaits this time." I'd seen the wicked urge flicker behind her hairdresser expression.

"But you suit them." She started separating out strands of hair.

"Ha ha." I stopped her hands, "Come on, we'll be late. I don't want to miss any food." She'd given me a couple of plaits once in an idle moment when she'd joined us on tour, and, having forgotten all about them, I'd nearly walked on stage with two monstrosities bobbing out from my head like a pair of droopy horns. Only a chance glimpse of my reflection in a glass door had saved me. I still liked her unknotting my hair, though, something I'd first let her do in the early hours of the morning after a gig, finding in this casual domestic intimacy a closeness which had eluded me with anyone else.

"Ok," she said, and stood up surveying me, "you look good."

She meant it, and my heart did a cartwheel. I touched her hand, "Oh Liz, I. . ." The sharp ring of the phone downstairs halted my attempt at a poetic declaration.

"I'll get it," I said, "if you sort out some of that wine I brought back, and some nibbly things to take." I took the stairs two at a time, ending with a gazelle-like leap, and picked up the phone with a cheery greeting.

"That Kate?" It was Mac from the pub band, and he sounded dreadful.

"Yes, how's things? Are we on for tomorrow?" I'd let him and his band down once when Liz and I were having a crisis, and I wanted to demonstrate my keenness and reliability.

"No." There was a despairing silence, and then a choking noise, "Suzie's left. She's left me and the band, and I can't face doing tomorrow night. We've cancelled."

"Oh God, I'm sorry." I was, too. I didn't know Mac and Suzie that well, but they'd always struck me as a stable couple who, like Fred and Jo, the mainstay of our band, had a musical compatability worth hanging on to. With a guitarist, Spiff, they formed the core of a loose group which I'd found easy to fit in to when I had nothing on with the band. "I'm sorry," I said again, "can I do anything?" It was only one of those things you say, without expecting to be taken up on your rhetorical offer.

"Yeah," he gave a bark of sarky laughter, "find us a singer. We're going to carry on, we just need a few days to get our heads round this."

Something in his unhappiness moved me, "All right, I'll ask around. Fred and Jo might know someone, can I tell them?"

"Yeah, yeah, the more people who know I got dumped, the merrier. I'll be in touch, see you." The phone went dead.

"That was Mac," I said, watching Liz shove bottles and packets into a carrier bag.

"And?" She picked up her jacket and shrugged herself into it, "All set for tomorrow then? D'you want me to round up the girls, get you an appreciative audience?"

I found my coat on the floor, "Well, actually it's cancelled. Suzie, you know, the singer, she's walked out on Mac. He sounds quite cut up." I had a minor brainwave. "Would you like to go out somewhere? I could get an advance off Fred on the money I'm owed from the tour, and treat you to a romantic dinner. We could go to that poncy hotel with the leisure centre, and have a swim and a sauna first." I would lie in the jacuzzi and enjoy the sight of Liz swimming efficient lengths.

"Oh." She paused by the door, and suddenly I could sense a debate going on under her impassive features. She disguised it by tutting at the lock on the front door, which had developed a tendency to stick, and I waited until we were both outside, and she had slipped her arm through mine. She breathed out. "Um," she began hesitantly.

"Yes?" I asked in a bland, non-pushy way. It was like playing with a fish, sometimes, to get her to talk.

She started to laugh. "All right, I did get another invite for tomorrow night, but I wasn't going to go, with you just being back. I wanted to stay in town with you."

"What was it?" I took her hand and put it in my pocket, "Stalking another celebrity?"

Her fingers curled round mine, "No, it was a party."

I tightened my grip, "Really? Whose? Where?" Wasn't I invited? Had she developed a whole new social circle which she hadn't got around to telling me about?

She laughed some more, "No need to get jealous. It's an old friend from college in London. Brigitte. She's straight. It turns out she's been living somewhere outside Carlisle for ages, she found out I'd moved up here, and gave me a ring. She sounded like she really wanted me to come, and said that there was loads of room to stay over, but I explained to her about my life partner, and how I wanted to devote the weekend to her. Now you're free, though. . ." The calm pressure of her fingers made me sure she was telling the truth. I wouldn't ask how Brigitte had found our phone number, the less I knew about Liz's old network of disreputable friends and ex-lovers the better. I liked the life partner touch as well.

"Would you like to go?" I asked. Our matching footsteps were firm on the quiet pavement, and our breath formed two equal plumes in the patchy city night.

"I'm not that bothered. Yeah, it would be interesting to see her again and catch up. You've been travelling all over, though. I thought you'd rather stay at home, have a rest, get up to date on the gossip, mess up the house I kept so tidy while you were away, that sort of thing. I mean," she smiled winningly at me, "if it was a normal weekend, and you were playing out of town and not coming back, I'd probably go out of curiosity, but since you're going to be here, I'd prefer to have some more quality time with you and your luscious bod."

"You silver-tongued charmer. I don't mind going. I like parties, it might be a laugh. We can have quality time while drinking someone else's booze." Surely I must be secure enough by now to face someone from Liz's past.

"Sure?" She stopped under a streetlamp so she could see me properly.

"Sure."

"Ok, I'll phone her tomorrow, check that we can still stay. By the way, honey bun," she started striding on again, "don't ask Tom about his business unless he mentions it. He's having some kind of problem, and he's a bit down in the dumps. He's taken to muttering and glooming in the shadows. Pat's fed up with it."

"Aw no, what sort of problem?" I was immediately worried, and forgot to start regretting my decision to go to the party. I'd always thought that Tom's overcrowded not quite antique shop did well, and hated the idea that he and Pat weren't blissfully happy together. Even though I'd moved out of the flat at the top of their house, and no longer depended upon them for scrounged meals and undemanding company, I counted on them being a constant presence in my life.

"Who knows?" Liz squeezed my hand, "I dare say we'll find out. Let's walk a bit faster, I'm getting peckish."

Sitting at the big table in Pat's warm and familiar kitchen, I experienced a surge of gratitude for its unchanging welcome. This was where I'd spent hours pouring my heart out to Pat, weeping over my ex, Chloe, crying over Liz, and drinking cup after cup of tea from her old brown teapot with the misshaped cosy Ag had knitted in primary school. The surfaces were piled with the same clutter of papers, books and balls of wool, the same rag rug tripped me up as I made for a drawer to find a corkscrew and my hands went automatically to the right cupboards to pick out glasses and dishes for our contribution. Pat had met us with an apronned hug and her swift, silent, gimlet-eyed appraisal of the state of our relationship, then introduced us to the fair-haired woman nursing a chunky baby on my favourite crisis chair in the corner.

"I don't think you've ever met Pru, have you? She has the misfortune to be married to Dodgy. He and Tom are finishing off unloading some rubbish at the shop. And that lovely little bundle is Milly."

The lovely little bundle had fixed us with a beady glare, and gone back to her determined sucking.

Now I smiled across at Pru, "She's going for it." The baby hadn't paused for breath since we arrived, not even when Pat and Liz started clattering pans and crashing trays in and out of the oven.

Pru's mouth quivered with tenderness "If I fill her up now, she might possibly nod off while we're eating. She takes after Dodgy. In fact, I don't think she's a baby at all. She's an alien, sent to sample everything on earth with her highly developed tastebuds and report back to the mothership. She ate the phone bill yesterday."

"That's useful. Bring her round to our place, and I'll give her ours. Do you call him Dodgy as well? I thought it was just us."

Her laughter broke through the maternal fatigue smudged on her face, "It's stuck. It suits him down to the ground."

I hadn't known that Dodgy, the weather-beaten oddjob man who appeared to have some vague and semi-mysterious connection with Tom, had a young family. I'd seen him several times at the shop, engaging Tom in cryptic conversation or stuffing banknotes into his overalls before melting out into the street. I'd assumed that, along with some of Tom's other contacts, he inhabited that flexible margin between the stuffily employed and the downright villainous, unencumbered by ties.

The baby heaved a replete sigh, and I'm sure I heard a definite popping as she released her mother.

"Good Lord, Milly, are you sure you've had enough?" Pru

propped the solid body on her shoulder, where it preceded to give vent to some disproportionally loud belches before wriggling around in excitement at this social gathering.

"If you could hold her for a few minutes, I'll go to the loo. Do you mind?" Pru's request was tentative.

I held out my arms, "Of course not. How old is she?"

"About eight months. She might do her hurling herself backwards off your lap trick, so be warned. She likes to catch her victims unawares."

Podgy hands clutched at my hair, sturdy legs at the dawn of coordination bounced on my lap and I gazed into the impossibly blue eyes. "Hello, Milly," I said. "What kind of day have you had?"

Pru had come back and was sipping a glass of wine, and I was still admiring Milly's miniature teeth, keeping her from the olives and reassuring her that she too could have hair like mine one day, when a clumping and banging preceded Tom and Dodgy's arrival. Milly squawked, her eyes went even more saucer-like at the sight of her father, and I caught her before she could launch herself off my knees into space.

"That's what I like to see, women in their proper place, cooking and minding the baby." Tom's geniality was patently forced, and Pat squinted at him and gave a cluck,

"Just what is the matter Tom Pearce? Here's Kate safely back, Liz and me cooking away at a delicious supper, and you're still in a snit. Tell me," she waved a wooden spoon at him, "or it's bread and water and the spare room for you."

I wished I had the culinary skills and will power to use this technique with Liz.

"Keep your hair on, Mrs P.," Dodgy gave me a sweet grin and lifted Milly easily from my arms, "We're having a spot of bother with stuff disappearing when it shouldn't, and that, oh apple of my eye, makes us really pissed off." He hoisted a giggling Milly above his head, "That's right, have a good dribble on your ancient dad. Of course, we didn't want to worry the little women, did we, Milly old girl, but if they insist. . ."

We extracted the story from them while we tucked into the best lasagne I'd had for ages, and passed an obstinately awake Milly between us like a hyperactive parcel.

"In my line of work," Dodgy said, beating me to the biggest baked potato, "I come across more than one chronologically challenged person who needs an honest tradesman to do those little tasks which keep their homes in the manner to which they're accustomed."

"He means rich old ladies who pay him a fortune to mend their toasters," Pru translated.

"We live in a sad society," he murmured, "old folks living on their own, neglected by their relatives who only turn up when the will's being read. You won't be like that, will you Mil?"

"Don't give her garlic bread," Pru scolded, "you know the effect it has on her. I'll tell you what he and Tom do, otherwise we'll be here all night. They're ambulance-chasing ghouls. Dodgy cases all these old biddies' houses for valuables, and as soon as one of them pops her clogs and the relatives appear, he's in there with Tom's card, recommending him as the man they need to take all those old-fashioned possessions they've inherited off their hands."

I saw a new respect on Liz's face, "Oh Tom, I never realised what a ruthless operator you were."

Tom looked more cheerful, "It's business, isn't it? Dodgy's got a good eye for the kind of stuff I can shift. I mean, I do recommend that the really valuable items go to auction but you know," he refilled his wine glass, "your granny dies, there's a houseful of junk to dispose of, you've got busy lives and all your own furniture, it's far easier to take a few mementos and get a fair price for the rest, than have the hassle of moving it and sorting it and fighting over it with your siblings. It's a service, when you come to think of it."

Both Pat and Pru gave roars of derisive laughter, and Milly joined in, letting the bread she'd been gumming trickle down her chin. I decided that since I'd staved off the first major pangs of greed, it was probably my turn again, and scooped her away from Dodgy, dabbing at her face with my tissue. "Don't worry," I said as she became aware that she had lost her mouthful, "I'll get you another piece."

Pru watched me, then relaxed, "That's how I met Dodgy. I'm a nurse, and I was in charge of one of the geriatric wards.

I started recognising this voice ringing up regularly, asking how his aunty was doing, and I rumbled him. No-one could have so many aging relatives."

Dodgy reached over and patted her hand, "I got her on my side. It was a master stroke. Inside information on who'd been rushed in and how long they'd probably got. We were a team, and now she's temporarily out of action, we've trained some of the other nurses. A deathbed scene, a phone call, and we know to get moving. It gives Tom a competitive edge over his rivals."

I stroked the spun silk of Milly's hair, "That's the most callous thing I've ever heard. So what's the problem? Have you been banned from hanging around in the hospital car park waiting to ambush the grief-stricken in their hour of loss?"

"We're being gazumped." Tom was doleful again, "It happened twice last month, and again today."

"Mrs Cardew out on the valley road." Dodgy took up the tale, "Nice old lady, son lives away, always asks me in for a cup of tea when I've cleared her gutters or fixed her gate."

"Nice Clarice Cliff tea service, nice Lloyd Loom chairs," Tom moaned.

"Yeah, well, she passed on, God bless her, two days ago. I popped by today, 'cause I heard her son was stopping in the house until the funeral, and what did I find?" Dodgy stuck the last piece of garlic bread in his mouth and appeared to swallow it without chewing, "It had been cherry-picked. No Clarice Cliff, no Lloyd Loom, no Moorcroft. We got the rest, the son didn't seem bothered and we didn't like to bring it up. He'll probably only realise there were things missing when he comes out of his shock." He stopped, and I saw that he was neither unfeeling nor dim, "It is a shock, even for a grown man who hasn't seen his ma in months. We don't try to trade on it too much, just lighten the burden," he added piously.

"So, are you saying someone's been in there and nicked the best bits? And it's happened before?" Liz's nose twitched at the scent of trouble.

Tom cleared his throat, "The first times we thought we might have made a mistake, but today's confirmed it. There's a definite pattern. The house isn't cleared out, which would bring in the law, things just go missing. If relatives notice they've gone, they might assume they've been sold, or pawned, or given secretly to someone else to spite them. Since inheritances always cause bad feeling."

"Have you been to the police? Who wants seconds?" I'd been hoping Pat would offer.

Tom had the grace to look shame-faced, "No. I suppose we didn't want to let on we knew what was in these houses."

I took my fork from Milly's hand before she could poke her eye out with it, and replaced it with a breadstick. A memory from the morning pinged in my frontal lobes. "Hey Liz," I said in unthinking excitement, "that transit van. It was in the layby on the valley road at the crack of dawn when we were. . ." I stopped and Liz kicked me under the table.

Pat put the lasagne dish back on the table, and gave us another pointed look, "Oh yes? And what were you two up to there?"

"Um, business," Liz said unconvincingly, "Kate was. . . giving me a hand. Here," she tried to create a diversion, "give Milly to me. I've had enough, and I know you want seconds." I settled the unprotesting infant in the crook of Liz's arm.

I attempted to make amends, "What we were doing isn't important. But we did see a van. Oo-er," I spooned out a generous second helping, "that could have been the thief. The man who was driving."

"What did he look like?"

"Did you get the numberplate?"

Tom and Dodgy's questions collided.

"Duh." Liz moved the breadstick away from her right nostril, "Oh yeah, I've got a photograph of him and the van clear as daylight. Of course I didn't get the numberplate, you grave robbers, we didn't take any notice of him. Try that one more time, Milly, and you're in deep trouble."

Pat laid down the law, "If it happens again, you must go to the police. It's not fair on the relatives if they're being ripped off."

Tom smiled at her as if they'd just met, "What happened

to your socialist ideals and your objections to inherited wealth?"

"Destroyed by living with you for too long. Right, girls," I was fifteen again, and being interrogated by my mother, "what business took you out to the valley road this morning?"

Liz's lower lip stuck out, "Pa-at, it was boring. . .oh Milly," her expression lifted, "whatever's happening?"

We were saved. A puce wave suffused Milly's entire head, and her unformed features contracted into a startled scowl. There was a wind-driven rumbling, a surprised mew, and then the wave receded, leaving her face bathed in rapt satisfaction, and the rest of us holding our noses.

"I told you she wasn't up to five pints of lager and a vindaloo yet, Dodge. You have to wait until they can walk." Tom flapped his hand in front of his face.

"Your turn," Pru and Dodgy said simultaneously, and stared at each other to see who would crack first.

"God, I can change a nappy. I think I've got seepage on me anyway. Got a changing bag then?" Liz scraped her chair back and stood up, holding the baby at arm's length. I tried to conceal my shock.

Pat jumped up as well, "I'll help. I like to keep in practice just in case Ag lands us with an unplanned surprise."

They bustled out like a couple of nannies, and Tom pushed a bottle in my direction, "Good tour, Kate? Heard you fell off the stage in Cologne." Fred in the band was Tom's brother, and I knew I couldn't keep much under wraps.

"It was Dave's fault. He got over-excited, and snared me with his guitar lead. . ." We gossipped about the tour, and I retired into the front room for a cigarette, so as not to contaminate any air which might be sucked into Milly's delicate lungs. Faint giggles and exclamations wafted down from the bathroom, and I was stubbing out my smoke when I caught the tail-end of Liz and Pat's conversation.

"Ask her," Pat was saying, "you don't want it between you."

Liz sounded mulish again, "Oh Pat, it's a can of worms. If she doesn't bring it up, why should I? We're happy like this. . ."

Pat snorted, and I waited a while before following them into the kitchen for pudding.

"I am sorry about this morning," Liz said that night.

"Are you really?" Floating in heavenly suspension between love and sleep, I wasn't too concerned any more.

"Hm," her hand meandered to the back of my knee, "it was almost worth anything to see your little legs move so fast. Milly's cute, isn't she?"

"They all are at that age. I bet you a tenner that Pat finds out what we were doing this morning."

"I'm not taking you up on it. She will."

"I'll never live it down. She definitely won't approve this time. She'll tell us off something rotten. Do you think that man in the van was Tom and Dodgy's thief?"

"Could be. Still, it's not our problem." She yawned and gave me a last kiss, "I'm glad you're back. Thank God we can have a lie-in tomorrow."

I tried to stay awake, so I could hold the even rise and fall of her breath for longer, but sleep hit me like a sledgehammer.

3

We arrived at the party the next night far later than we had intended. Liz had phoned Brigitte, scrawled directions which bore very little resemblance to what was in the road atlas, and told me that the house would be easy to find. The problem with navigating for her driving was that she wouldn't pause to look at a map, preferring instead to press on and to shout at me when we got lost. I pointed this out to her while we were trawling the black country lanes somewhere to the north of Carlisle, and was very nearly dropped off at the mainline station to make my own way home.

"You're such a crosspatch sometimes," I observed when diplomacy had prevailed.

"I know. It's because I'm nervous, ok?" She gave me her sideways smile.

I hit my head with the tattered atlas, "Well why didn't you say, for God's sake? I might not have nagged you so much. Oh dear," an unwelcome thought struck me, "are you afraid I'm going to disgrace you? I won't get very drunk, I promise."

"You nit. Unless Brigitte's changed drastically, you're a novice at drinking compared with her. No, I suppose it's just that thing of meeting up with someone you used to know really well, and wondering if you'll still get on."

I surveyed her determined profile, "You did say she was straight?" I ventured.

"Yeah." Then I saw her white teeth again, "Don't worry. One woman's more than I can handle nowadays. I've slowed down dreadfully. I'll be darned," she peered out through the windscreen, "I think I've found the right turning."

We parked at the end of a line of cars on a verge, and walked up to what looked like a converted barn, streaming with light and vibrating with noise.

"This must be it," Liz said brightly, letting our overnight bag drop from her shoulder, "unless up here is the place to be on a Saturday night."

Through large windows we could see a heave of bodies gesticulating in a cloud of smoke, and I could already smell the alcohol. Deciding that knocking on the open door of a porch at the front of the house would be superfluous, we pushed our way into the melee past a bulge of coats on hooks, and stood for a moment, dazed by the heat and press of people after the private dark of the car.

"Omigawd Liz," a screech rose above the hubbub, and a woman peeled herself away from a cackling group to teeter towards us, "Liz, you made it. Jesus, girl, I don't believe it."

I felt the startled jolt run through Liz's body, before she was enveloped in a tipsy embrace.

"Brigitte," the lazy calm in her voice didn't fool me, "how nice to see you."

After hanging around her neck for longer than was politely necessary, the woman let Liz go, and made as if to give me the same treatment. "And this must be. . .Cath?"

"Kate," I said snottily, and in a pre-emptive strike stuck my hand out to shake hers. She took it, and gave it an exaggerated squeeze.

"My, someone with manners. Not your usual style at all, darling."

Her glancing comment and the look she gave Liz excluded me, and we inspected each other with the fixed smiles that conceal instant unreasonable hostility. She was not at all as I had expected. Her short blonde hair was expensively cut and highlighted, her strapless little black number showed off a distinctly unseasonal tan, and I made a bet with myself that the sheer flawless nylons on her seemingly cellulite-free legs were stockings not chain-store tights. The discreet make-up on her fine-boned face couldn't quite hide the dissolute lines round her mouth, or completely mask the impression it gave of having lived fully and probably corruptly. The gentle pressure of Liz's hand on my back made us a couple again.

"Ah well, I've developed good taste at last. Sorry we're a bit late, I got us lost. You're ageing well, must be all the chemicals." Liz may as well have said the subtext out loud. You can say what you want about me, just leave Kate out of it, and I glowed with a wild satisfaction.

"And you don't look a day older either. Must be your energetic love life."

Liz laughed, "It is," and Brigitte joined in, cracking the odd little tension between the three of us.

"Come on then," Brigitte's smile fell into something more natural, "I'll show you where you're sleeping, then you can get tanked up like the rest of us."

Ignoring shouts and outstretched hands from knots of her guests, she led us across the wide room to a broad open staircase. The carpet was springy beneath my feet, and Brigitte seemed blithely oblivious to the spills and crushed peanuts it was collecting.

"Help," she nearly tripped on one of the polished treads, and grabbed the smooth bannister, "those cocktails were seriously good."

We followed her skin-tight rear to the end of a pale passage, where she flung open a door whose immaculate paintwork was marred only by a sellotaped notice, "This room is taken. Keep Out!"

"The guest suite," she tittered, "or one of them." She snapped on a light switch to reveal an expanse of pricey carpet, a double bed with an ironed cream cover, and a few unobtrusive cupboard doors. She pointed at one of them, "Shower and loo's in there. I told the woman who does to stick some soap and stuff in. Look ok for you?"

We were impressed. I had half-expected to doss down on a mattress under a heap of abandoned coats.

"Fucking hell, Brigitte," Liz gave up trying to be cool, "the dole didn't pay for this lot."

I could tell Brigitte was gratified. "Hardly. We all move on. Rare books and such-like, darling, flog them on the internet to rich people all over the world."

"But you don't know anything about rare books." Liz was nearly being rude.

She smiled foxily, "Ah, but Harry does. And it's not hard to pick up a smattering."

"Who's Harry?" Liz sounded resigned.

She tittered again, "Business partner. He's around. My alcohol level is dropping. Hurry up, I'll show you where the booze is."

Obediently we left our bag, and trotted behind her back down the stairs and into the kitchen. Even groaning under bottles and crates as they were, I could tell the panelled units were top of the range, and so was the massive table, covered to my delight with a wide assortment of extremely edible looking food. Brigitte saw my eyes pop, and Liz put her arm around me,

"Kate's idea of heaven," she explained, "food, drink, and a double bed."

"Can we move in?" I asked with genuine warmth.

This time the smile reached her eyes, "Sure thing. Help yourselves, and I'll introduce you to some of these gate-crashers."

I didn't find it hard to enjoy myself. Through being in the band, I was used to socialising with people I didn't know, and sorting out the crowd into those to whom I knew I could natter merrily away, and those who would be hard work. Anyway, it was fun to notice who was flirting with who, whose partners were getting annoyed, and who was trying to escape from a bore to a better prospect. A bunch of women homed in on us, and after a while I left them so I could circulate, and make repeat journeys to the food or to pick up another bottle of beer. I felt no urge to drink more than enough to oil the wheels of my social chit chat, and I assumed that Liz was being moderate as well, so I was somewhat taken aback when she reappeared at my elbow, swigging from a bottle of ouzo.

"Excuse me," she butted into the discussion I was having with a jolly couple about their organic smallholding, "I hope you don't think I'm being too forward, but I wondered if I could ask you to dance?"

I rolled my eyes. I'd heard the music starting up, and now she was playing her favourite party game of pretending we were strangers.

"Please?" She gave me a doggy look.

"Um, I'm not sure, my husband. . ." The couple looked confused.

"Sod him." She pulled me through to the gyrating pairs at the far end of the main room, and we smooched discreetly. She wasn't so far gone yet that her hips were less slinky, or her hands less sure, and after a couple of tracks, the thought of us sidling across to the staircase and up it together crossed my mind.

"Kate, you must meet Chris." I cursed at Brigitte's imperious tone, and her finger poking my shoulder, "He's a musician too. As for you, Busy Lizzie, I want a proper girls' talk with you." She practically pushed Liz into the space under the staircase, and left me, stupid with thwarted lust, to make stilted conversation with a chap who was into ambient music created by electronic equipment.

By the time I was reunited with Liz, she was well past her sell-by date. A weird wariness flickered behind her eyes, then she flung herself over me, nearly knocking me out with her bottle.

"Let's dance some more," she burbled, "we don't do this often enough."

Our bizarre display culminated in an unwise stab at an athletic tango. I picked Liz up from the floor, herded her into the kitchen and poured her on to a chair at the table, making sure that the bottle was nowhere where her revolving gaze could catch sight of it. The party had reached that thinning out stage, where responsible citizens had already left, rumpled couples who had slipped off to quiet corners were beginning to emerge, and sensible souls like me were thinking of a nice cup of tea. Guided by unerring instinct, I sniffed out the teabags, and was wrapping Liz's hand round a mug when Brigitte staggered in with a man in tow.

"Aaah, the lovebirds, how sweet." She kicked off her shoes and sat down. "I think that went all right. You haven't met Harry yet, have you Kate? Harry, this is Kate." Each time, she gave my name a pointed emphasis. I didn't think she was after Liz's delightful body, yet she clearly didn't like me, and I wondered if it was only alcohol making her so spiky. Harry gave me a distracted hello, and carried on with the argument they'd been having.

"I can ring for a taxi, if you won't let me drive," he said mutinously. Brigitte was dangling a set of car keys from her little finger.

"Don't be ridiculous," she snapped, "no-one will come out here at this hour. See if there's some brandy left in this tip."

I studied him as he clanked among the bottles. He was one of those typically English men who seem handsome at first sight, but a closer look revealed that his greying straight brown hair was just a bit too thin, his blue eyes a little too pale and close together, and his head slightly too small for his body. I couldn't fail to notice the wedding band on his ring finger either. You naughty woman, Brigitte, I said inaudibly. Her intentions were plain from the way her eyes were fixed on him, like a tiger contemplating a foolishly straying goat. I was saved from having to summon up polite opening gambits with this uneasy pair by Liz's upper half folding on to the table, her head missing the remnants of a cheesecake by millimetres.

"I feel a bit peculiar," she whispered from among the crumbs.

"I wonder why?" I said solicitously, "Perhaps you should go upstairs and lie down."

"Need a hand?" The malice in Brigitte's offer was obvious to me.

"No, ta, I think I can cope. Thanks, thanks for everything, see you in the morning. . ."

Brigitte gave me a thin smile and, with several puffing false starts, I managed to haul Liz to her feet and up the stairs.

"Don't you dare be ill on me," I warned, dragging her along the passage, hoping fervently that people had taken heed of the notice on the door. They had, or they had left the room as they had found it, and we collapsed on to the bed.

"You're so sexy," Liz chuntered in a brief recovery as I

tried to get her out of her jeans, hampered by her uncoordinated attempts to take off my shirt, "I'm going to lick you all over."

I didn't bank on it, which was just as well, since as soon as our clothes were on the floor and her head on the pillow, her eyelids came down like steel shutters, her mouth opened and she was out. I made sure the bin from the bathroom was close by, slipped under the quilt beside her, and had a private moment of self-congratulation. She would never be able to criticise me again for getting drunk.

I was glad to find that Liz was still breathing when I woke up the next morning. Feeling affectionate, I propped my chin on my hand and had a good look at her. Even in such a wrecked state and emanating a faint odour of aniseed, she was still the most lovely being in the world. I marvelled at the way her unblemished skin ran smooth and enchanting over her even features, her strong shoulders and perfect breasts, the slight curve of her stomach, her divinely long limbs and the intricate tracery of bones in her hands and feet. I certainly didn't want to whisper endearments into anyone else's ears, to open up under any other lips, or to have anyone but me travel through that dark nest of curls. . . I sighed. She wasn't going to be fit for anything when she regained consciousness, so I might as well go downstairs and make some tea. And if I did that, I'd have to get dressed, so I might as well have a shower and make full use of Brigitte's facilities.

Liz hadn't stirred when I came out of the shiny tiled bathroom, although she did give a tiny twitch at my yelp when I stubbed my toe on a bed leg in my search for clothes in the half-light. I decided that opening the curtains would be too cruel, left a tooth glass of water by the bed, and passed silent as a shadow out of the room and down to the kitchen, which also hadn't altered in the night. I am far from being Ms Tidy, but even I blanched at the carnage of bottles, sticky glasses, dead cigarettes squished in plates of soggy food and puddles of spilt booze on every surface. I found some bin bags and a dishwasher while the kettle boiled, and made a start. I was on a second pot of tea and my second cigarette when the equilibrium I'd generated by virtuous activity was destroyed by Brigitte's arrival.

"Good God," she said, surveying the fruit of my labours, "the model house-guest. You needn't have bothered. Stella's coming in later. You could have stayed in bed frolicking."

I shrugged, and wondered if Harry had escaped, or if he was still trapped upstairs. Maybe he was tunnelling out at this very moment, or disguising himself as the milkman to sneak away unnoticed.

"Liz is barely alive," I said in what I hoped was a non-frustrated way, "I'm just filling in time."

"Ah." She started messing around with a coffee maker I hadn't been able to figure out. "So, anyway. You're the one who's finally managed to pin Liz down, and keep her on the straight and narrow."

"I wouldn't say that." I met her eyes. She was wearing a padded silky robe, and although her face appeared tired without its make-up, she showed no major sign of alcohol poisoning. She's a tough nut, I concluded, and then was nearly disarmed when she flashed me a smile of unaffected charm.

"You're a nice woman, Kate. It's good Liz has got happy. She was never as hard as she made out."

"No." An instinctive aversion to discussing Liz and her past with this woman made me change the subject with obvious abruptness, "Where do you keep all these rare books you sell? I haven't noticed any."

Her smile became condescending at my naivety, "Harry stores some. Although most of the stuff we get to order. People in the States or the Far East with money to burn hit our site and tell us what they want, and we search it out for them, then bingo, more household toys and vintage brandy for me."

"Oh, right." The urge to flee came upon me, and I thought I heard a thump and the sound of running water from upstairs. "I think I'll take Liz some tea, see if she's up to it."

When I tippy toed into the bedroom, I saw that Liz had pulled the covers over her head, and was moaning piteously.

"I've brought you some tea," I said in my best caring

manner, "or would you like some hot orange and honey?"

"Piss off," I made out. I sat carefully down on the bed, and gently pulled the quilt down to reveal a pale green face and bloodshot eyes. I stifled any suggestion of laughter, "Oh sweetheart, feeling a bit rough?"

She mouthed something obscene, and I stroked her hair where it stood up from her sticky forehead. "Have you thrown up?" I continued with my impersonation of a kind nurse. She nodded, and winced with her whole body. "That's good," I crooned, "just start replacing your body fluids, and you'll soon pick up. I'll get you something sugary, it's the best thing." I kissed her shoulder and minced out, bathed in an aura of benevolent concern.

At least ministering to Liz, and running up and down the stairs with a selection of my tried and tested hangover remedies meant that I could avoid being alone with Brigitte for any length of time. On one of my trips, I caught sight of Harry's back view skulking down the garden path.

"I think she's sleeping with him and he's married," I said to Liz when I had coaxed her into sitting up and trying a glass of flat coke.

"Wouldn't surprise me," she croaked, "she's changed, but not that much."

"Oh? How's she changed then?" In a way, I felt guilty that I didn't like Liz's friend, when she had made such an effort with all of mine.

She frowned, and I could see that it wasn't only her debilitated condition which made the right words difficult to find.

"We were all a bit wild, you know, when we left college. Hung out in squats and got up to all sorts."

I'd gathered that Liz's past was far from snowy white, and I knew I hadn't heard a fraction of what she'd done.

"She wasn't so heavy, though, was more of a giggle. I didn't think she'd be into having such a smart house and things. She always said that if she ever came into money, she'd give it to the homeless. After she'd bought a shedload of drugs, of course."

A chill touched the base of my spine. "Did you take a lot

of drugs yourself?" I'd somehow supposed that Liz had been relatively abstemious, and had devoted her considerable energies to having sex with lots of women.

"Yeah." Her eyes slid away from mine.

I pressed her anyway, "What kind?" I had never been brave or self-destructive enough to try anything much.

"God, Kate, everything. Everything except heroin." She gave an unconvincing smile, "I was too much of a snob to try that."

"Oh." How could I have lived with her for over a year, and not found this out before? What other secrets did she have? "Was it fun?" I asked dimly, my throat constricting.

Her eyes were shaded, "Yeah, it was mostly."

It had been a while since this old wall of silence had cut us off from each other. Then she reached out to touch me, and her eyes returned to something like normal. "It's gone, Kate. I'm too old to go back to all that now. Yuck," she sniffed at her armpit, "I smell disgusting. If I get into the shower, would you be an angel and make me some more tea? I won't chuck it up."

I released a shaky breath and hugged her. For a brief instant, I thought she was going to tell me something else, but she only hugged me back.

"I won't kiss you till I've cleaned my teeth again," she muttered, "I respect you too much to inflict that on you."

I let her go, and went down to put the kettle on once more.

The morning had changed. If anything, I'd been mildly amused and surprised that Liz had got so drunk, and had put it down to a combination of vague nervousness, and an impulse to let her hair down away from people who knew her as the more sober half of our partnership. Now, a creeping fear of things unknown and left unspoken wrapped insidious tendrils round my heart. Was there more to this fracture in her customary self-control? What had Brigitte said to her in their heart-to-heart? Come on, I told myself, her youthful excesses shouldn't make a difference. I believed her when she said that she wouldn't be into drugs now, and I was so used to her not saying much about her earlier life that

I'd given up pushing her. "It's who we are now that's important," was her favourite phrase to conclude any fragmented anecdote. Standing half-way down the stairs after yet another trip to leave a cup of tea on the bedside table, I was hit by a memory of a hot night in the summer, just before we went on tour. I had walked home from a gig in the city, with nothing more on my mind than the idle hope that Liz had waited up for me. She had, and I had paused on the pavement outside our house to see her lying reading on the settee, the curtains drawn back and the window open to catch any chance breeze. She was still, one brown hand holding her book and the other resting on her thigh, and her face under the ruffled nearly black hair was closed to the world. I slept skin to skin with her every night I was at home, and she had kept no part of her body from me, yet in those minutes with the glass between us, she was a complete and utter mystery to me, a beautiful stranger who, if we had never met, would have passed me on the street without a second glance. She had lifted her eyes from her book, seen me, and given me the smile I had fallen in love with, and the nightmare sensation that she would have never noticed if I had left and carried on walking for ever had disappeared. Poised on the wide treads, I suffered a bolt of self-knowledge. That was what I was attracted to. It excited me that this secretive woman with a whiff of danger about her found me desirable, apparently wanted only me in her bed, and went to such pains to please me there. Would the day I finally knew everything about her be the day I didn't want to be with her forever? Glued to the spot by this scary impasse, it was a while before my ears responded to a melodious humming coming from the kitchen. "My love, he bought a bonny boat and set her on the sea. . ." The humming burst out into full song, my solar plexus imploded, and I shivered from head to toe.

4

The hidden voice held all the richness of brown sugar mixed in cream, and all the sadness of a saxophone playing in a dim bar late on a rainy night, while cars driven by lonely people swish past on wet streets. I stood listening, my chest aching and a lump in my throat, until the song dissolved into more wandering humming. It wasn't Brigitte, I'd seen her through a door left ajar on the landing, tapping at a keyboard in front of a screen scrolling with figures. Holding my breath, I wobbled down the rest of the stairs, and peeped round the kitchen door. The apparition attacking a counter top with cleaner and a scrubbing pad shook me out of my introspection. She was big, taller even than Liz, and she carried her healthy weight on her large frame with ease. Her long red hair, crackling like fire in a beam of November sunlight, was caught up in a loose bun, held together by what seemed to be a chopstick, and the colours of her long patchwork dress shouted out against the muted shades of Brigitte's cabinets and bleached surfaces. She looked like Boudicea on a good day, tackling her domestic chores before setting off to wreak havoc on the Romans, and I found myself wanting to check the drive for a chariot with scythes on the wheels.

"If that's you behind the door, Brigitte, where do you keep your mop? I'll do this floor next." Her husky cadences made even these banalities into notes plucked from a harp.

"It's me. I don't know where she keeps it, shall I go up and ask her?" I walked in so she could see me, "I'm Kate. We stayed over after the party."

"No, don't disturb her while she's making money. I'll have a look round. I'm Stella." Her eyes were green, and one eyebrow quirked upwards, giving her an air of detached amusement.

"You're a singer," I said baldly, "do you sing professionally?"

I hadn't expected this great earthy bellow of laughter, "Get away, would I be cleaning up Brigitte's mess if I did? Where are you from, planet Fantasy?"

I laughed back, uninsulted, "Not quite. I'm a talent scout for a band whose singer has strayed. Tell me all about yourself, and I'll get my people to contact your people with a deal."

I wheedled information from her while we finished off the surfaces and washed the floor. By the time we were taking a break with some coffee and a tin of shortbread I'd hunted out, I'd learned that she mostly worked as a care worker for an agency, spending two week spells living in with someone who needed round the clock care, and then having two weeks off, and that she was lodging with one of Brigitte's neighbours.

"It's not the easiest way to earn money," she said, dunking her shortbread and then sucking it, "though it gives me plenty of time to get on with my other. . .interests."

"What are they?" I asked, glad to find someone whose table manners were on a par with mine.

"Ooh, eating, sleeping, chasing men. . .who's this?"

Liz was standing in the doorway, like the ghost of parties past.

"It's Liz, my partner." Delight at seeing her upright wiped out what was left of my worrying gloom, and I patted the chair next to me, grinning up at her pallid face, "Take the weight off, my love, you still look a bit peaky. This is Stella, she's an amazing singer, and I'm trying to persuade her to join Mac's band."

Liz sat down, and rested her forehead on her hands, "Jesus, I'm never going to drink again. If you feel like this after you've been on a bender, I don't know why you do it. Don't light that up in front of me, you foul person, have some consideration."

I put down the cigarette I'd rolled, and smoothed the lock of wet hair on the back of her neck, "You need to eat something. I think I saw some kippers in the fridge, fancy one with some scrambled eggs? Or a big slice of that gateau from last night with all the cream?" Whatever the books said, revenge was sweet, and I crunched another piece of shortbread with gusto.

She moved a hand to give my leg a feeble blow, "Yeah, rub it in. At least I wasn't sick on my shoes."

"That was food poisoning, and you know it."

Liz looked out at Stella from under her fingers, "Give this woman a wide berth. Leave now, while you still have your reason."

Stella's eyebrow quirked a little further, "Actually, I've had a thought. How long are you here for? I could do with someone giving me a hand with something this afternoon, and if you come with me, Kate, you can tell me more about this band. You could come as well, of course, Liz."

Liz shook her head, and tightened her grip on her forehead, "I'd rather not if you don't mind. As long as Kate's back here by evening to drive me home. I need to die in my own bed."

I was so happy that Liz didn't want to spend another night at Brigitte's that I forgot to be vengeful, "Sure you'll be all right? You don't mind me leaving you?"

"I think I'll cope. Just come back." This time, her hand was seeking reassurance, and I folded it in mine.

"I dare say I will. Unless I get a better offer."

"Is it another cleaning job you want a hand with?" I asked Stella as we whizzed round the sitting room with bin bags and damp cloths. I wished my mother could have seen me, and that Liz wasn't too sunk in discomfort to be amazed at my transformation into efficient char person.

"No. One of my other interests," she said, plugging in the vacuum cleaner.

"I'm no good at chasing men," I shouted above its roar.

"I gathered that," she yelled back, "this is quite different. You'll need a coat."

She wouldn't tell me anything else while we finished off our cleaning, collected a handful of money from Brigitte, who had come downstairs again, and left her and Liz sprawled over the furniture, obviously settling in for an afternoon of reminiscing about the old days. I was disappointed to see that, instead of a chariot, Stella's chosen method of transport was an old camper van complete with deep red curtains and matching padded benches in the back.

"You've got this very comfortable," I said, turning round from the front seat and noting the cosy gleam of a brass lamp hanging above the rear window.

"Well," she said, the steering wheel like a toy against her impressive frontage, "I practically live in it during the summer. Caring Hands has my mobile number, and they can call me and tell me where to go for my next job. I like being peripatetic."

"Caring Hands?" I asked, screwing up my eyes against the sunlight bouncing against the windscreen.

"That's the agency I work for." She changed gear with a flourish, and we shot off down the lane. "Actually, they're based in your place." She pulled a pair of 50's shades with winged frames from the front shelf, and perched them on her nose.

"Of course, I thought the name rang a bell." I remembered seeing the adverts in the local paper, "Caring Hands Care in Your Home," I recited. "They do home helps who just come in for an hour or so a day as well, don't they? They're always advertising for staff." On off days in the past when the band had hit a bleak spell, I had even considered putting myself forward as a potential employee, but luckily for their clients, I had always been rescued by a just in time booking.

"That's the one. The owners must make a mint, though I have to say," she turned us out on to a wider road, "we did get some training, not like some agencies, and they don't seem to mind that I'm of no fixed abode for a large part of the year."

"Don't you miss not having a permanent home?" I asked, thinking how fond I'd become of our unremarkable house and the scars it had accumulated from our tenure. The oil stains in the backyard from Liz's now departed motorbike, the chip on the sitting room doorframe where she had kicked it in a temper, the fading splodges on the carpet where I had knocked a mug of coffee over. . . Stella gave another bosom-shaking bellow.

"No. I was married once, you know, lived on an estate in Milton Keynes, can you believe it. I was so, so bored. I was manageress of a Little Chef, and one day, something flipped, and I ran away with a gang of bikers."

"No!" I braced myself as she turned the wheel rapidly again, and we hit a potholed track.

"Yes!" Her eyes shone behind her rhinestone studded sunglasses, "They came into the restaurant, I asked them where they were going, they said 'Scotland', and I said 'Take me,' so they did." Ignoring the next big rut, she took her hands from the steering wheel and clapped them together. I hung on to the door handle. "Mind you," her hands went back just in time, "they weren't real Hells Angels, they were a club from Brighton on their annual outing, and I did have to go back after a fortnight to pack up my life and ditch my poor husband. Then I was free. . .here we are, just want to pop in and fetch my things. Come in, you might need some better boots."

Beginning to wonder precisely what she was planning for me to do, I followed her into the low stone farmhouse crumbling at the end of the track. For the second time that day, I realised that my domestic standards weren't abysmally low. She led me into a back sitting room whose level of dishevelled chaos beat my most dedicated attempts hands down. The bare plaster walls and worn stone flagged floor did justice to untidy piles of kindling, scattered muddy garden tools, heaps of outdoor garments and a rickety table obscured by a stew of curling papers, scummy mugs and unemptied ashtrays filled with the shreds of burnt tobacco which betray a pipe smoker. The fire in the ancient range was unlit, and it was colder than outdoors. Stella smiled at my expression, "I've given up trying to tidy up after Oliver. I've got a stove in my room, and I keep that warm and clean, and that's as far as I'm prepared to go. See if any of these boots fit, and I'll get my stuff."

I blew on my hands, and eventually exchanged my treasured baseball boots for a pair which looked as if they had carried their owner to the Annapurnas. Once I had added a pair of hairy socks which I saw in a recess in the range, and which a smell test told me had been washed at least once this year, they didn't fall off my feet every time I took a step. I was stomping around to keep warm when Stella came back holding a couple of straight poles.

"Take these, would you? I've got this to carry." She gestured to the doorway, where I saw a clipboard and some kind of surveyor's instrument on a tripod.

"Stella," I said, unable to contain my bemusement any longer, "just what are we going to do?"

"It's the Constellation Map of Britain," she replied, hefting up the tripod and resting it on the shoulder of her vivid orange padded jacket. She almost filled the doorframe. "I'm part of the Sacred Earth Society and we're mapping all of the British Isles to produce a definitive map of how sacred sites correspond to the constellations, both over the country as a whole, and in specific locations. I'm a member of the North-West team, that's why I want to stay here for the winter. I need to finish off a site this afternoon while the sun's out."

I detected the gleam of a fanatic in her greeny eyes, and sighed, "Oh. Do you read music?"

"Huuh huh huh huh." A bantam pecking its way into the house reversed direction and fled at the onslaught of her laugh. "I'm used to dealing with a sceptical world. One day, our work will be accepted, and be in all the history books. Just hold the poles where I say, and I won't trouble you with explanations. It's not far to walk."

It was miles to me. Sliding around in the boots, I slithered and crashed behind her along a lane between two hedges, through a copse, down another lane and finally into a large field with a mound at one end.

"Right. If you get along to that barrow and stand on top with a pole, we can start."

"Barrow?" I puffed, dashing the sweat from my brow and wondering if I should cut down on the smoking.

She pointed at the mound, and I had the merest suspicion that she was enjoying herself at my expense, "There. It's a Bronze Age burial site. Among other things."

At least posing on the bumpy surface of the mound trying to keep the pole vertical while she faffed around with her tripod was more restful than hiking across the countryside and, warmed by my exertions, I took stock of my surroundings. November, with its moody rains and dark evenings, was my least favourite time of year, but this sunny afternoon contained the memory of a summer gone and a promise that spring would come round again. The last leaves flamed in the copse, hawthorn berries like jewels pricked the bare veins of the hedge, and from my vantage point I could see the quiet fields flowing down to the blue line of the Solway, with the hills of the Lake District rearing in the distance. I fancied I could see the first lace of snow on their tops and, outsize boots and all, felt a burst of thankfulness that I was alive on top of this grave, not a heap of bones beneath it.

The sun was falling, turning the sky into a cold crimson furnace, by the time Stella pronounced her satisfaction, and we started the trek back to Oliver's house.

"Well, do you read music or not?" I demanded, watching the sunset transform us into figures swimming through a luminous amber sea.

"You don't give up, do you? No, I don't. I just sing along to the radio and tapes. I've never sung in public either, so I'd be useless to this band." Only the modern instrument on her shoulder stopped me from the queer belief that when we reached Oliver's house, it would be a wattle and daub hall with smoke rising from a hole in its thatched roof, and that the van would have gone.

"No you wouldn't. You can easily learn the kind of songs they do. You have a really beautiful voice, it's a gift, and you're wasting it." I hadn't intended to come over so preachy, yet I found that I meant it, and I hurried on before she took offence, "I mean, it's taken years of practice for me to get where I am, which is a half-competent player. I love what I do, but I don't have that talent which you have. Surely you must have been told this before, I can't believe no-one's heard you and said something."

"All right," she broke her stride to confront me, "I'll tell you if it will shut you up. I know I have a nice voice, it's just. . . I've always been scared to sing in front of people in case I can't do it, and they think I'm rubbish, and there goes my adolescent dream of being a great undiscovered singer. Stupid, huh?"

This chink in her armour was one I understood, "Jesus, Stella, everyone feels like that to some degree. It's terrifying putting yourself out there. If you don't though, you'll never know how good or bad you are. And I think you're good, so there. I should know, I've heard some terrible singers."

She was silent for a while, and then she groaned, "Ok, I might come down and meet this band, unless they've found someone else. Although it's a bit far to travel regularly in the unlikely event that they want me."

My brain started firing on all cylinders. Pat and Tom had told me only on Friday that the tenant in my old flat in their house had left unexpectedly. "Ag won't take it," Pat had grumbled, "she thinks it's still like living at home."

"I think I might have a solution to that. . ." I piled on estate agent enthusiasm, and gave Pat and Tom character references which would make a saint blush. "And the flat is warm and so much nicer than that dump you're living in. . ."

"Enough!" She swiped harmlessly at me with her tripod, "Give me your number, I'll think about it and ring you next week. That's a maybe, not a promise. I wish I'd kept my mouth shut in Brigitte's kitchen."

"No you don't. This is your first step on the road to stardom. Just remember those who helped you on the way up and carried your poles."

The light faded, the countryside lost its unsettling half-world quality, and Stella drove me back to Brigitte's in a van which hadn't been magicked away.

"Where've you been? I want to go home, I was getting worried." It wasn't often that Liz sounded so anxious and unsure, and I knelt down to embrace her where she lay on a settee, a glossy magazine by her side.

"Oh sweetheart, I'm sorry." I wasn't used to this wave of protectiveness either, or the need to comfort her, "Stella's had me in a field all afternoon. I'll get our bag, and we can go."

"Have a cup of tea first. I don't want you flaking out on me on the motorway. You look bushed." Some of her usual self-possession reasserted itself, and there was even a suggestion of promise in her kiss.

I rested back on my heels, "Feeling a bit better?" I ventured.

"Don't build up your hopes. I was checking to see if I had any nerve-endings left in my mouth."

"And how about here?" I brushed her fingertips with mine, searching her eyes for that give away darkening. "Or here?" A pulse fluttered on the inside of her wrist. Her lips parted, and I bent my head, lifting it almost immediately with a neck-cricking jerk when a cough betrayed Brigitte's presence at the foot of the stairs.

"Fuck," I muttered, "we can't even play doctors and nurses in peace. I'll put the kettle on."

I think Liz was nearly as glad as I was to leave Brigitte with hearty assurances that we would keep in touch, although the journey home brought on a relapse, in spite of my efforts to keep her amused with a run-down of Stella's nutty enthusiasms.

"I need some beetroot soup," she whispered, slumped at our dining table while I briskly threw the dirty washing from our bag into the machine.

"Darling, if I had a beetroot, I'd make you some," I said absently, "the corner shop might still be open, I'll run and get you a tin of something."

"It's not the same. I made some while you were away, and I was going to freeze it, but I had to eat it all."

"Why?" I joined her at the table.

"Comfort food. I was missing you." Her eyes were sad, and a strange hurt gave my heart a wrench, "Must be hereditary."

"Mm?" Suddenly I hardly dared to breathe. The air closed solid around us, waiting for her next reluctant sentence.

"Yeah. My proper father's family originally came from Russia. They were what you'd call economic migrants nowadays. Ma and I stayed with his parents once, after he'd left. I suppose it was to sort out the divorce, he was abroad by then. All I can remember is this tall fierce woman making me eat beetroot soup, and hugging me when I least expected it."

This was country where I had never had the courage to tread. Her father's disappearance when she was two was a subject she almost never raised, and she had only mentioned once in passing that he had died years ago. I had never brought it up, out of a cowardice born from experience of the barriers she kept round what she had no intention of revealing, and of the way she could keep me out with icy wordlessness. Neither had she ever given a hint of this Russian connection. Maybe that was why she liked Mrs T.'s box so much.

"That must be where you get it from," I said, my voice as low and unthreatening as I could make it, "all that telling me to eat properly."

She covered her eyes with her hand, "We lost contact with them. Ma wanted to forget, and by the time I was old enough to think about it, I wasn't that interested. I think I take after my grandmother, from what Ma says, contrary and with a terrible temper."

I had to ask her before these minutes of suspended time passed, and we switched back into our everyday selves, "Liz, what happened to your father?"

I thought she was never going to speak, or was going to stand up and walk out of the house. I saw the tension clamp her fingers, and hold the breath stationary in her back, and I rested my hand on her knee. I wasn't going to back off now.

A defeated sigh pushed her head further into her hand, "Well, he died. He died in a car crash in Mexico the year after I left college. I don't know how my mother found out, but she did. She told me, and I was too out of my skull to care. Satisfied?" This last word was a harsh rasp, and in an involuntary reflex, I stood up and forced her into my arms.

"'S'ok," I murmured again and again into her hair, holding her as tightly as if I was keeping her from sinking into a nameless bog, "'s'ok, you don't have to tell me anything else. I don't mind, I love you anyway."

"Aw fuck." In the end she gave in, and sagged against me, "I don't know how you bear me sometimes. I don't want to talk about this any more. There's some vegetable soup in the freezer, I'll have a go at eating some of that. I don't think this hangover's ever going to go away."

She was fully recovered by the morning, though, judging from the way she disturbed my slumber by tugging at my curls, tweaking my nose and generally making a nuisance of herself. I unstuck my eyelids, and the air jumped in my throat at the look of purpose on her face.

"Hello, sweet thing." The softness of her voice and her first kiss were belied by the shivering urgency of her hands and body sliding over mine.

"Oh God. . ." The world would be a happier place, I thought randomly, if everyone woke up to this. Then the past three days, with Tom and Dodgy's trouble, the party, Brigitte, Stella, and Liz's unexpected revelations, all receded to pin pricks on my horizon and vanished as I shot off into orbit.

Only a nagging need for sustenance eventually brought me back.

"Oh my, I'm so glad I don't live in the Middle Ages," I purred, finishing off a slice of butter and marmalade with some toast attached.

"You're weird," Liz's eyes and mouth were languid, "what makes you say that?"

"You know," I waved at the radiators, the breakfast tray and the heaped quilts, "I'm sure women did this with each other, but it would have been on piles of smelly straw with no cups of tea or cigarettes afterwards, and they never washed and it would have been cold and dirty so they wouldn't have been able to take their time or even wanted to. . ."

Liz looked thoughtful, "They didn't have underwear, though. Maybe they had lots of nice quickies behind haystacks or in the dairy. . .mightn't have been so bad."

"Ok," I massaged her calf with my toes, "if you had to

choose to live in any time or place in the past, which would it be?"

She didn't hesitate. "Ancient Greece. On Lesbos. Getting smothered in olive oil and having hot sex on the sea shore."

"Ha! The beach would all stick to the oil. It would be like making love covered in sandpaper."

"Actually you're right there." Her voice went a bit dreamy, "I'll have to take you to Lesbos someday, see how it is with you."

I nearly spat out my tea, "You mean, you've been there?"

"Of course," she danced her fingers along my shoulder, "I'm sure I told you. I sort of went with a girlfriend and kind of swapped her half way through the holiday. . ." She sniggered at my expression, "Well, honestly, Kate, what would you expect? It was like being a kid let loose in a sweetshop, all these gorgeous things in bikinis or less. . .heh heh."

I tried to move away from her. "You're disgusting. Sometimes I wish I'd never met you."

She put her mouth to my collarbone, "Sometimes you tell whopping great fibs. Anyway, I love only you now, remember."

"Prove it," I muttered after a few minutes, hanging on to my mug, "help me move this damn bed down into the dining room, so we don't have to keep carrying food up the stairs. We can scrap that table."

"Can't." Her words were getting blurry, "I'm going to cook that special supper tonight. We're eating at the table. With candles. Jesus, Kate, you're lovely here. . ."

I managed to slide my mug on to the bedside table before I threw tea everywhere. This beat tree climbing any day.

5

Tuesday morning, and Liz was back at work. I gritted my teeth, girded my loins, let the iron enter into my soul and heaved myself out of bed while she was in the shower. I bumbled towards the bathroom, eyes still more or less closed, and met her half-way along the passage.

"Good Lord," she said reeling, "It Came From Outer Space. What are you doing up before lunch-time?"

"Practise," I mumbled, "I must practise."

"Hm." She strode swiftly on, not pausing to take me in her fragrant arms, and tell me that perhaps it wouldn't matter if she was a little late for work after all. Wiping the steam off the bathroom mirror, I could see her point. My hair, vertical in places, framed features squashy with sleep, and a fetching pimple had germinated on my chin in the night.

"I'm too old for spots, God," I complained, "send them to the teenagers and computer programmers where they belong." Ten minutes and a huge dollop of Liz's expensive shower gel later, the thought of going downstairs and picking up my violin was not quite so daunting, although I can't say that I was champing at the bit at the prospect of the day ahead.

"Why? Why me?" I bleated. "Why did I make this stupid arrangement?"

Months ago, I had had the misfortune of falling in with a couple of Ag's friends who fancied themselves as musicians, although what they produced wasn't music as I understood it, being some kind of electronic drum'n'bass dance-y trance-y hybrid. They renounced the use of old-fashioned techniques such as recognisable instruments and basic musical knowledge in favour of twiddling at banks of controls from which they could probably hack into the Pentagon and launch cruise missiles.

"Celtic riffs, man," they had droned at me, "come into the studio sometime and lay us down some Celtic riffs we can sample. Lune Sound, that's what we're creating here."

I had quoted an extortionate hourly rate for my precious time, and they hadn't raised their pierced eyebrows, nor had they been put off by my touring schedule.

"November's cool. Can't rush perfection. We'll be in touch."

Today was the day, at two-thirty in the local recording studio, and I had to get my hands and brain back from the ups and downs of the weekend into session musician mode. This is a psychic spot, I accused myself, a punishment for selling your soul to swell the coffers of the house fund. I was guiltily aware that Liz's contribution to our joint building society account, the symbol of our commitment to each other and the future, was many times larger than mine, and for the umpteenth time I made the promise that I wouldn't blow my tour money on high living, but would deposit it safely as soon as Fred coughed up.

Swathed in towels and virtue, I zipped back into the bedroom, where Liz was combing her hair, her face wearing the look of distraction which showed that her mind was already at the business. In a grey sweater, which looked suspiciously like cashmere, and spotless black trousers, she was every inch the successful photographer, and a terrible temptation to my baser instincts. I averted my eyes determinedly, and began rummaging in drawers and the wardrobe. A skirt, I thought, a short-ish dark skirt and woolly tights with one of my favourite multi-coloured jumpers from Pat, that should help me feel like a recording artiste. I felt her gaze on me all the same.

"I think you lost some weight while you were away," she remarked into the busy silence.

"Really?" I unwrapped a towel and surveyed myself. My stomach and thighs didn't appear any less rounded to me, so I stood up straighter and pulled in some muscles, to see if my ribs would emerge.

"Hunnh."

I turned round at her muffled groan, and fluttered my eyelashes. The look of distraction had dissolved into a smile.

"Keep away, evil temptress. I'm going to work. When will you be back from the studio?"

I gave up, and stepped into my knickers, "Seven at the latest, I hope."

"See you then, sweet pea. I'll try not to stay on beyond that." She jumped towards me, planting a smacking kiss on my lips, then raced out of the room and down the stairs. I heard the familiar sounds of her putting on her jacket, thumping through to the kitchen for the car keys, and swearing at the lock on the front door. Unable to resist, I poked my head out of the curtains to watch her march to the car and fold herself neatly in, swinging her fancy canvas briefcase into the back. I grinned at the sight of her scowl when she realised that I'd driven it last, and at her impatient shoulder-hunched adjustments to the driver's seat. I beamed even more when I caught her glancing up at the window and blowing it a kiss. She pretended she hadn't seen me, gunned the engine, and burned rubber down the street as if she was one of the local boy racers in a souped up love machine, not a middle-aged woman in a rusty Fiesta. Satisfied with my spying, I finished my toilette, scooped up odd plates and mugs from various surfaces and made for the kettle.

I had an unusually productive morning. After a nutritious breakfast, which included only a minimum quantity of leftovers from the night before, I washed up, searched out my violin case, flexed my fingers and went for it. By one o'clock, with a few hours of solid playing behind me, I felt ready for any musical challenge. I would give those techno freaks the meanest riffs they'd ever heard, and show them what true musicianship was. Now that my mind was back in gear as well, I decided to ring Mac and tell him about my discovery of Stella. Maybe that would bring some cheer into his life. The phone rang on for ages, and I was about to give up, when it was picked up at the other end with a bleary "'lo?"

52

"Mac? It's Kate. Is this a bad time for you?" Perhaps Suzie had returned, and I had interrupted a wild reunion, or perhaps he'd hit the depths in a grief-induced drinking spree. I heard a jaw-cracking yawn, and for a moment thought that he had swallowed the receiver.

"Guurgh. Nah, I was only working last night.."

From the disarray of my memory bank, I retrieved the information that to pay his bills, Mac sometimes did shifts as an assistant on a psychiatric unit.

"God, I'm sorry, shall I phone back this evening?"

"I'm nearly awake now. It was just the scrabble at three in the morning with the insomniacs which wiped me out. What. . .?"

If he'd been a woman, I would have started with sympathetic noises and questions about his emotional state, but since he was a man, I told him about Stella. I was still relieved and gratified by the rising enthusiasm in his voice.

"That's great. Listen, me and Spiff got together at the weekend, and we've booked the hall at Baker's from three on Thursday afternoon to have a good practice and try out any singers who want to come along. D'you think she could make it? We'd like you to come and practise with us as well, if you can."

Baker's was a social club I'd been known to frequent, especially in the days before I'd rediscovered domestic bliss. In fact, as far as I could recall, I'd been carried out of the bar on more than one occasion, although that would surely have been forgotten by now.

"I think I'm free, so I'll give her a call and see if she is."

"Nice one. I hope you don't mind, I asked Dave from your band to pop in. Give us the benefit of his expert advice."

Pernickety Dave, whose high standards were matched only by his turnover of women. I shuddered in sympathy for any naive young maidens who turned up.

"Good idea," I fibbed, praised Stella some more and rang off. On a roll, I searched my coat pockets for the packet of cigarette papers on which I'd written Stella's number. To my surprise, her melodious tones came through almost immediately, although she sounded less than thrilled to hear me.

"Oh, it's you. I thought it might be the agency. What do you want?"

After five minutes of pleading, I'd exhausted my powers of persuasion. "Dammit then," I said rudely, "don't bother. Forget it, they'll find someone else. There'll be enough wannabes turning up anyway, and some of them will probably be quite good." I couldn't think why I was so disappointed.

"Really?" There was a hint of injured pride in that one word, and I changed my line of attack.

"Oh yeah, there's a lot of talent around. Anyway, I won't rabbit on and keep you. . ."

"Not so fast." I heard the rustle of paper, "I've been meaning to come down your way sometime to look at a site, and I suppose if I came on Thursday morning, you could help me again, and I could put my head round the door of this hall thingy and have a listen. . ."

I had her, and even managed to negotiate a ten o'clock start, rather than the awful nine she wanted. Pleased with myself, I ate a large sandwich and left for the studio.

I was glad that I had sorted out something potentially worthwhile, because the recording session was worse than my darkest imaginings. Even the thought of the pounds mounting up as the hours ticked by didn't really compensate for the frustration of running through tune after beautiful tune only to be met by unimpressed stares and requests to play "that one you did at the Billhook." Since the band played at the Folk Club in the Billhook every Wednesday night when we didn't have a more lucrative offer, this wasn't much help. I tried jigs, reels, waltzes and hornpipes, and then started on my repertoire of Eastern European dances and some tunes we'd picked up on tour. Nothing suited them, and I spent interminable periods waiting while they messed around with the few snatches they'd bothered to tape and traded gobbledegook with each other. I was amusing myself in one of these interludes by attempting a passage of Bach, when I realised that they had both fallen silent, and were looking at me through the glass screen. I came to an uncertain stop.

"That's it!" The one I knew only as Ty clicked his fingers and spoke through to me, "Play that again."

"Yeah, yeah," his friend's eyebrows had lifted a millimetre, which was animated for him, "that's the riff."

I took my violin from under my chin. "You're not serious. That's not Celtic, it's Bach." They both looked blank. "It's classical, you can't sample that, and anyway I can't play it properly, if you want something like that, you need a real violinist. . ."

Ty cut me off, "Hell, sounded fine to me. Let's go for it."

I opened my mouth, and his pal gave me a supercilious smirk, "He who pays the piper. . ."

The evil spirit of Mammon on my left shoulder defeated the good angel of aesthetic and artistic integrity on my right, and by the time I escaped at six-thirty, I was in a fair old strop. I stood on the pavement outside the studio, the spot I'd forgotten about earlier throbbing on my chin, and had a dither. In the pre-Liz era, I would either have gone straight to Pat's kitchen for a moan, or, more likely, have made a beeline for Bill, my best friend in the band, and have persuaded him to help me drown my peevishness in a drink or six and a bitching session. I looked at my watch again. Even if Liz arrived home at around seven, she would be tired and preoccupied, and she wouldn't really grasp why I was so narky. It had come as a surprise to me to realise that she held an inordinately high opinion of my musical skills, and thought that practically everything I played sounded wonderful, nor would she appreciate the crime I had committed with a well known classical piece. I took a step in the direction of Bill's house. A wee drink and discussion with him would do no harm, and I could still be back at a reasonable time. Or I could phone Liz from the pub. Gripped by a nostalgic urge for a carefree evening of knocking back the vodka, I walked on for a few yards before groaning and turning round. Yeah, it had been such fun, I scolded myself, drinking myself into oblivion and staggering home to an empty flat, with no-one there to hold me in the night or wake me up with sexy little kisses. Of course I should risk annoying Liz for the sake of an expensive hangover. I picked up speed and almost power-walked home.

"Mmmmm." I leant my head back, eyes closing in ecstasy.

"Aaaah," Liz sighed. Her spare hand tightened on my knee.

I gurgled. "I can't bear it, it's so nice."

Her hand withdrew and sneaked on to the table. "I'll have the rest of yours then."

I snapped my eyes open, and clutched my bowl, "Not on your life. That was a figure of speech, my mouth having an orgasm. What is this, exactly?" I took another spoonful of the pale gloopy nectar, and rolled my eyes in appreciation. What a wise decision it had been to forego a visit to Bill.

Liz's eyes did the fetching crinkle which always made my heart ping, "Syllabub. It's a top secret recipe, which I had to wring out of my stepfather while you were away by promising to be nice to ma for the rest of my life. You see the sacrifices I make for you."

"I make sacrifices as well." I picked up the dish to lick it out, "I nearly went boozing with Bill, I was so pissed off with those clowns this afternoon."

The crinkles disappeared, and she watched me bury my face in the chinaware, her shoulders stiff against the back of her chair. She half-turned her head away, and suddenly found the grain of the dining table interesting.

"You could have gone. You don't have to come running back for my sake." Her voice was probably more clipped than she would have liked.

"Oh piffle." I put the dish down, and wiped syllabub from the end of my nose, "It was a close-run thing, but an evening with the best cook in the world was just a teeny weeny bit more enticing than sitting in a bar eating crisps. . ." I leant closer, and let my fingers touch the inside of her thigh, and my voice drop an octave, "Especially when the cook is so accomplished at. . .other things."

She gave a reluctant giggle. "Ok, ok." Her hand settled on mine with surprising firmness, "You would tell me though, wouldn't you?"

"Tell you what?" I wanted to see her eyes laugh properly.

"If you felt. . .tied, or wanted to be somewhere else and not come back just because I'm here." Her head had angled away again, and her words faded into a mumble.

"Grrr." I yanked her face to within an inch of mine, "Watch my lips. I-love-you-and-I-want-to-spend-as-much-time-with-you-as-I-can." I had a horrible thought, and dropped my hand. "Do you feel tied? Is that what this is about?"

"No!" she shouted, banging her fist on the table and going red, "I just want to be sure you're happy with us like this." She was never that easy with vulnerability.

"I'm deliriously happy, you fool," I yelled back.

"Good!" Cutlery danced.

"Good!" Glasses shivered.

Her smile reached her hairline, "You've got pudding in your eyebrows. I'd lick it off for you, but," she pushed back her chair and stood up, "I've got to show you these first. You distracted me with your nonsense."

She danced to her work case, and extracted a folder. "Feast your eyes on these, baby. Not only am I a fantastic cook and an awesome lover, I am also probably one of the finest photographers working today." She tapped me on the head with the folder, shoved it in front of me and sat down again, oozing self-satisfaction.

I pulled out the glossy black and white photographs, and goggled like a cod-fish. They were beyond good. It was as if Liz had been standing only a few feet away from Kristin Dale, not lying under a distant bush, to record the early morning light moulding soft shadows around her still, elegant limbs and the self-contained absorption on her famous features. Toni would love any one of these, but maybe the last in the pile was the best. Kristin must have been looking straight at the camera for Liz to have caught this perfect view of serene eyes and slightly parted made for kissing lips. I forgot how immoral it had been of us to intrude on Kristin, and cleared crumbs from the table before putting the prints reverently down.

"They're brilliant," I breathed, holding Liz's eyes with my own, "it's a pity they have to stay private, they're so beautiful."

She looked even more big-headed, "See, it was nothing to get so worked up about. Mind you," she pulled a folded paper from her back pocket, "I thought this would be one for the tabloids."

I snatched the paper from her, not trusting her air of affected casualness. I was right to be wary. It was a picture of me, standing on the lawn next to Kristin, my right arm outstretched so that my hand touched her breast. Liz cut through my stunned expletives,

"I'm imagining the headlines. How about 'Kristin Dale relaxes with Mystery Lover' or," she started to snort, "'Love-rat Kristin Stole My Girlfriend for Dawn Romps. Broken-hearted photographer, Liz Sharpe, wept when she told how world-famous lesbian star lured her ten-times-a-night girlfriend into her bed with promises of a place in her backing band. . . ow, ow, stop, you harpy." She fended off the blunt table knife I had plunged at her, "It's only computer trickery, I'm working on one with you both naked, we could make thousands for the house fund. . ."

Our fight took us to the floor in front of the fire I'd considerately lit earlier.

"We shouldn't be doing this," Liz's voice was still charged with laughter, "we've got to synchronise our diaries."

"Damn the diaries." Her skin felt even better than the cashmere sweater, "You're doing the sound for us tomorrow at the Billhook, I'm meeting Stella for a practice with Mac on Thursday, and I'm away to Birmingham with the band Friday and Saturday. That's all you need to know." If she didn't carry on removing my woolly tights, I would probably die.

"I suppose you can tell me later. . .oh Lord," her voice trailed away, "careful with that zip. . ."

I enjoyed myself far too much on Wednesday as well, with the predictable result that I was not at my best on Thursday morning. I had a jovial reunion with the band at our customary get-together on Wednesday afternoon in the upstairs room of the Billhook, and we marked our triumphant return from the tour by playing a blinder at the Folk Club in the evening. Liz, who was practising for our planned tour of the States the following year, when she would take six months off work and join us in the guise of roadie cum sound engineer, turned up on time to play with the sound deck, and was greeted by the others with an enthusiasm which banished my sporadic fears that this arrangement would end in tears and possibly bloodshed. They even understood when she left half an hour after closing time, pleading the pressure of work the next day, and made no more than token protests at her wimpishness in not contributing to our attempt to drink the bar dry in a celebratory lock-in. I made myself leave after a couple of hours, and rolled home to spoil Liz's rest with contented vodka-flavoured snores. I barely registered her departure in the morning, and sank back into a dream of drinking espresso with her in a beachside cafe, while the band tuned up on the sand within yards of a warm surf. I could taste the sweet grainy coffee in my mouth, and feel my heart swelling at the adoration in her dark eyes. . . A vigorous banging at the front door ruined my delight. Crossly, I prised my eyes open and tried to focus on the alarm clock. It was ten o'clock. Stella. If I had followed my instincts and burrowed back under the quilt until she went away, I would probably have been better off. I was foolish, though, and made an uncoordinated lunge for the window to croak down at her to stay.

6

"I see you're ready, then," Stella said by way of greeting, taking in my old robe, bare feet and bird's nest hair. "You must tell me the name of your hairdresser."

"Ha di-ha." I closed the door behind her, and ushered her into the sitting room, "I'm afraid I overslept. If I can have some tea, I'll be with you in a jiffy."

"Not to worry. I guessed you weren't an early bird. How about some toast with the tea?" She sat down on the settee, and looked happily around, "You know, one reason I do the care work is that I love seeing in people's houses. You can tell all sorts about them once you're inside."

"Jesus. Don't tell me if you work out that we're axe murderers. I'll make some breakfast." I wanted to shield my eyes against the glare from her outfit. Under her bright orange jacket, she appeared to be wearing a shocking pink fluffy sweater, and her large legs were encased in a generous pair of crimson corduroys. She looked like some kind of giant sundae.

"Don't go to any trouble. Tea and toast will be fine."

I tottered to the kitchen and drank some water.

"Where's your friend?" she asked when I had finished bringing through piles of toast and the big teapot. "Is she the photographer?"

"Yup. Full marks for observation. She's at work." The tea was perking me up.

"I like that." She pointed to one of Liz's current favourites, which hung near the window. She had been hanging around in the new shopping arcade, and had surreptitiously snapped three elderly women having a breather on a bench, clearly being entertained by an equally elderly gentleman who was standing facing them. I think he was telling them a string of risque jokes, because they were leaning against each other, faces creased with helpless shocked laughter, and the bulging discount store plastic bags lying unguarded at their feet. When left to her own devices, Liz was not overfond of photographing people, favouring instead strange landscapes and abstract images which she soon ran out of patience in explaining to me. She had told me, though, that she liked this scene because she imagined that the man had slept with each of the three women when they were all young and was now reminding them, which had left me to ponder the workings of her mind. I brought myself back.

"So do I. What other conclusions about us have you drawn from our decor?" Actually, the sitting room wasn't as untidy as it sometimes was, and the radiators were free of drying underwear.

She smiled and pretended to check under the settee for fluff-balls. "I'd say you were two busy artistic people who preferred not to spend too much time on home improvements when you were together."

"Fair enough." The distinctive patter of raindrops against the window made me raise my head, "Oh God, Stella, do you really want to go out and play with your poles in this? Why don't we just stay here, and practise for this afternoon?"

"Hm, I wonder what your rising sign is, marked as you are by deviousness and low cunning? No, I haven't driven all this way for something which might be a waste of time. It's only a few drops, don't be soft."

Deviousness and low cunning indeed, I thought, as I mutinously showered and dressed, if I had any of that, I would still be snoozing in comfort.

"What are you going to sing this afternoon?" I asked bossily once we were chugging out to the north of the city. I'd decided not to waste breath on asking her where we were going, telling myself that a magical mystery tour in the rain would be much more fun.

She gave a patient sigh, "I haven't a clue. I'm not

promising anything, I might still give it a miss."

"Don't you dare. We've got a deal. Why don't you sing the 'Lowlands of Holland' like you were in Brigitte's kitchen? When we've finished with your site, we can go back to our place, find out what key you sing it in, and I can work out a dinky accompaniment. We'll be the business."

"Did anyone ever tell you, you're a terrible nag? Let's just see how we get on out here."

"Here" turned out to be what I had always thought was a private road, branching off from the A6 beyond the city outskirts. The narrow newly-tarmaced surface, bordered by white railings, glistened under a steady drizzle, and I became less and less enthralled with the idea of prancing with poles across these muddy fields.

"Are you sure it's all right for us to be here?" I asked nervously as we went round a tight corner and headed for the roof of a large house surrounded by trees, and hidden by a fold of land from the main road. "We might be trespassing."

Stella, her gaze sweeping round from side to side, wasn't paying me or her driving much attention.

"So what?" she said carelessly. "The land belongs to everyone. Bugger!" She narrowly missed ploughing us into a pair of mock baronial cast-iron gates set squarely across the lane. Beyond them the metalled track gave way to a gravel drive and disciplined shrubs, and no-one could miss the officious sign wired on to the black gatepost, "Private House. No Uninvited Callers." If we hadn't got the message, we could take a hint from the strands of barbed wire wound around the fierce spikes at the top of the gates. Brilliant, if I couldn't get into trouble with Liz, I had to find it with someone else. I put my foot down.

"I'm not going in there," I said, in what I hoped was an assertive, yet not aggressive, manner.

Stella gave me a pitying look, "Of course not. We've come too far. I'll just turn round. Look out for a field with a bump and some exposed rocks in it."

After about ten minutes of Stella swearing, we were crawling back the way we had come, the needle on the speedometer barely flickering above zero. All the fields had bumps in them, and it was difficult to tell if the grey shapes visible in the murk were rocks or depressed sheep.

"Aha!" Stella stamped on the brake, "I can see it. There, the field over that wall." She pointed to a field which looked identical to all the others, apart from the sturdy barn crouched in one corner. "See, that's not too bad. We only have to climb over the railings, cross that little paddock and find a way over the wall. Some people think there's an ancient burial site here, but I'm not convinced. I need to give it a once-over." She saw my expression, "Remember, Kate, you're adding to the sum of human knowledge. Think on that, my little helper."

"It's an honour and a privilege," I snarled, and pulled up the hood of my waterproof.

"What's it like, then?" Stella asked suddenly while we were tramping towards the wall, feet squelching in the water-logged turf.

"What's what like?" The rain was dripping from the bottom of my waterproof on to my jeans, and in a minute would penetrate the fabric to my skin. Soon my wellies would start to leak. I hadn't dried my hair properly, either, and my head was getting clammy in my hood. This wasn't the way I usually liked to treat a slight hangover.

"Tss. Being with a woman of course." She appeared unaffected by the wet, and there was nothing more than interested curiousity in her voice.

"Bloody hell," I shifted the poles on my shoulder, "don't ask me, I don't know any different. Normal, I suppose. You know," I relented and smiled at her tiny frown, "Liz drives me mad sometimes, but I seem to be in love with her, so I put up with it."

"Oh, right." She glanced along the length of the wall, "Ooh look, there's a gate." We veered off in the right direction. "The thing is, I like men," she said as if she was stating a preference for dark, rather than milk, chocolate, "but I get bored quickly because they're such hard work. Being so different. It's a waste of time to try and get them to understand you. I don't know if I could fancy a woman, though." She gave me an innocent smile, "Maybe I should try. See what I'm missing."

I started to giggle as I slopped through the mud, poached by what must have been a herd of very heavy cows, at the gate. "Keep me out of it, I'm married. Mind, I could fix you up with a couple of dates if you like. Offer you a selection from the single women of my acquaintance." I revved up a notch and climbed over the gate, narrowly missing a heap of dung on my descent, "Have a think about your requirements. Height, weight, hair colour, that kind of thing."

She landed beside me, her trousers splashed with mud up to her thighs, "I don't trust you. You'd set me up with some scary woman into black leather and chains, and I'd end up trapped in a dark basement with hot wax being dripped on to my delicate places."

I turned to face her, "Sounds good. Wouldn't you like to broaden your experience? Don't stand there too long, you'll sink. It's like a bog."

She put her hand on my shoulder, and extracted her right leg from the mire. Weighed down, I didn't jump at the unmistakeable crack of a shotgun snapping out from the direction of the barn. Someone must be shooting rats, I thought vaguely, that's what they do in the country. There was another thump in the air, and out of the corner of my eye I saw flakes of stone fly off the top of the wall. Powerful sound waves, my mind said, I wonder if this is a common phenomenon. Stella hitched her tripod up again, and I trudged on behind her. I only lifted my head when an indistinct bellowing seeped through my inadequate hood.

". . ..Orf my land. . .pheasant shoot. . ."

Stella had stopped. "Is he shouting at us?" she asked politely.

I saw the barbour-coated figure at the corner of the barn, red face under a flat cap, thick stick under one arm, waving his fist at us. I pushed away a clump of hair which had draped itself in front of my right eye, and wiggled my toes in my wrinkled socks. "Um. . ." Then I saw him raising the dull stick to his shoulder, and at last the alarm went off in my slumbering alcohol-numbed brain. Shotgun, flakes of stone, a rush in the air. . .

"He's fucking shooting at us!" My voice hit its highest register. For a terrible half-second, panic turned my digestive system to water, and my legs to plasma. In the nick of time, life-saving adrenalin kicked in. I grabbed at a handful of Stella's sleeve, screamed and started running.

"What are you. . .Kate, the poles. . ." I took no notice, just screamed some more and hurled myself through the mud to the gate. At least the deep gunge made for a soft landing when I fell over on the other side and crawled like a commando to the shelter of the wall. Stella wasn't beside me. I tried to stop screeching like a banshee and start breathing. Oh Lord, I couldn't leave her here. Where was the silly cow? I inched my head round the massive stone which formed the gate post. My face would be less of a target if I kept my right cheek pressed firmly to the ground. The man would have to be one hell of a shot to wing me from the barn. . . Against the laws of physiology, my heart leapt to the roof of my mouth at the sight of Stella, still yards from the gate and as inconspicuous as a double-decker bus, looking aimlessly around. Buttocks clenching like nutcrackers in anticipation of the next shot, I attempted to shout.

"Stella, get moving, he's going to. . ." There was a crump and I ate dirt. It didn't matter any more that I was about to pee or worse.

"Aw shit." The gate rocked and clanged above me, and I opened my eyes. Stella sounded miffed. "Not very friendly, is he?" She twisted acrobatically to miss jumping down on top of me, "That last shot was up into the air. I think he's gone now, and I picked up the poles."

I spat out mud and God knows what, "You bitch, you bloody, bloody bitch. We could have been killed." I put my fists to my eyes, and tried to push back the springing tears.

"Oh Kate." She crouched down, put her arms under my shoulders and propped me up against the wall. "Oh Kate, I'm sorry." How many times had I heard that from Liz as well? Her hand went to my cheek, and her big body breathed strength and sanity into mine. "I don't think he's trying to kill us, he just wants us to clear off so he can bang at his pheasants." Her hug was as safe as houses, and I stayed there until I thought that, from the absence of further shots and cries, it might not be fatal to come out. I moved to pat my hair. It was like a primitive kind of felt, embedded with a mixture of rain and field, and would require a major cleaning-up operation to be returned to its usual messiness. I dislodged a blade of grass from under my tongue.

"Sorry too. I didn't mean to shout at you, I was really scared." I could even speak semi-normally.

She helped me to my feet, "Not without reason, I suppose. Although a shotgun at that range is rarely deadly for a person wearing lots of clothes."

"I've no more swear words left. Are you sure he's gone?" If I got piles from sitting on the wintry ground, I would sue.

She pretended to scan the horizon with a telescope. "Can't see him. Let's get back to the van."

Only her bulky presence and her arm round my waist made me brave enough to cross the paddock and climb into the van. I was horrified to see how much my hands shook while she laid down the tripod and poles in the back. Safe, you are safe, I forced the mantra round my shattered system. We would soon be home, I would have a hot bath and a gallon of sweet tea, and I would ring the police and have that madman arrested. Stella started the engine, and broke through my reassuring fantasy of picking out the gunman in an identity parade and hearing a judge in a wig send him down for a long time, with stern warnings about the wickedness of firing on defenceless ramblers.

"Er, Kate, how strong are you feeling?"

"Not very. I want you to take me home." If she was planning to do anything else, I would knock her unconscious and hijack the van.

"I'm going to. I only think you should know," she crashed up the gears, "I don't think he was shooting pheasants."

"No? What makes you think that?" Now we were in motion, my hands were calming down.

"Well, you usually beat them out of a wood and try and shoot them when they're flying, don't you? There were no woods there, no other people joining in the fun, no sign of beaters, just one angry jerk with a gun."

I curled and uncurled my fingers automatically, "I don't care, I want to go home. Danger and me don't mix."

I shouldn't have said that. We were approaching the corner, engine straining, escape to the civilised main road nearly complete, and I was delving in pockets for my tobacco.

"Eeeek!" Stella let rip with a scream to rival mine, and swerved us off the tarmac. Bull-bars on the front of a four-wheel drive in the middle of the track clipped our mudguard. I had a glimpse of a face I thought I recognised, and then the side of my head whacked against the window.

"Bastaaard," Stella wailed, as we skidded along the rough grass before hitting the raised lane surface with a filling-loosening jolt. She fought for control and subdued the machine, which wanted to crash us into the railings on the other side, "He's taken my wing mirror!"

I cradled my ear, "Don't stop! I'll buy you another, I'll get one from the scrappy, I'll have one hand blown for you, keep going!"

The engine gave up complaining at being reined in, and resumed its air-cooled rattling.

"Saints preserve us, I knew this trip was a bad idea." Stella smacked the steering wheel and rounded on me, "You could have warned me about the locals."

"A Hearty Northern Welcome Awaits You," I quoted the Tourist Board's slogan, and thought it was the wittiest thing I'd said for months. Stella looked dispassionately at my heaving shoulders and kicking feet.

"Ever thought of getting professional help? I think you're overwrought."

I had my hot bath, and a big mug of tea to accompany it. With my filthy jeans flung into the wash basket and bubbles popping away the chill on my skin, I reduced the morning's horror to an unfortunate incident with which my psyche could cope. We hadn't been in any great danger and Shotgun Man had only been over-zealous in keeping us off his land. I held my nose and submerged myself, feeling the regular beat of my heart, and my body, reliable once more, basking in the luxury of heat and perfumed oils. I rose up, if not smiling then at least on an even keel. I was nearly myself again. Now I could get on to persuading Stella to have a practice with me. I had been right not to seek out my secret stash as soon as we arrived home and take a medicinal joint into the bathroom, I needed to keep a clear head. For her part, Stella had refused the offer of a bath, pointing out that she had remained mostly upright on our little jaunt, and anyway, she had some dry trousers in the van. When I came downstairs, she was on the settee again, examining the contents of our sitting room as if she was filing them away for some version of the memory game. Her dry trousers were bright green. I wasn't convinced that they went with her pink sweater as well as the crimson ones had.

I rolled a cigarette, and sucked the smoke right into the bottom of my lungs.

"Isn't that bad for your health? How many instruments do you play?"

I let smoke trickle from my nostrils, "Not as bad as shotgun pellets. I play the violin reasonably ok, the whistles less so, the guitar a bit and the saxophone worst of all."

"You're so modest. What do you want me to do, then?"

Her voice was no less resonant in our house than it had been in Brigitte's kitchen, and she kept perfectly in tune. Once I'd found the key she was using, I worked out a simple arrangement for the song, and suggested places she could stop so that I could fit in breaks on the violin. I made her run it through with me until we were as note perfect as we were going to be, and then searched around for my file of miscellaneous songs. I thought I would see how quickly she could pick up a song she didn't know, in case Mac decided to try her out with one of his standards. Engrossed in my role as Svengali, I was recovering fast.

"You're so strict," she complained when I brandished a sheet of words in front of her, "I didn't think you'd be such a slave driver."

I employed the bribery system I used on myself, "If you give this a go, we can raid Liz's store cupboards for goodies before we leave."

"Meanie." She listened sulkily while I picked out notes on a whistle. In the event, I only had to play it a couple of times before she was trilling away like a songbird, and I led her straight to the kitchen and the chocolate cake which Liz thought she had hidden from me.

Pleased with my protege, I jumped in her van and directed her to Baker's.

"I still might not sing," she announced stubbornly, standing motionless in the lobby outside the hall. Through the double doors, I could hear instruments tuning up, a microphone being tested, a burst of laughter, the thud of someone jumping off the stage and all the other sounds which made my pulse lift and my blood sing.

I smiled sweetly, "Suit yourself. I'm going in anyway."

The door opened, and Dave's bearded cynical face peeped round it, "Thought I heard your voice, come in, we're about to kick off. . ."

Stella shifted behind me, and Dave registered that she was with me. It was like watching a frog turn into a prince. He came out into the lobby, ran his fingers through his hair, extended a hand and gave his best shot at a smile of boyish charm.

"Hello. I'm Dave. I play with Kate in the band, I'm helping Mac out. And you're. . .?"

"Stella," she said huskily before I could open my mouth, "I've come to sing for Mac."

They shook hands, and I could see the hormones jumping up and down and punching the air. Dave did a neat reversing manouevre, holding the door wide with his left arm, and guiding Stella into the hall as if she was the Queen of Sheba.

"Come and sit here," he crooned, "I'll tell you what's going on. . ."

Nearly letting the door bang into my face, I blundered in after them. By now, I wouldn't have been surprised to see Mac in drag, or Kristin Dale hanging around waiting to see if Mac would let her sing in his band. How hard would it be to force the lock on the door to the bar, and get myself a vodka? I stood like a lemon on floorboards discoloured from years of spilt drinks and stubbed out cigarettes, and cast my eyes round for Mac. Dave had obviously asked Stella how she had got to Baker's, and she was holding up her van keys, laughing girlishly. My sore ear buzzed, and I was back on the track with the four-wheel drive careering towards us. This time, though, I recognised its manic driver. It was Harry, Brigitte's lover and business partner, whom I had last seen creeping from her house near Carlisle a few days before.

7

"Kate! Are you all right?"

"Huh?" I looked slack-mouthed into Dave's hairy face.

"Bloody hell, you've gone all pale and interesting. Here, sit down." He shoved me into a chair, "Maybe you should put your head between your knees or something."

I obeyed, and kept my head down until the floor, and noises around us, came into focus again.

"Ok? Have a swig of this. You look like you did when you drank that pint of damson gin two Christmases ago." He handed me a bottle of water, and I chugged it back thankfully.

"She thought it was wine," he explained helpfully to Stella, "and none of us wanted to disillusion her."

I felt able to smile, now that the cold sweat and nausea had passed, "You were all completely vile, and anyway, it wasn't a whole pint, only a couple of glasses."

He still looked concerned, which was a novelty. "You're not ill, are you? You're not usually given to swooning. . ." He stopped, and very nearly blushed. Fear that I might be suffering from some embarrassing female complaint, which I was about to describe in gory detail, had obviously crossed his mind.

"She got shot this morning," Stella said bluntly, "I don't think it's done her much good."

"Oh yeah? Was it Liz with her machine gun?" Dave lost interest in me, and turned back to Stella, making his eyes twinkle humorously. It was disgusting.

"Seriously," I started, but I didn't stand a chance against

Stella's enthusiastic account of how we had come under a hail of gunfire, and had been forced to crawl for at least a mile to safety.

"It wasn't quite like that. . ." I made a futile attempt to butt in, and was ignored. I fretted. I desperately wanted to ask Stella if she recognised Harry as the driver who had nearly wiped us out. I was trying to get a word in edgeways, when Mac appeared in front of me.

"Kate dearie, stop gossiping and tune up. We're going to start with 'All around my hat' for this girlie to sing with us."

"Oh for heaven's sake." He was too nice a guy to be completely malicious, yet he was having a hard job keeping a straight face. He didn't look too bad, considering, although there were faint grey smudges under his eyes, and his jeans could have done with a wash. I caught myself wondering if he had a washing machine, and brought myself up sharply. I wasn't his mother. I wasn't the tragic victim of a drive-by shooting, either, so I should try to focus on the matter in hand.

"Who is she? Is she any good?" I asked, taking a first proper look at the various women and hangers-on scattered around the hall.

"There, over there with the long skirt," he flicked his hand discreetly. "She's called Melanie, and says she's sung in a band before. I've never seen her in my life."

I squinted critically at the young woman. She should lose the beads and that look of artistic suffering, I judged cruelly, and I bet she's adenoidal.

I was right. We all, even Dave and Stella, quietened down and paid attention while Mac explained that we would run through some tunes, that anyone who wanted could have a go at singing, and that we would try to accommodate requests. He ended with a plea for good behaviour and tolerance, disguising it as a jolly comment that this was meant to be a fun session, and it would be nice if everyone listened to everyone else.

"So, no booing or yelling 'next!'," I warned Dave on my way up to the stage.

He must have been sorely tempted when Melanie opened

her mouth, and I know I winced more than once when she strayed further and further from the consensus of which tune we were playing. As the afternoon wore on, I could sense Stella's confidence rising and Dave's patience wearing thin. The only singer who could keep in tune was terrified of the microphone, and I'd soon had more than enough of faithless blacksmiths, lecherous sailors and merry months of May. I was still nervous enough for Stella's sake to prise her away from Dave for a few minutes before her turn, and make her sing some bars in the ladies loo to warm up. I needn't have fussed. She sailed on to the stage like a seasoned professional, winked at Dave, hummed the note I gave her, shut her eyes for a second, then gave me the signal to start.

From the quality of the hush that descended immediately on the hall, I knew she had found her calling. There were no whispers, shufflings of feet or rummagings in bags, and the only thing that mattered to me was softly following her voice, and trying to echo it in the breaks. The end of the song came far too quickly. After years of performing, I still felt my heart kick at the rare moment of silence before the ragged wave of clapping, appreciative cries and stamping. Stella bowed, mouthed a genuine-seeming thanks into the microphone and, ten foot tall, walked off the stage. At the bottom of the steps, she turned and touched my arm.

"Why didn't you tell me it was like that? It's better than sex almost, I wanted to sing for hours, I wasn't scared at all, I felt I belonged on that stage, was I really all right. . ." The high had hit her, making her babble.

"You were fantastic," I began, then Mac was there, trying to catch her eye.

"You're not rushing off, are you?" he said quickly. "We'll have to hear these other two out, but I'd really like to have a talk."

She beamed munificently, "I'm in no hurry, honey. Take your time."

"Great." He gave me a comradely nudge with his elbow, "And thanks, Kate, you two sounded ace together." Composing his triumphant features so it didn't look too obvious that he had already made up his mind, he went to encourage a shy girl who had tried and failed to walk on the stage three times already.

"Yeah, thanks teacher," Stella put her arm round my shoulders. "Thanks for nagging and making me come here and everything. This could all be a lot of fun."

"You're welcome." I saw Dave hovering, slipped from her embrace, and shot him a smile. He didn't see it. He was gazing at Stella as though he had opened an ordinary-looking parcel and found the Holy Grail inside. Serves you right, I thought uncharitably, you thought you were flirting with some talentless bimbo, now see what you've got yourself into. I left him to his inarticulate congratulations, and went to chat with Spiff.

The last two hopefuls weren't a patch on Stella, and by early evening, everyone else had drifted off, leaving Mac, Spiff, Dave, Stella and me packing equipment away, with the men showering compliments like confetti on Stella.

"Bar's open," Dave said, folding up a mike stand, "let's leave this lot, and talk business over a drink. I'm buying, it's not every day I find such a pearl among swine."

"Yeuch," I muttered to Spiff, "he's overdoing it a bit."

"Don't blame him," Spiff moaned, his eyes dazed, "it's a shame I'm too young for her. Maybe she'll work round to me eventually."

I rolled my eyes, "Dream on, Sunshine. Tell Dave mine's a vodka, I'm off to powder my nose."

When I went into the bar, the four of them were ensconced round a corner table, Stella looking completely at home. Dave was slipping his mobile back into his pocket.

"Oh. That was your missus, you just missed her," he said with a leer, "she's on her way home, she sounded cross."

I let my hand slip lovingly around my vodka glass, "Why? She knew I'd be here."

"She only wanted to know if we'd finished and how your day went," he smirked.

I couldn't think of anything I'd done wrong that she knew about. I looked at Dave more closely, and my heart sank. "Oh Dave, you didn't," I implored.

"Didn't what? I mean, I might have mentioned your little

encounter with a crazed gunman, to make conversation." He poured half his pint down his throat, "We're thinking of going round to Pat and Tom's after this, see about your old flat for Stella. You coming?"

"You bugger." Foreboding settled in my intestines, "I'll have to go home. Stella, what did he tell her?"

"More or less what I told him, lovey. Why don't you come with us? I can give you a lift home later. If Liz has got the hump, it'll give her time to calm down." Great, she was already teasing me like the rest of the band did.

"Ha!" I downed my vodka in one. "You all know I'm better getting it over with. Let me know if you decide to move down here, Stella, and see you tomorrow, Dave, for the trip to Birmingham, unless I'm in casualty."

Pursued by their laughing entreaties to stay, I charged out of the bar. Bloody Dave, he would have made it sound as if I had been inches from death, and he knew very well that this would wind Liz up. I'd conveniently forgotten both my own belief, behind the wall, that I only had minutes to live, and also that I hadn't checked out with Stella about Harry. The weather had switched from rain to wind, and I battled through the streets to a house full of bad signs. The lights were off downstairs, the fire was unlit, and there was no Liz in the kitchen. I threw off my coat, left my violin in the hall and stomped upstairs. I had guessed right. Liz was in the spare room, which she had appropriated as an office, making out that she was doing something vital on her laptop. She deigned to swivel round at my panting entrance. She had a face like fat.

I tried to jump in first. "Don't believe Dave, it was only. . ."

"Why didn't you call me? What were you thinking of? How do you expect me to concentrate on the business if you're running round getting shot at every time I turn my back?" She was incandescent with rage.

I worked myself up. The vodka helped. "That's ridiculous. It was one old man with a shotgun, and Stella says. . ."

"Stella!" Her shriek rattled the window, "You're never going anywhere with her again. Stella, Stella, Stella, that's all I've heard since Brigitte's sodding party. I should never have taken you, I should have gone on my own like I wanted to."

I scented blood. "Oho! That's what it is, you're jealous, you stupid. . . Russian besom. You'd never say it outright, you're too bloody screwed up and. . ." I pulled a word out of a hat, ". . .and dysfunctional!"

"Don't make me laugh! How could I be jealous of that woman-mountain?" By now, her chair had toppled sideways on to the floor.

"Well, maybe you should be," I bellowed with alarming illogicality, "maybe it's nice for me to spend time with someone who shares my interests. . ."

"Interests? What interests have you got except for your band and physical gratification, you selfish lump?"

Her breasts rose and fell, her eyes widened, and I buckled at the knees under an avalanche of desire. It must be true what they said about danger being an aphrodisiac.

"Christ." I seized her hand, dragged her to our room, and threw her on the bed. The button flew off her fancy trousers, and I smashed my elbow against the headboard, but it was nothing in the drive to the moment when she gave way to a ferocious pleasure which nearly landed us both on the floor.

"Damn you." She rolled over on top of me, gave me a feral smile and lowered her head.

At the liquid brush of her tongue, I came apart at the seams. I was crying, her arms came round me, and her mouth, tender now, kissed at my tears.

"Please don't do this with anyone else."

"I couldn't."

We pulled the quilts over us, and slowly made up some more.

"I thought I'd stopped getting so angry with you," Liz said at last.

I could see right to the back of her eyes, "Why were you so mad? You called me a lump. That was mean." Entwined like this, it was difficult to tell where she ended and I began.

"Well you are." Her hand moved slightly, and another warm wave rippled through me, "A lovely, beautiful, sexy lump. I'm sorry, I didn't mean any of it. Especially about going to Brigitte's on my own. It would have been horrible without you. I just wanted to hurt you."

"Why?" It had almost been worth the row, to end up like this. Like wind in a field of corn, a sigh arched and fell under her skin.

"Oh Kate, you didn't seem bothered about how dangerous it was this morning, and you never came to me first after it happened. I couldn't bear it that I wasn't there to look after you."

"Ah." At any other time, I might have thought this was a bit rich, seeing as it was usually her that led me astray. The mad thing was, in that instant I believed her.

"You see," the affection in her small smile robbed her words of any sting, and completed the transformation of my heart into runny jelly, "sometimes I think you potter along in your own little world, thinking of music all the time, and you don't realise how concerned I get for you. Even after all the scrapes we've been in."

"That's not true," I was too involved in stroking her hair to be indignant, "I was really bothered by this morning, and I don't think of music all the time."

"Ok, maybe not when we're like this, or when you're eating, but the rest of the time you are. You're always humming and tapping and running things through in your head."

"Perhaps." I hadn't realised that I was so transparent.

"Of course, that's why I fell for you," she became less serious and started nibbling my eyebrows, "I saw you playing in a trance, and thought, 'I've got to have that woman, and make her want me as much as she wants to play her music.'"

I hugged her tightly, "And you succeeded, you clever thing. Now I'm completely in your power."

"Good." She bit my neck lightly, "If I go and make some sandwiches, you have to tell me exactly what went on this morning."

I was admirably frank with Liz, although I may have left her with the impression that the man with the shotgun hadn't fired straight at us. I didn't have to over-emphasise how cowardly I'd been, she knew the tiny limits of my courage.

"And it was rubbish me saying you should be jealous of Stella," I concluded, "I think she and Dave have fallen in lust. I can't wait to see what happens next, I'm going to have to ring Bill before we meet up tomorrow and tell him."

If I'd left it there, we would probably have finished our picnic supper and enjoyed a long untroubled sleep. As it was, some niggling prompting drove me to add a postscript, in the form of a graphic account of how we'd been forced off the road by a driver who I was convinced was Brigitte's Harry.

"It may not have been, of course." I wound up my tale and lit a cigarette, "But I'm sure I recognised him. What could he have been doing, visiting Shotgun Man. . .Liz? Liz, what's wrong?"

Her body had slipped away from mine, and her face had congealed into a mask of indifference. The hand which moved her plate from the quilt seemed to belong to another person, not to the woman who had been a part of me an hour before. She got out of bed in silence, and went to the bathroom. When she came back, she had put on a robe, and she sat on the very edge of the bed, as though she had never touched me.

I tried to smoke without choking. "Not again," my insides moaned, "what have I said now?"

Minutes ticked by. Finally, her hand reached out behind her, and she coughed.

"Give us a drag, babe."

I passed her the remains of my cigarette without a word, and she smoked it without comment. Then she stubbed it out on her plate, something I'd never seen her do before. Her mouth twisted in disgust.

"Oh fuck." Her shoulders shrugged once, and she sounded hoarse, "Listen, Kate, there's stuff I have to tell you. I didn't want to, but I can't put it off any more."

"What kind of stuff?" I prayed that I didn't sound as scared as I felt.

She shrugged again, as if warding off a wasp, "Stuff about

the past. Brigitte and me."

"Right." I was rigid on the bed.

"I'm not proud of this, but it happened, even if it was years ago and I was a different person then."

Relief tingled along my veins, "You mean, it's nothing that's going on now?"

She snorted irritably, "No, aren't you listening to me? Goddammit woman, I'm trying to confess here." The minute flash of her usual self encouraged me, and I flipped back the quilt.

"Well, get in here and confess away. You'll catch cold, sitting out there."

"Bugger it." She climbed in beside me.

"There's a lot about me you don't know," she stated, as if she was saying something new.

"Blow me, and I thought you were such an open book." Sarcasm was my friend in this hour of need.

She snorted again, "Look, shut up and listen, this is hard for me."

"I'm listening," I snapped, "you're just not telling me anything."

She cursed creatively, then screwed her eyes shut, the way she did when she was about to say something I wouldn't like. The words tumbled out.

"I'm not a nice person, like you seem to think, I've done some really bad things, criminal things." She opened her eyes, and noticed that I hadn't run wailing from the bed. She slowed down, and in a level voice, risked telling me the worst.

"I was friends with Brigitte all through college, and when we left, we went into this squat. We did all these drugs, and didn't have any money, so. . .so we were thieves, basically."

"Thieves?" I cheeped. I wasn't sure how shocked I was.

"Yeah. Well," her arms unfolded imperceptibly, "I was more of the thief. You know, nothing major or organised, just shoplifting and anything lying around, handbags, wallets, the odd car." She was getting more confident, "Not every day, only when we were desperate, and from people who could afford it, not like heroin addicts who rob their

79

neighbours and relatives."

"How quaint. So what was Brigitte's speciality? Blackmail? Arson?" The sense of unreality I sometimes used to feel around her had returned.

She hesitated, and sounded ashamed again. "No," she said quietly, "when things were really bad, she used to sleep with men for money." There was more than shame there, her voice held something I couldn't quite grasp, a barely audible counterpoint to her steady recitative.

"This is what happened. Brigitte brought a man back to the squat one night, and he started getting rough with her. I heard it, I was in the next room. I had this old truncheon I'd found, and I went through and beat him up with it. Then we got some guys to drive him out to the docks and dump him. He could have died, I didn't hang around to find out. A day and a ton of drugs later, I woke up in some strange woman's bed. I couldn't even remember what the sex was like. I knew I had to get out," she turned to me, her eyes shuttered, "so I picked up a few things from the squat, hitched to ma's in Bath, cleaned up my act and didn't go back to London for a year." A new wretchedness unnerved her calm, "I've warned you before that I can be violent, but you never believe me. Now you know. I'm not sure I'm worth it, Kate, underneath perhaps I'm still that awful junkie person, who's no good for anyone, let alone someone like you, who's normal and loving and. . ."

"No!" I put my hands to my face, and spoke against the swelling in my throat, "Stop a minute, let me just take this in." I lay there, a fog blanketing my heart and mind. The day had been too long, and overly traumatic, for me to deal rationally with this. I clutched at certainties. The only time I'd ever seen her violent was with someone whom she believed was going to hurt me. A ray of sunlight glinted through the fog, and the penny dropped.

I reached out to her unyielding thigh, "Liz, you were in love with Brigitte, weren't you?"

8

I had hit the bulls-eye. Her head jerked, and I touched her hand under the quilt. Our fingers curled together out of a habit which all that she had said could not break.

"No. . . I mean yes, in a way, I suppose I was." The shame she had tried to subdue overwhelmed her voice.

I tightened my grip, "Don't be so hard on yourself. You were only trying to protect her, like you do with me. Do you really think you killed that man?" I couldn't believe that I was talking so calmly.

She twitched, "Not really, no. I didn't hit him on the head, more on his back and arms, and I kicked him in the balls. I doubt it was fatal. But that doesn't stop me having nightmares every now and then." She pulled herself up against the pillows, and spoke more harshly, "I was crazy. Since I was a teenager, I'd known not to bother with straight women, and there I was, running after Brigitte like a lost puppy."

It was my turn to snort, "Yeah, and it's so easy to control who you fall for." Before I could stop it, the question I was telling myself I wouldn't ask jumped out of my mouth. "Did you never sleep with her then?"

Her hand contracted in mine, "She let me fuck her once. She was stoned and curious. I think it meant nothing to her."

It was as if she had slapped me. When she used that word in bed with me, it was with a kindly, desperate longing, not this vicious crudeness. I was going to let go of her hand, but stopped when I saw her mouth trembling.

"And to you?" However terrible the truth was, it could not

torment me as much as not knowing.

"I'd wanted her for years. It was the best ever until I was with you."

She knew how to pick her moment. I had waited over a year for this, and she had to tell me when I was in no fit state to respond.

"You mean. . .?" This had been a conversation which could spell ruin to our relationship, and I couldn't stop the smile leaking over my face.

For the first time since she had come back from the bathroom, she let me into her eyes.

"That's why I never tell you this stuff. It's so good with you, I think I'll lose it if I do."

"Why have you told me now?" I was whispering.

"Do you wish I hadn't?" It was almost a challenge, and I felt my smile fade, and my eyes shy away.

"Maybe." I hadn't had nearly enough time to work that one out. "So why?"

Through her hand, I could sense a tangle of fear, determination and bleak resignation snarling through her body.

"I don't know. When you mentioned seeing Harry today, it was suddenly. . .inevitable that I would. I thought of telling you the morning after Brigitte's party, but it seemed impossible to do. I suppose I hoped I'd stop remembering, and it would all go away."

I thought back to the party, and Liz's dive into the ouzo. "Did Brigitte talk about it when she got you on your own?" No wonder Liz had escaped into drink, with all this bubbling under the surface.

"Not in so many words." She settled back, as if I'd somehow let her off the hook, "Let's face it, however Brigitte's making her money, you can bet your bottom dollar it won't be a hundred percent legal. All she told me was that she was on to a good thing, and did I want in. I said no. When I went in with Ben, I made up my mind not to get involved in any more dodgy deals, you know that."

"No, I don't." I was astonished at how testy I sounded, "You never told me. You never tell me anything. I still don't understand why me seeing Harry should bring all this up. . ."

"God, Kate, work it out! You tell me that someone goes to the lengths of shooting at you to keep you off his land, and then along comes Harry down that private road as if he owns it. Harry's with Brigitte, I know Brigitte is probably incapable of keeping on the right side of the law. Fuck knows what you and Stella blundered into, I can't let you or her go back there again for another go, knowing what I know about Brigitte. She and Harry could be into drug dealing in a big way, for her to live like that. And if I just told you to keep away, you'd do exactly the opposite, to annoy me. I had to tell you. Besides," she went back to being wretched, "you deserve to know the truth about me. Even if it changes how you feel."

I didn't say anything. I privately thought she was being melodramatic about the likelihood that Stella and I had stumbled across a criminal rendez-vous. As for how I felt. . .

She threw the quilt aside. "I'm going to have a bath," she said abruptly. I didn't move. She stood for a moment by the bed, shaking out the creases in her robe. Her shoulders went up to her ears again, "Will you come in with me?"

Everything hinged on her mundane question. Following her would be an admission that I could forgive her anything. Staying where I was would open up a breach between us that I would have no idea how to cross.

I tried to pick out a middle route. "I don't think I'd have liked you when you were younger," I stated baldly.

"No, I don't think you would."

Our inadequate voices were the only link between us.

"I didn't know you had nightmares." It sounded as if I was accusing her.

"Only when you're away."

That holed me below the waterline, she fought so dirty sometimes. I reached for a tissue and blew my nose.

"I'll start running the water. I don't want you to see what I left in the bath after this morning."

"This is a bit nice," Liz remarked, all the nobbles along her spine relaxing as I sponged her back.

"It's more than you deserve. I should be using a brillo pad." Once more, hot foamy water was bringing me back into the land of the living. "Why don't you write down all the bad things you've done, and give it to me to read while I'm somewhere else with the band? Then I'll be able to see if I should stick with you or not."

She leaned back against me, and positioned my arms around her waist, "It would take me too long. That's the worst, I promise."

"No more nasty shocks?" I buried my nose in her hair. Whatever my mind said, my body went its own way to have this perfect fit restored.

"No." She jiggled her knees, and water swilled around us, "You're staying overnight in Birmingham tomorrow and Saturday night, aren't you?"

"That's the plan." None of us had volunteered to drive home in the early hours of Sunday morning. The organisers of Saturday's gig were famous for their post-performance parties.

She decorated my leg with a handful of bubbles, "Can I come down on Saturday night and bring you home? Or do you have to stay?"

As a rule, she never asked so politely. I gave in completely.

"That would be really good. So long as you don't mind putting in an appearance if they have a party afterwards."

"I don't mind." She hooked at the plug chain with her toes, "Just shoot me if I go anywhere near the ouzo."

By late Sunday afternoon, peace and stability had seemingly returned to the Sharpe-Halton household. The only side-effect of being shot at was a slightly worse than usual case of the jitters before we went on stage on Friday night. Moreover, I had solved the problem of the cautious atmosphere between Liz and me on the drive back from Birmingham by falling asleep. Now, with the fire lit, the curtains drawn against a rainy dusk, and a tea tray on the floor, we were pleasantly occupied in a rambling argument over Liz's proposal that we should re-decorate the front room. I was working on the principle that if I acted as though nothing had changed, nothing would.

"I can't see what's wrong with a combination of these yellows. I think they'd be tasteful." I held a couple of the paint charts Liz had picked up at a DIY store towards the light.

"But they're so common nowadays," Liz complained, "I think we should go for something more dramatic, like a deep red at least on one wall. It'll be really warm."

"What about in summer? It'll be too much."

"Plants," Liz said enigmatically.

"Plants?" I inspected her more closely, to see if she was serious.

"Yeah. We could have some nice big plants instead of all this junk. They'd be very cooling. We could aim for a conservatory effect."

She saw me glance at the only plant in the room, a dessicated lemon geranium, and began to laugh, "Oh, well, maybe we could try some cacti."

"Sort of a New Mexico desert effect?" I flipped the paint charts on to the floor, "It'll be a struggle anyway to clear out this room so we can actually reach the walls."

She fished the magazine from the heap of Sunday newspaper. "But we'll have to sort it out if we want to sub-let the house while we're in the States, so we can kill two birds with one stone. . .Good God, these fashions are unbelievable, would you pay three thousand pounds for that mess?" She showed me the picture of a model wearing what looked like an enlarged dishcloth, "Nice boobs and legs, though, wonder who she is. . .?"

We were playing tug-of-war with the magazine when there was a timid knock at the door. None of our friends were so restrained, so we assumed the worst.

"Jehovah's Witnesses," I gasped, relinquishing my hold on the ruined pages, "you get it, pervy."

"Get it yourself, prudey. Tell them we're beyond saving."

I put on an unwelcoming grimace, and yanked the door open. "Mrs T.!" I remembered to change the grimace into a smile, "Come in, it's horrible out there, Liz is just putting the kettle on. . .Is everything all right?" Her normally placid face was oddly tight, as if her hair was hurting her.

"I. . .oh dear. . .it's probably nothing. . .shouldn't disturb you. . .spoiling your free time. . ." She wasn't usually incoherent, either. Mind you, she might have dreaded interrupting whatever we did on a Sunday afternoon.

"Sit down," I said firmly, sweeping newspapers, a book and an ashtray from our best armchair, "sit down, have a cup of tea, and tell us what's wrong."

"It's Edna," she said, perched on the edge of the chair like a worried budgie, "I always ring her about this time on a Sunday to discuss changing our lottery numbers, and I did, and there was no reply. It's not like her, she wasn't going out that she told me, and I know you'll think I'm a daft old bat. . ."

"Not at all," Liz said diplomatically, "you said she hasn't been too good lately."

"That's it. She's been having this girl round from that agency to do some cleaning, what with her heart being dicky and her legs all to pot, not that she couldn't get someone from the social if she wasn't so bloddy proud and insisting on paying, the silly madam. I said to her, I said, I'll ring the bloddy office for you and fill in the bloddy forms, but oh no, she wouldn't have any of it, accused me of being tight as a crab's arse and went ahead. . ."

She could always curse with the best of us, but the faint Slavic intonation, which I hadn't heard in her voice before, was a measure of her agitation.

"Would you like one of us to nip round to her house, and see if she's there?" I didn't want her to work herself up into a frenzy of fearful speculation, nor to voice what I was sure Liz was thinking as well, that Edna might be lying at the foot of her stairs with a broken hip or worse.

Mrs T. looked more uncomfortable. She hated asking for favours. "Of course, I'd walk round if it was fine. . ."

After the ritual of offers and counter-proposals which etiquette demanded, all three of us piled into the car and drove the few hundred yards to Edna's street. Her unlit windows confirmed my suspicion that all was not well with her, and I took Mrs T.'s arm when she insisted on getting out of the car, and pounding futilely on the blank front door. Liz peered through the window facing the street,

"I can't see anything. Maybe I should go round the back. . ."

The door of the next house along popped open, and the warm smell of chips wafted out. "She ent there, so piss off.. Pardon, Mrs Tweddle, didn't recognise you love. Sorry duck, she's int 'ospital. They cem and tek 'er an hour ago. Right poorly she looked. The wife would 'ave rung you if she weren't at work." He was a big man, with a shaved head, and tattoos snaking out from his rolled up sleeves.

Mrs T. swayed and shrunk beside me, and Liz quickly took her other arm, "Which hospital?" she snapped. In the streetlamp, rain glistened like tears on her cheeks.

"Infirmary. Not to worry, Mrs T.," his tone was more awkward than confidence-inspiring, "they'll have her right in no time." He cleared his throat, "So shall we feed that cat of hers for while she's in, or do you want the old bugger?"

"Cat?" I asked blankly.

"Ay, that big hairy effort. Dainty she calls it."

Mrs T. was still unable to speak, and Liz evidently couldn't deal with any more complications. "Fucksake, who cares about the cat," she muttered under her breath. She raised her voice, "If you could feed it till tomorrow, we'll decide then."

"Fair do's. Chin up, Mrs T." He disappeared back into his house.

Liz, far better than me in a crisis, put an arm round Mrs T.'s bowed shoulders, "Come on, we'll go back to ours, have a tot of something medicinal and phone the hospital. It might just be tests, we don't know yet. . ."

Sadly, all our hot toddies and soothing clichés counted for nothing in the scheme of things. I saw from Liz's set face when I returned on Monday evening from a long session of polishing up new material with the band, that not even the Infirmary had been able to keep Edna with us.

"Yeah, she died this lunchtime," she said, and carried on sorting through a pile of bills, as if she didn't already know which were paid and which needed urgent attention.

I made some tea, warming the pot and measuring out the

leaves with concentrated precision, then took the tray into the sitting room with enormous care. You never knew, slopped milk could be an invitation to death to linger in our streets.

"How's Mrs T.?" I asked, to stop my vision blurring.

"Not brilliant." She tried to fit the telephone bill, with its pages of itemised calls, back into its envelope. The uneven pages bulged, the envelope creased and ripped, and she hurled the lot against the wall. "Jesus Christ!" her broken shout jolted my arm, and sent hot tea on to my jeans, "we didn't know her that well. I can't think why I feel so shitty. . ."

I abandoned my mug and opened my arms, and for the first time ever, we mourned together for someone other than ourselves.

"It's all your fault, I never cried until I met you," Liz accused eventually, throwing a wad of tissues with unnerving accuracy into the bin in the corner.

All my remaining self-control went into making one of our jokes, rather than embarking on an analysis which might take us further than I was ready to go. "You see, you've found your inner child."

"Inner drip, more like." She poured herself some tea, "Mrs T.'s got the card school round this evening. I think they're going to all get tiddly on sweet sherry, and badmouth Edna's eldest son, Brian, who never visits, not like Ray. . ."

". . .Who comes all the way from London for her birthday and takes her to a show, and one year flew her down for 'Phantom of the Opera.'" I completed the familiar refrain.

Liz slurped her tea, "Did you notice anything different about the kitchen?"

I quaked. Had she bashed a hole in the wall, and I hadn't realised?

"Um. . ."

She put me out of my misery, "Go and look at that corner by the washing machine."

I obeyed meekly, and charged back again.

"Where is it? Where did you get it from, is it. . .?" Liz had always refused point-blank whenever I had so much as hinted at how nice it would be to have a cat, yet there on the floor was a litter-tray, and on one of the surfaces, now I was paying attention, was a carrier bag full of cans.

"Don't get too excited," Liz was doing her best to look nonchalant, "it's only Edna's. I said we'd mind it till one of her sons claimed it. It's under the armchair. It's probably stuck, it's so fat."

I dropped to the floor, and put my face on the carpet. A pair of amber eyes looked balefully into mine.

"Dainty, Dainty," I sang softly, "come on out and have some milk."

I spent most of the rest of the evening in the same position, shoving delicacies in front of a disdainful nose, and then pulling them back a few feet to see if the object of my attention would emerge. Success came with refusing to surrender. The smell of a tinned sardine was finally too much for Dainty, there was a resigned mew, an undignified squeeze, and out she came. She may have been dainty in her youth, but the name was hardly appropriate for a mature, long-haired tortoiseshell, about the size of a small child. She gulped down the sardine without so much as a thank-you, licked her lips, hiccupped, and began a stately tour of inspection of the accommodations. A protracted scratching and displacing of cat litter from the kitchen told us that she had located her tray, then she reappeared, sniffed her way on to the hearthrug, and commenced a noisy wash.

"It's got a comb," Liz said, in a tone which managed to convey how absurd a notion this was, "you have to comb it every day. Mrs T. can't have it, she's allergic. So don't go thinking I've gone completely soft, or that I'm trying to make up to you for being a bad lot in my youth."

I tore my eyes from Dainty's supple contortions. I recognised the opening and sighed internally. I really didn't feel up to a heartfelt discussion of whether Liz's admissions had led to any profound emotional shift in me, not least because I still hadn't figured it out. Benign nature intervened, in the shape of one of our largest resident spiders taking an evening stroll across the hearthrug. Of course, Liz wasn't afraid of spiders; they were just not her favourite creatures, and she didn't see why she had to be the one to remove them from the bath or the kitchen sink. We both watched mesmerised as Dainty stopped her ablutions, crouched like a tiger, wiggled her behind and pounced. The murder was over in a flash. The cat swallowed delicately, gave a feline smile, and resumed grooming her stomach.

"Oh my," Liz was genuinely moved, "I think she can stay for a while, then."

9

Edna's funeral was on the Friday of that week, and the few days leading up to it were not the easiest of times. I was vaguely aware that her death was a final weight, tipping the scales to alter the comfy balance of the life I had left before I went on tour. If I pictured Liz's confessions, Mac and Suzie splitting up, and Brigitte's party, not to mention getting shot at and being stuck up a tree, as a line of stationary cars, waiting for the lights to change, then this tragedy was the vehicle which ploughed into the back of the queue, causing a multiple pile-up. Like a passenger in shock, I stood helplessly on the roadside, unable to react apart from agitating that this would make me late for my next appointment. I could see that I should be facing up to what Liz had said, and in between keeping an eye on Mrs T. and playing with the band, I made various attempts to focus on what was going on in my emotional mudflats. It wasn't much good. I had become so hopelessly used to the idea that Liz and I were together for the long haul, that I couldn't quite reconcile the capable, beautiful and funny, if moody, irritating and amoral, lover I knew with the picture she painted of an out and out lowlife criminal. Lying against her sleeping warmth at night, I poked at my different fears to find out which one jumped up and scared me the most. Since there was no way I wanted her not to be there, I ticked knowing more about her making me bored off my list. Neither was I particularly afraid that she would ever be violent to me: everytime I had provoked her, recently and further back in the past, she had invariably taken out her fury on inanimate objects. Maybe I was still most uneasy about how much she regretted renouncing her former carefree life of casual affairs and shady sidelines to settle down with me, and how much a small, unrepentant part of her might have loved to team up with Brigitte again. The killer blow, though, was a persistent voice reminding me that since she had now risked telling me what she was most ashamed of, I was going to have to reciprocate if we were to move on. I resisted for as long as I could, and we spent the week tiring ourselves out with work and worrying over Mrs T., both of us steadfastly refusing to acknowledge that we were heading for the meaningful conversation I dreaded.

It wasn't all doom and gloom, however. Poor orphaned Dainty took quite a shine to me, and I devoted time to lowering my blood pressure by combing her fly-away locks and stroking her as she sagged into my lap like a purring sack of flour. I was also cheered up by a summons to Pat's kitchen for a gossipfest on Wednesday morning. I arrived to find Bill already there, setting out Pat's coffee cups and saucers, and whisking croissants out of the oven. Bill and I had been very disappointed with Dave so far. All over the weekend in Birmingham, and on Monday, he had refused to rise to the hints about Stella which we had expertly cast like lures in front of him, and had professed ignorance when I asked directly if she was going to move down to the city. We had surreptitiously studied him, like professors observing the subject of a psychological experiment, but had seen none of the conclusive signs of a man in love, unrequited or not.

"He'll crack soon," Bill had murmured optimistically at one point, "didn't you see how he nearly came in late on that last set? He's got his mind on other things, you mark my words."

This morning, he was setting the scene for whatever Pat wanted to discuss with all the fussy care of a designer for one of those photo-shoots of the happy home lives of the rich and famous.

"No! Wait!" he commanded, as my hand, pulled by an invisible force, shot towards the croissants, "Pat's on the phone, we mustn't start until she comes through."

"Aw, come on, they'll get cold." My mouth was drooling

at the thought of those golden buttery flakes, melting like ambrosia on my tongue.

He slapped my wrist. "You're not good with delayed gratification, are you? Liz'll have to stop satisfying your urges on demand."

"Oooh, do I detect a tiny touch of envy? 'Im indoors having trouble with his back again?"

"You can get lost. I'm not giving you details of my private life."

We wrangled on happily until Pat appeared, bursting so much with news that her mouth was shaking with the effort of keeping it shut.

After the necessary sober exchange of condolences for Edna, and an update of how Mrs T. was bearing up, Pat could contain herself no longer.

"Well, that Stella's moving into the flat upstairs. She came down to see Mac again yesterday, and guess who called round with her last night to check the offer was still there?"

"Dave!" Bill and I shouted simultaneously, causing a minor snowstorm of croissant crumbs.

Pat's face fell. "Bum. How did you know?"

"I was at that practice, remember," I said smugly, "wasn't it obvious when they came round afterwards?"

"I wasn't paying much attention to him," Pat said, clearly mentally kicking herself, "I was trying to weigh her up. What d'you think then, she seems nice. . .bit of a snappy dresser."

Like vultures at a carcase, we dissected everything we knew of Dave's romantic past: his failed marriage; the minutiae of his many encounters since; and his tally of conquests on the recent tour.

"Only four definites," I concluded, counting on my fingers, "because we can't be sure about his movements that night we left Cologne."

"He was gone for at least fifteen minutes after we'd finished packing up," Bill pointed out.

I guffawed, "Surely that wasn't long enough. I'd have asked for my money back."

"Fifteen minutes would do me fine at the present moment," Bill refilled his coffee cup, and tried to look sex-starved.

"And me," Pat joined the ranks of the deprived, "take me to Manchester one day soon, Bill darling. You can cruise the bars, and I'll pick up a travelling salesman in a hotel for a night of cheap champagne and depravity."

She had requested this so often that I ignored it. I brought the meeting to order, "We're getting off the point. I'll tell you something about Stella. . ." I recounted what I'd learned about her proclivities, finishing with my considered judgement, ". . .So I think she'll have Dave for breakfast, and spit his bones out down the fire-escape."

Pat smiled, "Do him good. I've missed having someone crying at my kitchen table. He can take over your role, while Stella breaks his heart anew by leading a string of different lovers up the stairs."

We imagined this pretty scenario for a while, then my mind hopped to another topic,

"How're Tom and Dodgy? Have they come across any more cases of disappearing valuables?"

"No, thank goodness, it all seems to have gone quiet on that front. Though I suppose I'm duty bound to tell them that Mrs T.'s friend has died, so they can hover at the wake. Still," she gave me a sly dig in the ribs, "Stella's promised to pay the rent regularly. She's carrying on working for those Caring Hands people, but she's just taking on local jobs, instead of going away, so she can practise with Mac's lot. We might be able to pay the gas bill this winter, and I can't think that Stella will eat as much as you."

I looked down my nose at her, "Oh pardon me. I was under the impression that you liked having an unpaid babysitter, assistant for Tom and confidante."

"Needs must when the Devil drives. Why don't you put the kettle on again, and tell us about this friend of Liz's where you met Stella?"

Fortified by this restorative session, and congratulating myself that I had succeeded in describing Brigitte and her party without arousing Pat's suspicion that it had been anything more that a straightforward social event, I made it to Friday. The band had no engagement, and Liz had decided to take a couple of hours off work, so we were both free to drive Mrs T. to the crematorium and to give her moral support. I hadn't foreseen that the funeral would be so touching. Since I had expected a brief, platitudinous converyor-belt service, conducted by a minister who'd never met Edna, and attended by a few of her contemporaries, I was surprised at the turn-out, and by the fact that we weren't the youngest present. The majority of the company may have been dressed-up pensioners, torn between the sadness of the occasion and the impulse to socialise, but there was also a bevy of young women, and a row of uncomfortable teenagers squished into an approximation of formal garb.

"They're from the Day Centre," Mrs T. told us in a stage-whisper, pointing at the young women, "and those are her boy Brian's children and their half cousins. Let me see, Edna's brother married a woman from down Keswick Avenue, and they had two sons and a daughter, so that one there with the spots must be the daughter's eldest, and. . ."

Nodding in the right places, and trying not to look at the shiny coffin on its sliding plinth, we let her derive what comfort she could from her genealogical exposition.

"Which is Ray? Doesn't he have children?" I asked, when what was left of my consciousness was overloaded with information about exam results, achievements on the football field and unplanned pregnancies.

Mrs T. looked faintly shocked, "Oh no, dear, didn't we tell you? He never married, there he is in the front pew with his friend, Walter, next to Brian and his wife."

"Ah." I had wondered who the middle-aged pair in matching black overcoats were. Was it my imgination, or was there really a distinct gap between these two men, and the pompous-looking couple next to them? I smiled at their backs. The piped music died away, a shuffling sigh ran through the chapel, and the service began.

I held out through the minister's kind jokes about Edna's love of gambling and the hopeful assurances of the Victorian hymns. It was only when a scarlet-faced adoloescent shambled to the front, and announced that he was going to read "me gran's favourite poem" that I succumbed. Struggling to weep quietly and respectably, I hardly heard a word. I didn't want to be reminded of my mortality and the passing of love. Liz, her features shored up by sub-standard concrete that might crumble at any time, put one hand under Mrs T.'s elbow, and passed me a tissue with the other. The end of the service came not a moment too soon. I left Mrs T. to murmur with Ray, while I stood outside, breathing in great chestfuls of cold, traffic-fumey air.

"All right?" Liz demanded, eyes narrowed in her rigid determination to remain unaffected, "Ray wants Mrs T. to go back to Edna's house with them for a drink. There's space for two in his car. You can go with her and make sure she's ok, and ask if anyone wants that cat."

"Fine." I could be as businesslike as her, "You get back to work."

She moved swiftly off, and I went to do my duty by Mrs T. For a while, this required me to do nothing more than wait while she and Ray carried on hushed conversations with departing mourners. Finding myself standing next to Walter, we struck up one of those tip toe-ing exchanges, by which strangers who are thrown together try to find out if they have anything in common.

"So you've come up all the way from London," I said, after we'd swopped names and the connections to Edna which had brought us here. "Do you like living there?"

"Oh good heavens yes. I'm an urban animal. I couldn't live without my theatre and ballet and art galleries and dinner parties. I can't think how people like us manage in the provinces."

I caught his drift, "It's not so bad. There's enough going on. . ."

"But darling, how do you get to meet anybody new? There can't be much variety."

Mischief darted out from under his apparently sombre expression, and I sensed that he was longing for some light chat to diffuse the heavy gloom which hung like cigar smoke over everybody.

I giggled behind my hand, "Well, I'm with someone, so I'm not looking any more, but I suppose you don't have a lot of choice if you're single. It's headline news in the local paper when someone different arrives on the scene. Everyone lines up to view them in the pub."

"Stakes out the supermarket to catch them behind the chiller cabinets?"

"Works out when they go to the Post Office to stand behind them in the same queue."

We nattered inanely, in danger of forgetting where we were, until we realised that the last grey and black couple had said goodbye to Ray and Brian, and it was time to retrieve our grief and head for the wake.

Not everyone had made it back to Edna's house, but it was still a struggle to find Mrs T. a comfortable seat, and ensure that she was reinforced with a glass of sherry and an egg roll. Brian and his wife held court, graciously soaking up all the lovely things Edna's friends were saying about her, while at least half their minds, I suspected, were totting up the value of the house and its contents. I went into the kitchen, where Walter had appropriated the kettle.

"You look like you could do with one of these," he said, and handed me a beer glass filled with what looked like black coffee.

I took a mouthful, and nearly honked it back up, as it exploded in my throat and the top of my skull lifted several inches.

He winked, "Funeral special. I came well prepared. I think Ray'll need a few of these to get him through, poor lamb. Let me get him started, then we can embarrass the young folk by joining them for a smoke outside the back door."

We stood in Edna's tidy yard, tacitly not trying to engage with the grandchildren, who were passing round lager cans and cigarettes and communicating in grunts and swear words in that youthful mixture of furtiveness and ostentation.

"Ray and his brother don't get on," Walter observed sotto voce, "I foresee ructions if we don't get out of here before sundown."

I was mellowing rapidly, and the funeral special was heating me from the inside out. "Everyone here's on Ray's side, really. They think Brian was a Bad Son."

"Yes, but Ray didn't produce any grandchildren, did he? It'll all come out in the will. I bet she's left the lot to those fine examples of today's youth. Not that we need the money, it would just help him to have something special from her. . . time for a refill, I think."

I checked on Mrs T., and was relieved to see that in the sitting room ties had been loosened and tight shoes slipped off under an anaesthetising tide of sherry. The guilty yet irrepressible laughter of survivors was breaking out in jokes about funeral disasters and Edna's sharp card-playing. Having reached the bottom of my second glass, I remembered Liz's instructions, and thought the logical thing to do would be to conduct a survey to find out if anyone wanted to give Dainty a more permanent home. I would start with those who had a special claim, and looked around for Ray and Brian.

"They went upstairs, dear," Mrs T. said in reply to my hissed question, "Brian was coming over all bombastic. It isn't a proper funeral without an argument, even at Frank's, that niece of his, who's no better than she should be, tried to flit off with the copper coal scuttle. . ."

Pushing this unlikely image to the back of my mind, I climbed the stairs. Thank goodness they had a strong bannister, they were terribly steep. I paused on the landing to catch my breath. The carpet was pattterned with vivid swirls, and, following them with my eyes, I felt a bit dizzy. Perhaps if I sat down for a minute or two, I would get over what was plainly an emotional reaction to the stresses of the past week. Raised voices from behind a half open door halted my slide to the floor.

"How the hell should I know where they are? Maybe she put them in the loft." That was Ray.

"Why should she do that? They were here last time I visited. Look, you can see the marks on the walls where they were." What must have been Brian's fist banged against the offending plasterwork.

"And when was that? How many months ago was it that you bothered to call? Hasn't it crossed your tiny blinkered mind that if you'd come around more often, you might have caught her before she got so ill. . ."

"You little shit. It was you being a queer that did for her heart, and you know it. I wouldn't put it past you to have taken those medals, they're worth a mint, more than the rest of everything in the house put together. I'm going to look in your car right now, rent boy."

"You fucking bastard. . ." There was a wheezing, scuffling noise. This was escalating into a fully-fledged fight well before Walter's prediction of sundown. It didn't appear to be an appropriate moment to mention the cat. Should I go into the room anyway, and diffuse the conflict with my womanly diplomatic skills? I was prevented from giving this bizarrely confident notion a try by Walter pounding up the stairs and sweeping past me like the Charge of the Light Brigade.

"What the hell's going on, you two?" he snapped, throwing the door wide, "haven't you any respect?"

Normally, it's true, my inclination would have been to sneak away from such a confrontation, yet now I was moved to peer round into the room, so that I could give a full account of the proceedings to Mrs T. It was a spare bedroom, and the two brothers were squaring up to each other in an incongruous clutter of lace-covered dressing tables and chests of drawers. Violence cloaked them in a dangerous gas which one more word could ignite. Temporarily outflanked, Brian backed off minutely.

"It's Dad's medal collection," he barked, "he had them in those special frames on the walls in here. They've gone."

Walter leant heavily against a wardrobe, which rocked unsteadily. "Oh," he said.

I watched fascinated as he lurched first one way then the other with the piece of furniture, regaining his balance only after some fancy footwork. The gas level fell a fraction, and I finally realised that the funeral specials had done a disservice to everyone's powers of reasoning. I poked my head further into the room, to add my razor-sharp logic to the mix.

"Have you looked anywhere else? Your mother might have packed them away. . ."

Ray snarled at the room in general and me in particular, "They're not up here or downstairs. I'm going to check the loft, and if that git there accuses me one more time. . ." He raised his hand to shove at Brian's chest.

Walter grabbed at his arm, and uttered the immemorial phrase heard all over the city centre at closing time, "Come on, he's not worth it." He started tugging his partner out of the room, "We'll have another drink, and go in the loft if you have to."

They exited with the bravado of punters ejected from a club. I sniffed haughtily at Brian, and avoided falling headlong down the stairs by sensibly descending step by step on my behind. I needed to sober up. Fragmented suspicions were leap-frogging about in my head, and I wanted to piece them together. When Walter and Ray re-appeared in the sitting room, brushing cobwebs from their clothes, and stiffly informed a whisky guzzling Brian that the medals weren't in the loft, I was convinced. Somehow, Tom and Dodgy's thieves had struck again, and had made off with the most valuable objects Edna had left behind.

10

I was in a dilemma. I stood in the kitchen, diluting the funeral specials with glasses of cold water and handfuls of left-over sandwiches and cake, considering my options. If the medals had been stolen, it wasn't fair to leave Ray and Brian in the dark, where they could add another sour layer to the legacy of bitterness and distrust which lay between them. Telling them right now that I thought Edna's house had been burgled, however, would lead to a host of questions which I didn't want to answer. Suppose they called the police? I would have to produce evidence to back up my suspicions, and explain about Tom and Dodgy's scheming, and the other houses where valuables had disappeared, and what if steely-eyed detectives went straight round to hound Tom before I'd had a chance to warn him? I weighed up the choices. Tom was my friend, whereas Ray and Brian were little more than strangers. Their sad sibling rivalry wasn't my problem, but Tom's welfare was. Therefore, I summed it up pedantically in my head, I would keep mum until I'd talked it over with Tom. I would discuss it with Liz when she came home this evening, if she was in any mood for rational conversation, and she would surely agree with me. I finished off a synthetic-tasting apple pie, and my heart sank. The evening was not going to be one of billing and cooing by candlelight, and I regretted ever wanting to know anything about her past. Being honest with one's partner was such a struggle, it was a pity I wasn't a better liar.

For once, my instinct was partly right. Assured by Walter that he would see Mrs T. safely back to her house, I went home to complete my sobering up. From her observation post in the window, Dainty gave me a disdainful look as I tripped over a loose edge of carpet and collapsed on to the settee, where I promptly fell asleep. After about an hour, she must have decided that it was high time for some more entertainment. Through my dazed slumber, I became aware of a sumo wrestler crouching on my chest, batting at my face with a tickly padded hand. Groggily I came to, saving my ribs from being permanently crushed, and pushed and croaked at Dainty to get off. My mouth felt like her litter tray, and I was shivering all over. Creaking and groaning, I made it to a vertical position, cleaned my teeth, filled the coal bucket like a put-upon Victorian scullery maid, laid and lit the fire, and poured litres of tea down my grateful throat. Thus slightly better prepared, I awaited Liz's key in the lock. She came in with the cheerfulness of someone sent unjustly to the scaffold, threw her canvas briefcase on to a chair, and backed out of the room, mumbling something about needing to lie down for a minute. I scowled at Dainty, who was stretched out on the hearth rug, toasting her furry underside and twitching her whiskers in some ecstatic dream of salmon steak with mouse garnish. If I became a Buddhist, maybe I could be reincarnated as an over-indulged domestic cat, instead of a scruffy human forced to endure a pivotal moment in the struggle to maintain a stable relationship. I fought back the temptation to join Dainty on the rug, made two more mugs of tea, and took them upstairs. Good timing or not, Liz and I were going to have to talk.

She was lying flat on the bed, with a hand over her eyes, and as relaxed as a hardwood log. I plonked one mug on the bedside table and walked round to sit up next to her, mustering all my powers to deflect the get away from me rays she zapped at me from every pore.

"What's the matter?" I asked, forcing the words past a dam of anxiety in my oesophagus.

She moved her hand, and pinched the bridge of her nose, as if contemplating some abstruse point of theoretical physics, "Do you want us to split up?"

The tea scalded my mouth. "What makes you say that?" I

hawked, my voice hitting an upper register, as it always did under stress.

"Well, do you?" She moved her hand again, and studied her nails.

"Can we stop talking in questions? Do you?"

Her head tilted in tiny acknowledgement, "No."

I wriggled myself into a more comfortable position, "Neither do I. Why should you think I would?"

She reached for her tea, and glanced at me so I could see the little relieved smile in her eyes. The rays retreated into her body, her tension subsided, and she gave me a companionable kick. "Dunno. It's just that usually you want to talk and talk about how you feel, and you haven't really said anything about what I told you last week. I'm not sure where I am with you, that's all."

I flapped around, rolling and lighting a cigarette, buying time to round up the straying sheep of my thoughts.

"I suppose. . . I think. . . it's like. . ." I inhaled and exhaled, and started again. "Basically, I suppose I think it should make a difference to how I feel, but it doesn't not really." I wanted to kiss her jawline, and where her hair rested on her ear. I made do with touching her ankle with my toes, "I mean, I wouldn't like it if you behaved like that now. I suppose I'm scared that part of you finds me boring, and still wants to. . .go off with Brigitte and stuff."

"Fuckinell." She put her tea down, pulled at a clump of my hair, and mashed my cigarette in an ashtray, "What can I do to convince you? I mean, I'm never going to be Ms Pure, this is about as far as I can go, but I never want to go back to that again. I love you, I like our life together. . . what is it now?"

I had turned my lips away from hers. This was where I had to go for it.

"Um. I've got to. . . got to tell you something about me." Damn and blast to the needles of conscience which were keeping me from the distracting heat of her body.

"My oh my." She had made a characteristic swift recovery from the doldrums, "What dreadful secrets can you possibly have that I don't know about?"

"I'm serious. I don't want to tell you this." I sat upright again and hugged my knees. My stomach was doing peculiar things, and I didn't think it was just the abuse to which I had subjected it that day.

Her fingers danced on the back of my neck, "Speak. It can't be that bad."

I rounded on her, "Ok! I told you that Chloe and I split up because we drifted apart, and I slept around a bit and all that."

"Yes. And?" Her fingers stopped dancing.

I gripped my knees tighter, "That wasn't the only reason." I had been rehearsing this speech all week, and had forgotten every single well-chosen word.

"What else was there? Did you ruin her career by seducing her students, or pursuing her naked through the lecture halls?" She was even going to start giggling if I let her.

I spoke into the quilt, "Nothing like that. It was more personal." I rescued the cigarette, straightened it, relit the misshapen end and sucked vigorously. I didn't want to look at her face, and watch lurking amusement transform into blank horror.

"You see," I said between puffs, "in the year before I joined the band, something. . . strange happened to me, and I started wanting. . . I started wanting. . ." I still couldn't say the word. If I did, that almost forgotten ache in the pit of my belly would rise up to overwhelm me, and I would go out of my mind.

"Wanting what? A party frock, a private jet. . . a man?" Her voice changed.

"No!" I gave up on the cigarette, and shouted out in despair, "A baby, I wanted a baby." I buried my face in my knees. I wasn't going to see my words, as solid as the real thing, hanging in front of me.

Nothing happened behind me, apart from an interested "Hm?" A muffled thumping came from below, as Dainty woke up and began her evening spider hunt. I would have to lift my head soon, my face was getting hot.

Liz yawned, and stretched her arms till they cracked, "Right. Fancy another cup of tea, then?"

I called her a terrible name. This was my most hidden secret. How could she treat it so lightly? She responded with a patient sigh and a tug on my shoulder, and I was pulled down into a calm embrace, and made to look into eyes as soft as caramel. "Tell me," she whispered.

So I told her everything. How, without warning, the physical longing had possessed me entirely, how I had fought and fought Chloe's refusal to consider the possibility, pointing out to her that with a solid relationship and her steady income, we would be ideal parents, and how the desire had been subdued with alcohol, the band, flings with strangers, and finally the crushing weight of my misery when Chloe and I had split up.

"It was unspeakable," I finished, "I was so. . . helpless with it. I never want to feel that again, and I try never to think about it in case I do."

She pushed wisps of hair from my cheeks, "Why would that be so awful?"

"Oh come on," I snapped, wondering why she failed to grasp the obvious, "it's a nightmare. The trouble is, I'm not so far off forty, and I'm dreading that bloody biological clock waking up, and making me go through it all again. It's totally impractical, it's not what you want, and I've never told you in case you pack your bags right away to avoid being saddled with a hysterical, broody, hormonal wreck." She still might, warned the gloomy voice which had made me never breathe a word of this to her before.

"Why do you think I'd do that? Do you want a baby now?"

I gawped at her, "Not this evening. But. . ."

She dropped a kiss on to my nose, "Well, honey-pie, if you get the urge any time, just tell me, and we'll discuss it properly." She laughed at my stricken silence, "Or am I totally unfit to be a co-parent or whatever the correct term is nowadays."

"But. . ." I looked around and pinched myself, to check that I wasn't still dreaming on the settee. Of all her possible reactions, I'd never anticipated this unruffled acceptance. Her eyebrows flickered, and the complacent smile I'd seen so many times before beamed benevolently at me. No, there was no way she could have. . .

"You knew!" My voice was cracked with animosity, "You knew, you sneaky, smug, superior scum." This broke all my records for being made a fool of. All her previous concealments were mere blips compared with this massive deception, and I knew I was within inches of smothering her with a pillow.

"It's not my fault that I know," she said with maddening reasonableness, "Pat told me when you were away. She said you told her years ago when you were miserable and pissed. I think it's pretty amazing she's kept it to herself for so long."

"I'll kill her. I'll kill her, and then I'll kill you. I loathe and despise you."

Her teeth bared in anticipation, "Yeah, I know. Come and show me how much. It's been a long week."

"I see the cat's still with us," Liz said, dropping another chunk of chocolate cake into my mouth. We had adjourned downstairs, to have supper by the fire.

I swallowed, "It's a bit of a long story." I continued with Dainty's jaw massage, and her slitty eyes rolled back in delight. The settee was just the right size for the three of us, if I lay like this with my head in Liz's lap and my ankles hooked over the arm-rest, while Dainty slumped on my front, head-butting my chin when I forgot to pay her enough attention.

"Am I going to like this?" I wasn't surprised that Liz sounded so weary.

"I think so. It could involve crime. Don't do that, you'll put my neck out." She had started bouncing my head up and down on her thighs. "I suspect, oh robber queen, that Tom and Dodgy's house thieves have struck again."

She listened, intently for a change, to my account of the wake, and Ray and Brian's spat over valuable medals which had gone astray. I played down the role that the funeral specials might have played in impairing my judgement of events, and she ended up as convinced as I had been that persons unknown were doing the dirty on the recently deceased.

"You didn't say anything to Ray and Brian did you?" she demanded. "Oh God, that's gross, isn't she fat enough already?"

I carried on letting Dainty lick butter icing from my finger, "She's been bereaved, she deserves a little treat. No, of course I didn't say anything. I could land Tom in it if Ray and Brian called the police, and they wanted to know how I knew stuff had gone from other houses."

"You did right, my little accomplice." Her voice became thoughtful, "I think that maybe I should have a discreet word with Mrs T., to see if she knows anything about these medals. In any case, we'll have to speak with Tom." She wasn't too worn out to get excited at the prospect of intrigue, and my head was bounced up again, "This could call for a Council of War!"

The conference convened on Sunday afternoon at Pat and Tom's house. Liz had generously informed me of this arrangement when I dropped into bed in the wee small hours of Sunday morning, tired and put out because an out of town engagement with the band had made me miss Toni's birthday party. From the way she pretended that she'd been tucked up virtuously in bed for ages, I knew that Liz had only just made it home before me.

"Wonderful, marvellous," I grumbled, "was the party good? What did I miss? Did she like her picture?" We had forged Kristin Dale's signature on the best print, and had it expensively framed.

Liz rubbed her eyes to make it clear that I had woken her up, "She absolutely adored it, she thinks I'm a genius, and she gave me a big, big kiss. I was chatted up by this beautiful woman and. . ."

I turned over, "Oh go to hell. I'm going to sleep."

She put an arm over me, and snickered into my neck, "Darling, don't you want to try for a baby now?"

I didn't have the energy to rise to the bait, "Go ahead if you like. I'm going to lie back and think of Kristin."

Her laughter popped through me like iridescent bubbles, "That makes two of us then. . . sweet dreams, grumpyface."

Supremely warm and safe, I went to sleep smiling.

I still took the opportunity to collar Pat in the afternoon, and to drag her into the sitting room, away from the babble in the kitchen where Tom was clearing the table, ready no doubt for maps with coloured pins and little models of burglars carrying bags of swag, and Pru and Dodgy were tossing a soggy nappy to and fro.

"You told her!" I accused Pat, planting my feet squarely on the carpet, and jabbing my finger at her, "I swore you to secrecy about the baby stuff, and you went ahead and told her. How could you? I thought you were my friend, how can I trust you now? I'm never telling you anything ever again."

Pat didn't bother to try and look ashamed, "Ah, bollocks to that. She doesn't mind, does she? Anyway, you should have mentioned it to her by now if you're serious about her, instead of making out it's some deep, dark secret. And don't shout, you'll wake Milly." She pointed to an armchair, where Milly lay in a nest of cushions, tiny eyelashes fluttering and pink fingers clutching a sticky plastic spoon.

I gibbered a little longer, then couldn't prevent myself from replacing the knitted blanket that had slipped to her knees back over her chubby shoulders.

"Liz doesn't mind, does she?" Pat repeated more gently.

"She says she doesn't." I whispered back, "She says we can talk about it if it happens again."

"Well there you go. She really wants to make it work with you, you know." She patted my arm, "She was so down when you were away, and came here all mopey that she didn't deserve you and rubbish like that. I said that Chloe hadn't deserved you either, since she was so hard with you over the baby business, and that's how it kind of slipped out." She nobly refrained from pointing out again that I could have brought it up with Liz myself, and I put my hand over hers.

"All right," I mumbled ungraciously, "I'm sorry. It just felt such a big thing, and I was working up to telling her in my own time."

"Yeah, when you're arrested for shoplifting in Mothercare, you twit. You never know, you might not feel that way again, it might have worked its way out of your system."

"Perhaps, though I find myself thinking. . ."

"What are you two gossips doing now?" Tom's head came round the door, "Hurry up, the committee's assembled, and the tea's brewing."

The committee included Stella, who sat at the table and handed round tea as if she had lived in the house for decades. She was wearing her patchwork dress again, and a sweater I recognised as a reject design of Pat's, the one with purple sheep floating in a psychedelic landscape. Liz was wary in her company, until she extracted a small alarm clock from somewhere on her person, and made a harumphing noise.

"Dave's coming round for me in about an hour. We're going to Mac's to have a serious practice." Even she began to turn slightly pink under Pat's immediate x-ray scrutiny. "What the hell," she gave a hooting laugh, "I know you're dying to know. I think he's cute, but nothing's happened. . . yet."

Pat smiled, Dodgy and Pru wolf-whistled, Tom averted an embarrassed face, and Liz and I competed to sound the most revolted.

"Cute?" We spoke together, "You're nuts."

She gave her head a little toss, like a lionness about to go for a turn around the veldt with the leader of the pride, "Well of course you two wouldn't think so, but I have different tastes." Her voice was amiable, and Liz grinned,

"Tastes for a different species, I think," she said equally amiably, "when we could introduce you to so many nice women. . ."

Tom tapped his mug with a teaspoon, "Order, order. Kate, tell us properly what happened at poor Edna's funeral, Dodgy and I want to hear it from you."

I obliged with a succinct account of Ray and Brian's row over the medals, and my conviction that their disappearance was connected with the thefts which they had noticed previously. Pat, Tom and Dodgy seemed singularly unimpressed, until Liz jumped in to my rescue.

"Allow me." She whipped out a notebook from her jacket

pocket, licked her finger, flicked through the pages, and started droning in the manner of a stolid policeman giving evidence in court.

"Following up the suspicions of the witness, Kate Halton, musician extraordinaire, I interviewed Mrs Tweddle of 24 Buccleuch Terrace, a known associate of the deceased. She broke down under questioning and said, and I quote, 'Now, dearie, let me have a think. . . the medals were definitely there the last time I was in Edna's house, when was it. . . it was one day in the week before she died, was it Monday or Tuesday. . .? What? The exact day isn't important? Well it can't have been Wednesday because I stayed in for the window cleaner, and it maybe wasn't Monday because that was when I went for the bus and it was late. . . Don't fluster me, young lady, you'll soon know what it's like when your memory goes. . ..'" She had Mrs T.'s accent off pat.

"I'm on the edge of my seat here," Pru laughed, "can't you just give us the gist?"

Liz put the notebook down, "Aw, I was enjoying that. Ok, she basically said that the medals were there the week before Edna died, because she saw them when she went into the spare room to check that her home help had dusted in there. And there's more." She glanced expectantly around. I hadn't realised she'd been so busy while I was away on Saturday.

"Yes, yes, you missed your vocation, you should have been in the CID," Tom said rattily, "get a wiggle on, we're not getting any younger here."

She tapped her head, "Ungrateful so-and-so. I used this, and tracked down Edna's next door neighbour, you know," she nudged me, "the one who told us to piss off. I had a brilliant hunch, and found him in the Angel where you get your tobacco, watching the football with his mates. I asked him, very tactfully, if he'd noticed anything unusual at Edna's, and d'you know what he said?"

"Piss off?" I suggested.

"No, oh ye of little faith." She puffed up her chest, "He said he'd been on nights from the Monday when Edna died, and he was coming home early on Wednesday morning, and had just turned into the street when he was nearly flattened. . .

by. . ." She slowed down, to build up to her climax.

Tom grabbed Pat's arm, "I feel senile dementia coming on. Get her to tell me, before they put me away."

"A transit van, shooting out of the back alley behind the houses. There, what do you all make of that? Smart work or what." Liz slapped the table, and waited for our applause.

11

Tom looked bemused, "I'm sorry, have I missed something here?"

"The van, the van!" Liz slapped the table again, "Don't you remember, noodles for brains, Kate and I saw a van out on Valley Road the morning Dodgy found that things had disappeared from Mrs Cardingle's house."

"Mrs Cardew," Tom said automatically.

"Right. So it's obvious. Someone's nicking the stuff and whisking it away in a van. Edna's medals will have gone the same way as Mrs Cardew's Clarissa Cleft tea-cups. God, do I have to spell everything out?"

"Clarice Cliff," Dodgy said, equally automatically, "have you no culture?"

Liz leaned back in her chair, and gazed beseechingly heavenwards, "Whatever. The point is, picky thieves are at large, and," she was becoming stern, "having devoted my valuable time and not inconsiderable brain power to what is, after all, your problem, I have come to an inescapable conclusion, which you should have arrived at yourselves."

"And that conclusion is?" Pat asked in her defusing Ag voice. "We're not all as sharp as you, ignore the men, they wouldn't recognise a logical conclusion if it jumped up and bit them on the bum."

Liz let herself be mollified, "Don't you see? All these houses that have been robbed must have something in common. They must all have been visited by someone, apart from you Dodgy, who knows what's valuable, and who is able to act quickly when the owners die to slip in and get what he or she wants. What about your business rivals, Tom? Are any of them so unscrupulous?"

Tom scratched his head, adopted an expression of deep thought, and started counting off something on his fingers, his lips moving slowly.

"No," he said after an age. It was difficult to tell if he was taking the piss or not. Liz thought he was, and I saw a wisp of smoke escaping from her nostrils. Pat made a slight movement, and Tom jack-knifed as if he'd been stabbed in the stomach.

"Oof!" He came upright, his eyes watering. "Ok, thanks Liz. You're right. But who else, besides Dodgy, can get invited into old people's houses and clock their possessions?"

We all gave it some thought.

"Meter readers."

"Those old-fashioned insurance agents who go round collecting the money once a month."

"Double-glazing salesmen."

"Postmen? They can look in the windows."

"Hairdressers who do home visits."

"Home helps like me," Stella proposed, "though you can fit what I know about collectables on a postage stamp."

Her suggestion was swamped in the flood of other far-fetched ideas.

"It's hopeless," Pru moaned eventually, "I can't think of anyone who'd be so organised about it all. I mean, to sniff out things that are worth money, find out when the owners had died, and whip in and out before the relatives appear."

My well-honed graduate brain kicked in, "Doctors might," I said, nearly leaving my seat I was so thrilled with myself, "doctors. They're educated, they visit old dears at home, they sign death certificates. . ."

"They devote their lives to helping others, they're selfless, hard-working, noble, and well-paid." Pat thought very highly of her GP, who was a great believer in the health-giving properties of moderate amounts of alcohol and butter.

"They also have enormous rates of drug addiction, alcoholism and stress," Pru interjected, with all the authority of one who had had to work with them.

Liz tilted her chair back, her eyes gleaming, "I can just see it. A conspiracy of doctors, who supplement their income and relieve their stress by stealing antiques."

"Maybe it started out small," I took up the story with enthusiasm. "A conscientious GP was tempted by a lone Faberge egg in a dying patient's sitting room, he put it in his pocket, no-one noticed, he got hooked on the thrill of getting away with it, he couldn't stop, he recruited colleagues, they found fences to dispose of their ill-gotten gains. . ."

"Before they knew it, they were locked in a dark world of crime and deception, their morals corrupted, their Hippocratic oaths long forgotten," Liz finished, her voice rising deep and dramatic from her boots.

"It could fit," Pat said agreeably. I noticed that she had given up on her principled stance that Tom and Dodgy should call the police if further thefts occurred, "And Mrs T. is bound to know who Edna's GP was. Old people always like discussing their doctors. Ask her, Liz, next time you see her."

Liz took up her notebook, "No problem. What will our next move be after that, though?"

"Surveillance," I said, getting a bit carried away. "We can find out where he or she lives, and who they associate with, and search around for clues that they're living above their income. It needn't be that hard, people love gossip and spreading rumours in this town."

Stella joined in, "I know, I could register with him or her, since I've just moved down here. I mean, I haven't seen a doctor for years, but I'm sure I can get an appointment and keep him talking to suss him out. I'll think of a suitable ailment."

"Colour blindness perhaps?" Liz suggested under her breath.

Sensing restiveness in the ranks, Tom cleared his throat, "Good. I think that's the only possible line we have. We'll pursue the doctor thing, and I'll keep my ear to the ground to see if there's any talk of medals in the air." He considered his mixed metaphor, and let it pass. "I could even pretend to one or two dealers that I've a customer who's after medals, and see if they surface. I wish we knew what medals Edna had, it would make it a lot easier."

"Can't help you there," Liz pronounced, managing to imply that she had single-handedly solved enough of the puzzle already, "Mrs T. just said there were loads, with lots of different coloured ribbons. Could be a rare VC among them, you never know."

"Great. Did you notice anything else nice-looking at the wake, Kate? It might still be worth my while to get in touch with this Brian." Tom shifted out of Pat's reach as he spoke.

"Not really. The truth is, I got a bit squiffy. . ."

Dave's shout from the hall brought my feeble response to an end. "Anyone in?" he bellowed, as, like an unsuspecting lamb to the slaughter, he walked confidently into the kitchen. He stopped short when he saw our array of nosy faces.

"It's the vetting committee," Pat said brightly. "We have to ask you a series of questions before we let Stella out with you."

His discomfiture almost cancelled out the trouble he'd obviously taken with his appearance. His hair was clean, his beard was neatly trimmed, and it looked as if he'd introduced his jeans to an iron for the first time. He hadn't been nearly so well-groomed at the gig last night.

Stella stood up, and treated him to a smile which had probably reduced grown men to adolescent rubble, "Pay no attention, honey. I'm ready if you are. Let's go."

She winked at us behind his back, then led him out, reminding me, rather uncomfortably, of those wildlife programmes in which female spiders ensnare their mates, only to devour them after the deed is done.

"Wonder how much singing they're actually going to do?" Tom asked with such untypical cattiness that the conference dissolved in impolite cackles and ribaldry.

Liz and I stayed on for a while, then walked peacably home, where we astonished each other by having a mature and coherent discussion over my potential broodiness. Liz started it while I was giving Dainty her grooming session, kneeling in front of the fire where Dainty could rub her head on the settee leg as I combed and fussed.

"I suppose I'd better get a cat-flap and fix it in the back door if Twinkle Toes is stopping here," she observed neutrally from round the side of the newspaper.

I stopped combing and flicked a mass of hairs into the fire, "D'you hear that, pretty girl?" Dainty swished her tail, "That'll be nice and convenient for you when you're ready to go out." So far, she had only ventured into the back yard once when I had accompanied her, and had shown no particular interest in the great outdoors again. Secretly, I had been relieved, since her reluctance to leave the house dispelled my fretting that she would try to return to her old home, and be run over, or catnapped by animal experimenters. I turned her round, and tried to give her a back-combed hairstyle, "There. That looks divine. Would you like a ribbon?"

Both she and Liz gave me pitying looks, and Liz opened her mouth. I waggled the comb at her, "If you so much as breathe the word 'child substitute', I'll walk out of the door and never come back."

Liz smiled, "I wish." She put the paper down, with all the pages mussed up the way I hated it, and looked at me more kindly, "How does it make you feel then, seeing Milly?"

I was so taken aback by her mildly concerned question, that I answered honestly.

"A bit odd. I mean, I think she's absolutely beautiful and fascinating, and when I pick her up I want one just like her, to look after and watch grow up. Then common sense hits, and I think of the reality. No sleep, no drinking, no smoking, no sex and a worry for the rest of your life."

Liz slipped off the settee and joined me on the hearthrug, "So you think about it, but it's not an overwhelming desire at the moment."

"That's about it. Anyway," I shovelled some more coal on the fire, "it wouldn't be practical. I'd have to give up the band, I couldn't afford it and. . ."

She took the shovel from my hand, chucked it in the coal

116

bucket, and wrestled me to the floor so she could hiss in my ear. "I'm not going to keep saying this. If it was what you really wanted, we'd manage somehow financially. Just don't not tell me."

I worked out her double negative, and the assumption underlying her abrupt phrases. That we were a couple, and she would be there to support me. I clutched at her shoulderblades, with the sensation that a golden stream had poured into my heart, turning me into a blancmange of love and gratitude.

She growled into my hair to hide her scarlet face, "I love you. I'd love anyone who was a part of you. Your happiness is important to me. Now go and peel some onions, I want to cook supper."

By Monday afternoon, I felt that life was at last settling into some new equilibrium. I had intended to spend some time with Mrs T. in the morning, but found that she was about to set out on a trip to a winter market with the Day Centre.

"They're picking me up at the bus stop," she announced, stoical and smart in her thick coat and gloves, "Edna wouldn't want the world to grind to a halt because of her." She gave me a determined look, "She was weary, you know. She would have hated to linger on, being a burden or having to go in a home. It's hard, and I'll miss her, but it was her time." She paused, and pulled herself up to her full four foot eleven and a half inches, "And don't come the miserable bugger with me. I've got plans. Do you think these shoes will murder my feet, or should I put my old lady boots on?"

I glanced down at her matching court shoes with a definite heel, "Keep them on. You won't have a chance of pulling in those furry boots."

"That's what I thought. No harm in keeping the competition on their toes. Don't bother sending out a search party if I'm not back tomorrow, I might have hit the jackpot."

I walked her to the bus stop, waited until the coach arrived, then strolled home to ring Pat and see if there was any hot gossip from the Dave and Stella front. I was treated to an exhaustive account of how Pat had happened to come across Stella, still in her patchwork dress, climbing the fire-escape to the flat's private door at nine in the morning.

"She's out at work now, so I'll have to nobble her this evening and get the full story." Pat sounded as if she was counting off the hours until Stella reappeared.

We frittered away another chunk of time in speculation and soothsaying, before, bored with blowing cat hairs off the receiver, I resolved to apply myself to some cleaning.

"I can't help it," I shouted at Dainty, as she beat a miffed retreat from the vacuum cleaner, "it's the price you have to pay for your general gorgeousness."

Mission accomplished, I practised my technique of playing the violin whilst lying on the floor with my feet up on a chair. This had little practical value, but over the years, I had found it conducive to thought. Eyes shut, I wandered my way through familiar tunes, probing the inner recesses I usually preferred to leave undisturbed. Was it possible that I had been making a song and dance about nothing? Maybe my memory of how it had been for that year when I had wanted a child was faulty, and it hadn't been that bad. Or perhaps, my thought processes became convoluted, it hadn't been a child I had wanted: it had just been a trick of my subconscious, foreseeing that Chloe and I were not going to last the distance. I tried this theory on for size, and, liking it quite a lot, made up my mind to stop agitating and concentrate on how I could earn some more money. The band didn't have a great deal coming up before Christmas, apart from a booking to go to a private recording studio in the wilds of Dorset in a couple of weeks time, to spend around seven days laying down some tracks with an up and coming singer. We were very pleased with ourselves at securing this prestigious opportunity, yet I let a few brain cells dwell on the notion that giving the odd lesson, to rigorously screened adults only, of course, might be a bearable way to bring in some easy cash. There were always enthusiastic amateurs keen to learn from seasoned professionals like myself. . . I practised a faster tune, and wondered if we could find a piece that the whole band could play lying down.

Elevated to a higher plane of benign placidity, I greeted Liz on her return from work with a pot of tea and a cat-fur free hug, and was relatively unperturbed by her frazzled demeanour, set off by hair which had plainly been tugged at all the way home.

"Haven't we got any beer? I'm distraught," she twittered, descending on to the settee, and attempting an imitation of a well-bred heroine having a fit of the vapours. "This might call for smelling salts."

"Have you gone bust?" With supernatural efficiency, I handed her a chilled can and a glass.

"No. It's much, much worse." She picked ineffectively at the ring-pull, chirruping with frustration.

"Here, let me." I poured the beer, and pretended to be a fifties housewife, "Drink that darling, and I'll run for your slippers. Would you like me to rub your temples?"

"No I would not!" She knocked back half the beer and gave me a Gorgon stare, "One teeniest snigger from you at what I'm about to tell you, and I'll never do that thing you like so much again for as long as I draw breath."

"What thing?" I figured I'd better gauge the magnitude of her threat.

"That thing with the massage oil."

"Oh heck." This was serious. "What about the thing with the whipped cream?"

"That as well." The rest of the beer disappeared.

"And how about. . .?"

"All of it!" she shouted, and threw the empty can at me. It bounced harmlessly off my curls.

I put up my hands, "Steady on. I'm only trying to get it clear."

She punched a cushion and put it behind her, "Do you want it in writing? Don't make this harder than it is. I've won a competition."

Her deadpan face gave me no clues. "What kind of competition?" I asked reedily. She wasn't the sort to play "Spot the Dog" in the local paper, I'd never known her to phone in inane answers to the City Radio, karaoke down the pub wasn't really her style. . .

She covered her mouth, "Remember my warning. You are looking at the north-west regional finalist of the Professional Photographers' Association mumble mumble mumble of the Year Competition."

I cupped my hand to my ear, "The what of the Year Competition?"

She screamed in agony, "Wedding Photographer! I've won a bloody wedding photography competition!"

Her tortured words sank in, and I leapt up from my seat, "But Liz, that's amazing! I always knew you were brilliant, oh God, you must be so proud, I'm so proud, the best in the north-west!" I began to edge my way towards the kitchen, "I must just. . ."

"Where are you going? Come back!"

I scrabbled frantically at the back door, "I think it's going to rain, I put a rug out to air." My words were distorted, as if I was speaking under water.

I didn't stand a chance. She gave chase and caught me in the yard. I chucked the rug over my head.

"You're laughing!" she yanked at the rug, "I knew it, you swine."

I tried in vain to keep my mouth concealed. "These are tears of joy and pride," I hiccupped into the smelly fabric. Of all the different facets of Liz's job, taking wedding photographs was the part she'd always professed to hold in the deepest contempt.

Her lips wavered, "I thought at least you might support me. What am I going to tell our friends? I'll never live this down, my reputation will be ruined. It's all Ben's fault. He entered a set of my pictures without telling me, and now this has happened."

"Look on the bright side," I advised through the rug, "you'll be so much in demand from anyone who wants a gay wedding." I flung an arm round her, "Oh Liz, I really am proud for you. You must be pleased somewhere in your stony heart."

She disentangled me from the rug, and began to giggle, "I don't know whether to laugh or cry. But there's more. Brace yourself, this is the real killer." She began to waltz me in the direction of the back door. "I thought that the PPA would post me the prize certificate, but Ben is getting ideas above his station. He's joined the Chamber of Trade, and the little tyke's arranged for someone to present it at one of their dinners this Thursday." She hoisted me up the step into the kitchen, "I wasn't going to go, but Ben gave me a mouthful at work today. I don't see why I should be the only one to suffer in this, so I've got a double ticket. You're not doing anything else on Thursday night, and therefore, my spouse of choice, you're going to put on your best dress, come with me, and be civilised with the stuffed shirts. So ha ha to you and your cruel, mocking laughter." She draped the rug back over my head and pranced off, her "I'm simply the best", sung at the top of a triumphant voice, ringing hollow in my ears.

12

Having dumped me deep into sartorial crisis, Liz reverted to being obnoxiously chipper over the next three days. Her front only dropped when the band played the "Wedding March" for her on Wednesday evening at the Billhook, and she treated us to a series of vulgar gestures before subtly undermining our performance with obscure technical glitches on the sound deck.

"All right, you've made your point, can we have a ceasefire?" Jo asked her in an interval.

"What?" Liz did injured innocence quite well, although not well enough to fool us.

"You know. We won't mention weddings again. We want to impress Stella, not make her wish she'd never moved down here."

Bill sniggered, "I don't think our performance in the musical sense is her main criterion at the moment."

We looked over to where Dave and Stella sat, slightly apart from us, their fingers just touching across a table. Stella had turned up before the evening started, and Dave had introduced her to the rest of the band with a formality which told us that, this time, he actually cared what we thought of his companion, and she of us. Fred and Jo, as ever, had been unreservedly friendly, but Bill had revised his earlier opinion that a reversal in love, for a change, might do Dave some good.

"She'll destroy him," he had whispered agitatedly to me, "she'll crush him and sap his strength and turn him into a shadow of his former virile self, and then where will we be?

Without our dynamic source of artistic tension, that's where. We're doomed."

"You old drama queen," I had scoffed. "It might work the other way, and he'll be driven on to even loftier heights of cranky genius, whether she dumps him or not. Besides," I had glanced over my shoulder to check that Liz was out of earshot, "don't waste worrying time on them. You should be concentrating on planning our shopping trip tomorrow, and being my fashion guru. And don't even dream of suggesting that I should ask Stella to come with me instead."

I was in a style pickle, and Dave and Stella were not uppermost in my mind. A trawl that day through every cupboard and old suitcase had confirmed what I already knew. I had not a stitch of clothing that was remotely suitable for a Chamber of Trade dinner. I could barely fit into my one decent skirt, I had somehow mislaid the dress I had worn to my brother's wedding ten years ago, and everything else was too scruffy or too obviously bought for making an impression whilst jigging about on stage. In reply to my plaintive "But what are you going to wear?" Liz had only put her finger to her nose and smiled inscrutably. This added to my angst, and drove me to the unpalatable conclusion that I was going to have to break the habits of my adult life, and go shopping in a proper shop with a support team, namely Bill.

He laid down the ground rules on Thursday morning over complicated cappuchinos in the new downtown branch of a chain of trendy coffee shops.

"No charity shops. You've been paid from the tour, you can afford to treat yourself for once in your dungareed life and look glam."

I put my hand up, "Can't I just look in a couple, see if they've any retro. . .?"

He was hard, "Definitely no. No detours. We've got six hours to complete this mission, and I think we'll need every minute." He peered under the table at my legs, "I hope you're wearing tights under those jeans."

I stopped scooping foam into my mouth, "Ugh, of course I'm not, that's really unhygienic. I've got socks on."

He smote his brow, "So how are you going to tell properly what the dresses look like when you try them on? And please don't tell me you're wearing one of those enormous vest-y bras as well."

I had a squint under my layers of fleece and Oxfam shop stretchy cotton, "Er. . .sorry."

A vein bulged on his forehead. I cut off his screech with a well-placed amaretto, lobbed into his open mouth, "I'm not going for a low-cut number, so stop nagging. Where shall we try first? The Army and Navy stores?"

Retail therapy had never appealed to me, and after two hours with Bill, I was feeling all the hysterical boredom and frustration I thought I had left behind in my teenage years, when I traipsed round town on Saturday afternoons with my friends, marvelling at their insatiable appetite for trying on outfit after identical outfit. It was cold outside, but all the stores were boiling hot, and I quickly became light-headed and feverish with overloud music and with peeling off my comfortable clothes to squeeze into dresses that were variously too prissy, too tarty, too strappy, too tinselly and too full of static from their artificial fibres. Seams were even more prone to splitting than they had been in my youth, and zip technology had apparently gone backwards.

"Are you sure you haven't got that on back to front?" Bill enquired, as I stood flushed and sticky in front of him, looking like a sausage bursting out of its skin.

"Would it make any difference? It's a travesty of a dress." I manouevred my breasts around a bit, "Who in their right mind would buy this? You're useless, Bill, you haven't shown me anything that makes me look like a sexy woman, not a drag queen."

He pawed the ground, "Even I can't make a silk purse out of a sow's ear. Perhaps you should face facts, barring liposuction and major plastic surgery, you're always going to look like lard."

I relaxed my stomach muscles, and there was an ominous creaking in the dress's engineering, "Don't throw a hissy fit on me now." I twirled round and my boobs escaped, "If I can get out of this, I'll buy you a tofu bun at the hippy caff, and we can re-group."

"You're not looking at the clothes in here," Bill commanded loudly as we entered the blessed alternative sanity of the Singing Dolphin Fair Trade Cooperative Shop and Eating House, "I'm not letting you represent the band at the Chamber of Trade in a smock hand-woven by Bolivian peasants from mung beans."

"Ssh." I smiled ingratiatingly at the lovely woman with wild braids who was bagging up muesli behind the counter. Before I met Liz, I had amused myself by coming in here and buying stuff I would never eat, in order to engage her in politically correct conversation, and to fantasise about her dragging me through the "Staff Only" door to some exotically furnished love-nest, even though I knew she was straight, and lived with a soppy guy who ran men's groups.

"Go upstairs and order what you like and a bun with mush-rooms for me. I'm just going to get some spices for Liz. . ."

I shot towards the clothes section as soon as his back was turned. Beyond the racks of hemp shirts and baggy trousers, a row of dresses called out to me, and from the middle, one was shouting my name. I pulled it out, and was sold. It was some kind of heavy purply silky material, shot through with blue, it had a waist, it had proper sleeves, it felt like it wouldn't disintegrate in a mild breeze, and it had a v-shaped front that would show enough cleavage without requiring me to buy an underwired bra precision-tooled by rocket scientists.

"Can I try this on?" I asked my former object of desire.

"Yeah, if you don't mind coming through here." She opened the door I had dreamt about into a chilly, concrete-floored space filled with sacks of beans and polythene bags of pungent spices, and left it ajar in case I absconded with a year's supply of alfalfa.

The dress slipped over my gooseflesh like a second skin. "What does it look like?" I hissed through to her.

She popped her head round the door, blinked, and came in. "Wow," muesli trickled on to the floor. "That really suits you. It makes you look. . . different. In a nice way." I couldn't miss the appraising shift in her eyes.

"I'll have it," I said loudly, before the wopping price tag bludgeoned me back into my normal stingy self and consciousness of the house fund, "and a bag of cumin while you're at it."

She gave me a spine-tingling smile, "I'll chuck that in for free. I knew that dress was waiting for someone special."

Now I understood the point of shopping. "You're too kind," I simpered, "do you take credit cards?"

Wings of allure and seductive power carried me upstairs to the caff, where Bill's table-thumping tantrum was water off a duck's back.

"I've got me a babe magnet," I said, dipping his largest chip into garlic mayonnaise, "I have no need for your magic powers any more. I'm ready to go forth and woo Chamber of Trade wives in their hordes."

"Get your bum pinched by their husbands more like. Just swear in blood that you won't wear your baseball boots."

I gave him a greasy kiss, "You love me really. I'll wear Liz's old motorbike boots, will that do? All I've got to do now is find some tights."

Back home, I hung the dress carefully on a hanger out of Dainty's reach, and devoted the rest of the afternoon to primping and self-beautification. I brushed the ton of dust off my proper shoes and polished them, had a serious bath and a shower, cut my toenails, and trimmed my hair with a pair of nail scissors. I basted myself in baby lotion, and pumiced away every trace of nicotine stain from my fingers. Dainty watched in awe as I filed my nails with a piece of fine-grade sandpaper. "Il faut soufrir pour etre belle," I told her, and she yawned in understanding. Liz came home while I was having a tea break, pink legs protruding from my bathrobe, and my unnaturally clean feet protected with a pair of her thickest socks.

"You smell nice," she was buzzing with a mixture of tension and elation, "are you going like that?"

"No. I bought a dress." I had ripped up the price tag, and buried the shreds in the rubbish bin.

She grinned guiltily, like a child caught with forbidden

sweets. "I bought something as well. I know, I'll get changed in the spare room, so it'll be a surprise, and we can meet down here and have a cocktail." She produced a bottle of my favourite Russian vodka from inside her jacket, "Let's do this in style."

I felt a peculiar nervousness, waiting downstairs while she thudded from the shower to the spare room. I sat carefully on the edge of a chair, so as not to crease my dress, imagining that I looked like the female lead in an old movie, just before Cary Grant made his entrance.

I stood up when the door opened, my heart did a gymnastic double flip, and my eyeballs bulged cartoon-style.

"Blimey." It was the best I could come up with.

"Oh my." One finger stretched out and touched my waist.

She had bought a suit. Not a clumsy man's suit, nor a polyester chain store effort, but a dark tailored creation in fine wool, with a flash of satin lining when she moved. A long jacket with a cream shirt underneath, and trousers which made her legs go on forever.

One corner of her mouth lifted, "You're drooling. Does that mean you like it?"

I gulped, "I want to take it off you, very slowly."

Her lips on my neck sent tremors to every cossetted extremity, "Your dress has the same effect." She withdrew, "We'd better have that cocktail. We're the perfect couple. We don't want to be late."

We played the perfect couple brilliantly for the first half of the evening. Heads held high, we swept into the old-fashioned ballroom of the Grand as if we attended such functions once a week, and everyone should know who we were. The space was set out like a home-grown version of the Oscars, with a sea of tables for eight, and a dais with a microphone standing at one end of the room.

"That's where I've got to walk to, to get my prize," Liz murmured, "I've thought up a little speech."

Stage-fright for her set me jangling. I had been treating this evening as something between a joke, a wearisome duty and a free dinner with complimentary wine, and now the enormity of her achievement finally hit me.

"Aren't you scared? I'd be beside myself." That wasn't the most supportive remark I could have made.

She straightened her shoulders under the handsome jacket, "It's work. Let's find Ben and our table, then I must schmooze."

I sat at the table, ogling the array of glasses and serried ranks of cutlery, and making the acquaintance of Shirley, Ben's housekeeper girlfriend, while our partners worked the room.

"Talk about Mr Smooth," Shirley said, jutting her chin towards a dinner-jacketed Ben, "you wouldn't think he calls them the Chamber of Horrors. Got a light?"

I passed her my lighter and relaxed, "I think you're the youngest person here. What a collection of mutton dressed as lamb. I don't know how Liz is keeping a straight face."

I watched her listening, head to one side, to a hefty battleship of a woman tricked out in a triumph of black velvet. I'd never seen her like this, so polite, attentive and civilised. Meeting her here for the first time, no-one would have an inkling of her delinquent tendencies, her rumbunctious past, or her wildness in bed. . . I pulled myself together. That suit was really getting to me.

Shirley picked up a bottle from the table, "She looks dead cool. I could fancy her myself. Shall we see if we can find a waiter to open this wine?"

With the headstart of a cocktail and a couple of glasses of wine, I had to watch my step through the stately passage of several traditional courses. I reminded myself not to slurp the soup, eat salad garnishes with my fingers, steal the best bits from Liz's plate, or bolt everything down so quickly that I couldn't talk sensibly with the other two couples on our table. I also had to hide my guilty worries at the thought of Liz walking alone to the microphone and addressing this self-important conventionally prosperous throng. Suppose she forgot her lines, and started swearing, or launched into an anti-capitalist tirade? Or what if she used the occasion to air her views on marriage (a bad thing), and expensive weddings (a worse thing)? I worked myself into such an internal state that I even found myself responding to the loyal toast, before lighting up with Shirley, and numbing out the tedium of the following speeches with a massive glass of port.

"It's now," Liz's spasm next to me broke my contemplation of a frieze of lively cherubs on the ceiling, "bloody hell, Kate, help. . ." Her desperate hand jumped in mine.

The mayor, no less, his chain winking and gleaming on his puffed out chest, approached the microphone, and I unglazed my eyes to stare into her dilated orbs. She was as terrified as I was after all.

"You'll be fine, my love." I sounded a lot more sober than I was, "Whatever you do, whatever you say, you're the best and I'm so proud to be with you." It came out with a sincerity I hadn't forced.

She grunted, "I'm going to have Ben killed for this. If I dry up, cause a diversion by fainting as loud as you can."

I didn't need my acting skills. The mayor finished his description of a paragon of civic virtue, and Liz, straight as a die, glided to the dais. Her speech was a model of its kind: modest, gracious and short, and I found myself wishing that the band, her mother and all our friends had been there to see her professional glory. Next time she won anything, I would make sure we invited them.

"Will you still want to go out with me, now you're famous?" I asked her, not entirely frivolously, when she had glad-handed her way back to our table.

"As long as you carry on wearing that dress." The same naughty Liz was behind the suit, and I experienced a delightful frisson under my wise purchase.

An overstuffed businessmen with a cigar in his hand shoved his face in front of hers, "Damn good show, Mrs Sharpe. Come and have a word with m'wife. Very keen on photography. . ."

Shirley tittered in my ear, "You've lost her now. . . hell, my old boss is over there. Quick, come to the bog with me, I'm not drunk enough to speak to her."

Using me as a human shield, she guided me through the tables.

"Which one is she?" I was regressing into giggles.

"There. The repulsive bag in the flowery dress and too much jewellery, next to her slimy husband. She's Mrs Brewster, she owns Caring Hands, the domestic help agency, and she sacked me."

"Why?" I caught a side view of a tall, overbearing-looking woman, fractionally too old for so much make-up on her horsey upper-middle class face, standing in a loud group of red-faced men.

"I was too cheeky for her. She called me an undisciplined gel. Don't let her see me."

Good Lord, how had Stella managed to keep her job with the agency for so long?

"Hide behind my skirt, and I'll push my chest out."

We were sidling past, eyes averted, when a bray rose above the group's haw-hawing, "Orf with his head, I say, damned peasant."

The intonation, joking as it was, was an icicle piercing my heart. Cold sweat beaded my hairline, and my head swivelled involuntarily towards the speaker, like a rabbit caught in car headlights. It was Mrs Brewster's consort who had spoken. His pugnacious stance brought the taste of mud to my mouth, and the shrinking fear of hot metal pellets to my flesh.

"Kate, get a move on," Shirley had bent her knees to reduce her height to below mine, "my legs are giving way."

I pulled a veil of hair over my face, dropped my knees as well, and, two demented crabs, we scuttled to the ladies.

"Get Liz," I neighed, hugging a tampon machine to stay upright, "get her to come in here, I need her now."

A portly matron exited one of the cubicles, and raised an eyebrow at us.

Shirley examined her face in the mirror and reached for her handbag, "You can't be that desperate. I'm staying in here for a while. Ben and me are going on to a club after this. Do you and Liz want to come? What do you think of this eyeliner? Is it too much?"

The matron washed her hands quickly and departed. I utilised my pre-performance trick of bringing some saliva to my mouth by visualising biting into a lemon,

"Where do the Brewsters live?"

"What? Some big place out to the north I think. They're rolling in it. Why?" She stuck her tongue out of the corner of her mouth, and applied some more eyeliner.

Some big place out to the north. That fitted in with where Stella and I had been fired upon. "He shot me once." I tried to say it, and it wouldn't come out. "Oh nothing." I let go of the machine, "Won't you get Liz? There's someone out there I don't want to see as well."

"Half a mo'. I'll finish this, then sneak out and find Ben. If I see Liz, I'll tell her you're here." She dabbed at her face with some unidentifiable unguent, "Is it an ex?"

This was so unlikely, it was almost plausible. "Something like that."

"You girls. Is she married?"

I took the path of weaving a tangled web, "Yes. Her husband can't stand me, and I don't want a scene."

"Ooh hoo hoo," now she was getting far too interested, "go on, tell me, who is it?"

"I couldn't possibly say. It was a real secret. She's got children and everything." I would believe myself if I wasn't careful.

She rested her bum on the wash-basin surround, "This is brilliant. I'd never have guessed all that went on here. Does it happen a lot?"

The web drew tighter, "More than you'd think. You know that Greek girl in the deli. . ."

I fed her the fruits of my fertile imagination, whispering whenever someone came in, until, her mouth wide open, she remembered Ben, and charged out to pour my untruths into his ear. Beyond conscience, I locked myself in a cubicle. Think, girl, think, my history teacher's snarky bark came back to me. Mrs Brewster, head of an agency which sent dozens of workers into old people's homes, Mr Brewster, shooting at me and Stella to keep us off his field, Harry, who sold items on the internet, driving to the Brewsters'. . .

A pair of shined boots topped by trouser leg materialised at the cubicle door.

"Kate, what the fuck are you playing at? What's all this about a married woman? Can't you act your age for one evening?"

I unlocked the door, and dragged the pillar of righteous wrath inside.

"Liz, the man who shot me, he's here, he's Mr Brewster, Stella's boss's husband, I can't go out there, I think they're Tom and Dodgy's thieves."

It was a long five minutes of saving my bacon with higgledy-piggledy explanations.

Liz began knocking her head on the cubicle wall, "God Almighty, I don't care if Mr Brewster is Jack the Ripper. You're going to come out and help me say polite good-byes to all these influential potential customers."

"Can't I slip out through the kitchens? What if Mr Brewster sees me?"

"He's not going to recognise you, is he, you fruitcake! He's only seen you lying down in the mud in an anorak, and here you are, a voluptuous woman with legs in a fuck-me dress. I hardly recognise you myself." The line of her mouth was a little less grim.

"Oh."

"Get a grip, Mata Hari," she led me out of my refuge, "which one is your married woman then?"

With a rictus of a smile, I shook a million sweaty hands, mimed "ha ha, wonderful evening, how lovely, goodnight" a million times, dodged the Brewsters like a jumping bean, and made it outside to the pavement with my secret identity as a trespasser intact.

"Don't you want to go on to this club with Ben and Shirley?" I asked Liz meekly. Her nose was in the air, and I was still in the doghouse.

"No way. I want to get home and have a nice cup of tea. I rang for a taxi. Here it is, get in, you baggage."

She stretched her legs out in the back seat, and massaged her forehead. I played the remorseful sixteen year old, who had been expansively ill on her parents' new carpet after experimenting with snakebite.

"Liz, I'm so sorry. I didn't mean to ruin your evening. I'm a cow, you always support me, and now I've spoilt your big moment. . ."

Her shoulders wobbled, "I can't believe I said that," she was impotent with laughter, "a nice cup of tea. Save me, I've turned into an old maid, oh lawks, golly gosh." Her private joke made her incoherent for the rest of the way home.

I had left the central heating on for Dainty, and the sitting room was toasty warm.

"Shall I make some tea?" I put my shoes neatly in the hall, wanting to redeem myself.

Liz gave me her enigmatic look, "You might as well. Don't start combing that cat, though."

Prim and proper, I sat next to her on the settee, hyper-aware of her quiet swallowing, and the way her mouth kept relapsing into the memory of her laughter. I jumped when she took one of my curls, and wound it lightly round her finger.

"Calm down, babe. I never expect things to go smoothly when you're involved. Not everyone will have realised that you spent three quarters of an hour in the loo."

"Was it that long? I was scared. I'm sure it was that Mr Brewster who shot at us."

Her fingertip was a centimetre away from my ear-lobe. I could casually adjust my head, and. . .

"Let's not talk about that now." Her eyes were dark, hungry and misted with a strange novelty, "Play along with me. I feel like I met you for the first time tonight, and I want to seduce you."

A Mexican wave spiralled through me. "Try it," I suggested, in less of a willing to be seduced purr and more of an unladylike command. Yet I did my best in the careful exploratory kisses, and the artless hesitations in her caresses, biting back the moan torn from the base of my spine when at last her palm cupped my breast, still in its demure silky sheath.

"I've wanted to do this all night," she said thickly, and moved her thumb.

My throat opened and I lost it. The tensing and flexing of muscles under those trousers was as erotic as I had guessed, and so were the sounds she made when my fingers reached the seam at the top of her legs. The settee was agonisingly

133

restrictive, and we ended up being unusually acrobatic on the floor.

"I'm sorry," I panted into the collapsed body, "I couldn't hold back."

She rose and fell one more time, "God, I love it. I love it when you do that to me."

Satiated in every cell, we rolled around for a little while longer.

"Damn good show, Mrs Sharpe, that wasn't a very old-maidish performance," I said when we had reached the giggling in disbelief stage.

"I might have to see a chiropracter tomorrow." She gave me a love bite high on my neck where it would show, "You didn't spoil my evening at all. I think we should dress up more often."

13

Since I was off with the band again from Friday until Sunday afternoon, I didn't have a lot of time to brood over the connection between this Brewster couple and Tom and Dodgy's thefts. It turned out to be a niggly weekend, when an accumulation of little things going wrong made it a struggle for us to maintain our usual good nature. The weather was unremittingly foul, a tyre blew on the van, thankfully not when we were on the motorway, and, chilled to the bone, we arrived a fraction late at the venue on Friday evening to find that no-one seemed to know where I could get a cup of tea. I sniffed out a MacDonald's a street away, and had to abandon my principles for the sake of restoring my system to the point where I could perform. Our B&B was underheated, and Bill swore that he had taken down the curtains in the night and wrapped himself in them to keep warm. Saturday and Sunday morning followed a similar trying course, and I was almost tearfully glad to fall in through our front door after a journey home dogged by roadworks, flash floods and drivers with a death wish. My weepy relief was increased by the welcoming sight of Liz on all fours with Dainty's comb in her hand, addressing the underside of the settee.

"Come out, you mouldy old beggar. You let Kate do this. I'm just as nice as her."

She dropped the comb, and stood up to hug me, "I wanted her to look smart for you, but she won't cooperate."

"She hates her tail being done," I sighed into the familiar sweater, hoping against hope that she wasn't intending to go out to the business and spend a few hours planning the week ahead, as she sometimes threatened to do on a Sunday evening.

"That explains it. You could have told me." She kissed me with just the right amount of undemanding affection, "You look like the dark undead. Rough weekend?"

"Mmm." I shut my eyes, and felt the silly tear trickle down my cheek.

She wrapped me up in her arms again, "Sweetheart. What would you like? Tea? A sandwich? Bath? Go to bed?"

I brightened up, "All four?"

"It can be arranged. The water's hot. You go on up, and I'll bring your tea." She wiped my cheek with her sleeve, "I don't know how you managed without me."

I have the perfect woman, I reflected, trying not to get bubbles all over my sandwich or in my tea, and drinking in Liz's absorbed face as she leaned on the bathtub and tickled my toes under the water.

"Aren't you getting in?" I asked, my inviting tone spoiled by the mouthful of crusty best loaf.

She grinned, "Wouldn't you prefer me to massage those terribly stiff shoulders of yours when you get out?"

A partial recovery was setting in, "I thought you were never going to do that for me again."

She positioned a mountain of foam on my head, "You shouldn't take me so seriously. I didn't mean it. I'm sorry about Thursday evening as well."

"Whatever for?" I didn't have any criticisms of the way the evening had ended.

She grimaced, "If that Mr Brewster was the man who shot you, I should have bopped him on the nose, not been so horrible to you."

"That wouldn't have done your business much good." I blew at the foam sliding down my face, "Pass me a towel and break out the massage oil. I'm on my way to forgiving you."

I woke up to the reassuring scent of cooking floating along with light from the landing through the open bedroom door, and to the ecstatic rumble of Dainty's purr as she tasted my hair.

"What are you doing here, bad cat?" She kneaded the quilt with her front paws, and turned heavily over so I could scratch gently at her stomach, "Liz'll turn you into a hat if she finds you like this." Her purr went up the scale to include a soprano trill. In harmony, my oiled and soft-jointed body hummed at the recollection of unhurried hands, and the soporific lullaby of Liz's voice, rocking me off into charmed sleep. It was possible that her nurturing mood would stretch to coming upstairs with more tea, and I gave her another five minutes, which I spent cuddling the cat and rejoicing at the complete disappearence of the weekend's tension.

"She's not coming," I complained into Dainty's transported expression when the time was up, "I'd better get dressed and go down."

"You're back with us," Liz remarked, chopping up mushrooms with scary rapidity.

I leant in my regular stance against the kitchen door jamb, "In every sense." Her smile was the one I'd scale mountain peaks for. "What are you cooking, precious jewel?" I asked smoochily.

"A very hot curry, to restore your chi, and balance your yin and yang." She dipped a spoon into a seething pan, and licked at it reflectively, "Pretty bloody good. So you're ok with my plan, then?"

"What plan?" I snatched at a piece of mushroom, and ate it with a smear of mustard from an open jar on the worktop.

"The plan I told you about after the massage."

"I didn't hear a word," I said cheerfully. After she had reached the parts a professional aromatherapist could not, she couldn't have expected me to be a good listener. "Is it about work?"

She looked at me obliquely, "Hell. Maybe you'd better sit down."

There, in the unlikely setting of our kitchen, I had a minor revelation. The sensation in my innards resembled the feeling you get when you are sitting in a descending jet, the undercarriage locks into place, and you know you are going to land safely. It didn't take a genius to work out that she was about to launch into a justification of some hair-brained scheme of which I wouldn't approve, and that she expected me to respond with my usual squeals and remonstrations. She was never going to change, and I would have to like it or lump it. The ground was rushing up to meet me, I tightened my safety belt, and went for liking it.

"You can't shock me any more," I said confidently, "I'm sure it's an extremely sensible plan."

She steered me towards the settee, "Sit down anyway. The curry needs time to brew."

I listened placidly while she sidled up to the part of her spiel she believed would be the most contentious.

"The more I think about it, the more I think you might be right about Mrs Brewster being a thief." She checked my face for signs of disapproval. I didn't let on that I had given this matter very little thought since Thursday night.

"So, over the weekend, I did some more detective work. I asked Mrs T. if Edna's home help had come from Caring Hands, and when she said 'yes', I went and had a word with Shirley, seeing as she used to work for them."

"Why didn't you just talk to Stella? She's worked for them for longer."

Liz sucked air in through her teeth, "Dunno, exactly. I don't like to think that Stella's in league with the bad guys, but I wanted to be careful. Just because Mr Brewster took a pot shot at her, and she herself mentioned home helps that afternoon at Tom's, doesn't mean she isn't playing some kind of double-bluff. And don't look at me like my lifts don't go quite to the top, I'm following my instincts."

I re-composed my features into their smiling calm, "And where did your instincts lead you with Shirley?"

"A long way. Listen to this." She began tapping my leg to make her points, "Mrs Brewster personally visits every new client, supposedly to check on their needs, so that gives her a chance to case the joint for valuables. Every client hands over a front or back door key, which is kept in the agency office for home helps to pick up and return, so Mrs Brewster can easily have copies made. And last but not least," her tap became a grip, "Shirley said that all the employees were under strict instructions to inform the management as soon as they found out if any client was in hospital or had shuffled off the mortal whatsit. I think, my loyal sidekick, that we have established beyond reasonable doubt that Mrs Brewster has the means and the opportunity to carry out these hideous crimes. We just need to find out if Tom and Dodgy's Mrs Cardew had a Caring Hands home help. If she did, I'd say we were home and dry."

"What about motive, chief inspector? Why should an apparently wealthy and successful woman stoop so low? You haven't mentioned your plan yet, either." As long as it didn't involve visiting the Brewster's palatial spread again, I thought I could cope.

She looked pleased with me, as if I had asked the right question. "Yes, the motive puzzled me. But I think Shirley gave me the answer."

"Pray enlighten me Miss Marple."

"Ok. Beneath her somewhat hedonistic exterior, Shirley is in fact quite an acute observer of social behaviour and the class system. In other words, she's dead nosy about people and where they come from. She told me that in the good old days, Mrs Brewster's parents lived in Kenya, where they sipped pink gin on the verandah while the Africans toiled in their fields. After independence, they upped sticks with their children and went to Rhodesia, as it was then, to continue enjoying their colonial lifestyle. Shirley got the feeling, though, that they weren't quite as well off as they had been in Kenya, and that Verity, that's Mrs Brewster, rather married beneath her when she tied the knot with Billy Brewster. He worked for the railways, high up and on a good salary, of course, but still not quite our class darling."

"So he's not the country gentleman he pretends to be? How did they end up here with that big house?"

Liz looked pleased with me again, "Well, Shirley says they retreated to England after Zimbabwe became independent, and she reckons they sold up what they owned in Africa, and smuggled the proceeds out as gold to give them a nest-egg. Mrs Brewster started her business, it flourished, and hey presto, a few years later they were able to buy their dream home outside the city, where squire Brewster could make out that he was a retired coffee planter or some such."

I had a think, "That still doesn't give them a motive for theft, does it? They must be comfortably off as it is. Stella once said that the agency made a mint."

Liz adjusted an imaginary pair of specs, "The motive, my dear child, lies in the realms of psychology. From what Shirley said, my theory is that Mrs Brewster, in particular, has a huge chip on her shoulder. She thinks she deserves an upper-class lifestyle, she resents having to work for it, and so she nicks stuff from clients she despises to buy little luxuries that otherwise she couldn't afford. What with the upkeep of that great pile and all."

I ummed and aahed, "I'm not quite convinced. . ."

Liz looked me full in the eye, "Kate, I know I'm right. It takes a thief to catch a thief. I've been there, I know the mindset. Only in my case, I thought I was an artist, expanding my mind with drugs and living the low life, so that one day I could astound the world with my photographic genius. I didn't see why other less talented drones shouldn't subsidise me by surrendering their wallets."

I had no reply to this. She laughed, not entirely comfortably, "The difference is, I realised that I wasn't a great artist, and I would have to go partly straight or I'd end up inside. I only broke the law for the fun of it, to relieve the monotony of a steady job, after I left London that time."

I was stumped. No matter how well I thought I'd come to know her, she still had the capacity to startle me.

Her laughter changed to an easier chortle, "I'll modify that. I'm a whizz at photography, and I can be amazingly artistic, but I don't have that thing which makes a top-notch photographer."

"Like me," I said, before she could say it, "I was about sixteen when it sunk in that I wasn't going to be an international soloist, playing concertos with the Berlin Philharmonic. It took several years after that for me to find my level."

"Precisely. That's why we're so well-matched."

"We're getting off track, here," I said, a few well-matched kisses later. "Have you spoken to Tom about all this? It's his

140

problem really."

She sighed, "No-o. I'd like to have some hard evidence to give him, so he doesn't think I'm tripping. That's where my plan comes in. The curry must be done by now, I'll tell you while you're eating."

She hadn't lied about the curry's adult-only strength rating. It was like eating a slice of the Indian sub-continent, and a perfect antidote to a northern British November evening. Liz still couldn't force herself to be direct.

"Shirley's aunt does our cleaning at the business," she pointed out, chewing on a mouthful of lime pickle without flinching.

I tried to reduce the temperature of my tongue with yoghurt, "Does she?"

"Yeah. And by a curious coincidence she happens to clean the building where Caring Hands have their offices. On Tuesday mornings, she does the ground floor, and on Tuesday evenings, she does the first floor, which is Mrs Brewster's empire."

I thought I could see where this was leading, "I don't suppose she has keys to all the offices?"

"Strangely enough, she does."

"And is she going to acquire a tall, dark, snoopy assistant one Tuesday evening?" Industrial espionage might be a step up from storing drugs, transporting smuggled booze, stalking singers and all the other misdemeanours she had previously favoured.

Liz looked wary, "Not quite. She's actually going to acquire a bad knee, which will mean that one of her other kind employers will volunteer to do her evening stint, so she doesn't run the risk of losing her contract."

I abandoned the indirect approach. "Let me get this straight. You're going to disguise yourself as a cleaner, break into the Caring Hands offices, and see if you can find any evidence of Mrs Brewster running a burglary operation?"

Her wariness became outright apprehension, "That's about the sum of it. Of course, I'll cover my tracks and won't do any damage or anything. It shouldn't be that risky, and I've got a valid excuse for being there. I'll wear an overall and rubber gloves."

She watched me pick out a chilli, and put it to the side of my plate, "Kate. . ."

"There's a flaw in all of this," I said mildly.

"What?" She braced herself for a torrent of abuse.

"It'll take you too long if you have to clean and then hack into Mrs Brewster's computer and ransack her filing cabinets. You'll need a look-out as well. I'd better come with you." I showed how hard I was by swallowing the chilli whole, refusing first-aid when my top half burst into flames, and not rushing to the freezer cabinet to cover myself in frozen peas.

Subjected to the water torture of my agreement with her plan, Liz broke at bedtime.

"What's wrong with you?" she shouted, tearing my book from my hands. "Are you on tranquillisers?"

"Darling, whatever can you mean? I've never felt better." I'd been silently practising this transparent voice and expression all evening.

She had no choice but to continue her bull in a china shop blunder onwards, "So why aren't you screaming and yelling at me, and trying to stop me getting into those offices? I thought I could depend on you." Her twisted logic sometimes baffled even me. I took her hand, and did my utmost not to laugh into those thwarted, peeved eyes.

"Ok, Liz. I think it's an utterly terrible plan. In a lifetime of dire plans, you have exceeded yourself with this one. It's worse than anything thought up by Mr McBadplan of Badplan city. I have no vocabulary to express how loopy it is, or how awful it will be when we're caught. But," I brought her fingers to my lips and kissed them, "I know that whatever I say will make not an iota of difference to you, and you'll do it anyway. I've decided to preserve my blood vessels and save my energy by taking the path of least resistance. There, is that better?"

I'd never seen such a kaleidoscope of emotions cross her face. They finished with the grudging amusement and admiration of a conman who has been out-conned. She sank back into the pillows.

"Ah so, grasshopper, I have taught you too well. You are

as wily as your master. Cow." She plumped up the quilt and whined, "You see, it was always such fun persuading you to agree with me."

The skin around her lips was still a faintly lime pickle flavour, which was by no means a turn-off. I stopped kissing her for a moment, "Never mind. Let's do it the other way round, and I'll try and persuade you of something." I heard Dainty give a scratch in passing at the closed door which kept her downstairs. "How about me trying to persuade you to let Dainty sleep here with us?"

"You'll never succeed. . . don't let me put you off trying, though."

We went to sleep with the honours even. I had her verbal assent that Dainty could go upstairs in the daytime, and I had somehow agreed to do all the cleaning in the Caring Hands offices on the coming Tuesday evening.

14

Tuesday night was perfect for expeditions of a cloak and dagger nature. A cold mist, smelling of smoke and the sea, fuzzed the streetlamps, and the scattered, muffled figures on the pavements huddled, heads down, towards the vital heat of homes and pubs. My sang-froid about our foray into the nether world of bogus cleaners had been dented by the discovery that Caring Hands' offices were up near our historic castle, which was probably the oldest prison in the country, having been in continual use since at least the middle ages. A few hundred feet away, behind black walls and dimly lit windows, lay a world as unknown as Mars, from which I was protected only by the permeable barrier of good luck and circumstance. I had a quake under Shirley's aunt's nylon overall, which comprised my disguise, and tried to flit lightly over the cobbles. On a night like this, all the sickening tales of violent justice told to us by Issy, our amateur historian friend, seemed close and contemporary. I was breathing the same tainted air as those wretches who were dragged on hurdles from this spot through the stinking city to a horrible death, and beyond the mist, the same primitive shapes of ignorance and fear waited to return. I hummed to myself to keep them at bay.

"Why are you singing 'Zorba the Greek'?" Liz asked, rattling a bunch of keys like a ghost with its rusty chains.

"It's the theme from 'The Third Man', cloth ears. Is this it?" She had stopped outside a solid wooden door set into the wall of a fine stone building with sash windows, cast-iron drainpipes, and polished brass nameplates by the entrance.

"Yup. The ground floor is a firm of solicitors, very up-market."

"Thank goodness it's not Eleanor's firm." She was Issy's solicitor partner, and although a true friend, would not, I suspected, have wanted to know of our venture, "It would be a bit off if we were caught in her building, and we asked her to defend us."

"You're getting cold feet, you fraud." Liz was still struggling with my new-found tolerance of her villainy.

"No I'm not. I'm just planning for every eventuality." I smoothed my overall, shut my eyes and took some sighing breaths, "Let me get into role. Mm..mm. . . yes, I'm there, I have Mrs Mop's motivation, open up."

She selected a key, and in we went, the door closing behind us with a well-oiled clunk. By the diffused spectral glow of a streetlamp filtering through the fanlight, I found a light switch, and we were back in the 21st century, in a neutral cream passageway. Its faint odour of paper, box files and photocopiers reminded me of my ex, Chloe's, department at the university, as did its air of being a place where arcane yet serious business was conducted. Guided by a set of neat "Caring Hands This Way" signs, we passed through a pair of fire doors, up a carpeted staircase, through more fire doors and into the dragon's lair. The click of another light switch revealed it in all its unshowy comfort. We were in a seating bay furnished with well-upholstered chairs and a low table, which boasted a twee dried flower arrangement and a fan of glossy brochures in the dead centre of its waxed surface. A receptionist's hatch, closed for the night, ran along one wall, and reproduction watercolours of the Lake District adorned the others. Another passageway, to the side of the hatch, clearly led to the actual offices. Any worried relative seeking reliable help for an aged member of the family couldn't fail to be reassured by this clean, professional set-up. I messed it up a jot by throwing my coat, scarf and gloves on to one of the chairs, and sitting on another to read the list of instructions Shirley's aunt had passed on to me. Liz, meanwhile, methodically unlocked every door in sight.

"Cleaning store," she pronounced, opening a door opposite the bay, "now you've no excuse not to get busy. She usually takes about an hour, so we'll try not to spend longer up here."

I frowned at the list, "Start panicking. This is going to take me all night." According to my orders, I had to collect any dirty cups from around the offices, wash them in the little kitchen next to the store, scrub the kitchen floor, clean the loos, dust any uncovered desk space (without moving a single piece of paper), empty the bins into a refuse sack, vacuum the entire floor area and put the refuse sack outside the back door on the ground floor. I hoped they paid Shirley's aunt more than the minimum wage, and decided that I could only match her work rate if I ignored Liz altogether and got on with it.

This wasn't easy at first, since on my search for coffee cups, I saw her in action in the offices. These consisted of a large-ish open plan area behind the receptionist's hatch, complete with several desks, computer terminals, filing cabinets and rubber plants, and Mrs Brewster's inner sanctum, which could be reached both by a door from the main office, and a door from the passage. Across the passage were the loos and a less well-ordered room housing a photocopier and shelf after shelf of files. True to form, Liz made straight for Mrs Brewster's room, switched on the computer and had a go at breaking into the desk while the machine warmed up. Unnerved by her less than gentle tugging at a clearly locked drawer, I asked her courteously if she knew what she was doing. She replied with a curt burst of the techno-speak she knew would bamboozle me, and I backed out with my load of used cups, well and truly put in my place.

Three quarters of an hour later, and I had been taken over by the unquiet spirit of some cleaner who still haunted her old patch. My overall was damp and grimy, you could have eaten a three course meal off the kitchen floor, the loos reeked of pine cleaner and disinfectant, and I was sitting on an upturned bucket in the store, enjoying Caring Hands' chocolate biscuits, a mug of their tea, a crafty fag, and a read of a magazine I had found hidden near the photocopier. Bins, dust, vacuum, I repeated to myself when I had discovered more than I wanted about a starlet's fourth marriage, shouldn't be too bad. I pinched out my cigarette, slipped the tab-end into my overall pocket, had a quick spray around with some air-freshener, picked up a refuse sack and sallied forth. I left Mrs Brewster's bin until last, when my sack was nearly full with wads of paper, the unsavoury remains of office lunches, tea bags and coffee grounds. Dragging it into her office, I almost tipped out the lot at the scene before me.

"Whatchewdoin'?" The disembodied voice of an affronted domestic came out of my mouth, "Who's going to clear up this mess?"

"You're the cleaner," Liz grunted from down on her knees, and carried on sifting through the contents of a large waste-paper bin, which she had upended on to the carpet. "You haven't emptied all the other bins have you?"

I lugged at the sack, "What do you think this is?" She eyed it greedily. "Oh no," it was time to be strong, "you're not emptying this on my floors. If you want to look through it, you'll have to take it home. Anyway, why. . .?"

She put one hand to her face, and thumped the floor with the other, "I can't get into their fucking computers, their filing cabinets or anything. This is my last resort."

It was also time to draw back from suggesting that she might have thought of this before we set out.

"This sack is going in the store. Pick all that up, and put it in it when you've finished. I've got my dusting and vacuuming to do yet."

She looked surprised, "Aren't you going to help me here? Two minds will be better than one."

"Jesus Christ." I kicked at a screwed-up ball of paper, "What are you looking for?"

"Clues."

I bent down, and fished out a random till receipt, "Here's one. She bought, let me see, a salmon and cucumber sandwich and a bottle of mineral water yesterday. There's your evidence. She's spending money on expensive lunches, she must be a crook." I subsided at her most frightening glower, "All right. I'll give you two minutes."

I have engaged in much more fascinating activities than rifling through someone else's rubbish, even when that rubbish contained such thought-provoking items as circulars advertising office equipment and stair-lifts. What did Liz hope to find? A discarded letter from a fence, saying, "Dear Mrs Brewster, Thank you for stealing those medals. If there are any more where they came from, I'll have them. Your faithful servant, Thos. Rogue Esq."? Convinced that I was wasting cleaning time, I half-heartedly unscrewed the ball of paper I'd kicked, separated the sheets, and whinnied. It was hardly a smoking gun, but this photocopied article from a trade magazine was the nearest thing to a clue I'd seen all evening.

"Beatrix Potter Books, Ephemera and Memorabilia," I read the title out loud to Liz, keeping the pages from her grasping hands, "an update on recent prices." The print of the article was tiny, and its style was deathly dull, yet the prices it quoted for figurines of Mrs Tiggywinkle, let alone for early editions of the tales of Flopsy, Mopsy, Dropsy and co. made me gasp.

"See?" I gestured to my fellow spy, "She must have a client who has a collection of this tat, and she's been checking out what it's worth."

"Kate, you're fantastic," her faith in criminal nature restored, Liz fell on top of me, "I knew we'd find something if we kept at it."

I started trying to get her off me, "Don't get carried away. There might be an innocent explanation."

"Pish tush, the woman's a bad'un." She stood up, and looked at her watch, "We're running out of time. Give me that article. You finish off your cleaning, and I'll have a quick run through the rest of this. I'll put it in the sack when I'm done."

Heady with relief that the end of this charade was in sight, I ran around with a duster, and then a fierce vacuum cleaner which sucked at the carpets like a beast let out of its cage. Liz scooped paper into the sack, shot down the stairs to throw it out of the back door, and followed me round, turning off lights and locking doors behind me.

"Get your coat on," she ordered, giving the table in the seating area a cursory wipe with my scarf, "I'll stick the vacuum back in that store."

I turned off the last light switch while her key was still in the store lock, "I think you owe me a drink or two," I said bouncily, "not to mention a snack, like a takeaway pizza, for instance. . ." I was counting my chickens. The thunk of the front door closing, and two sets of heavy footsteps in the passage below reverberated through the building. My hair levitated with fright, and I didn't need to be a lip-reader to decipher what Liz was mouthing.

"Maybe it's the solicitors," I mouthed back, wishing I hadn't had that mug of tea.

It wasn't. The footsteps followed a relentless course through the fire doors and up the first few stairs. There was only one thing we could do, and we did it, shutting the store door behind us at the precise nanosecond the footsteps reached the second pair of fire doors at the top of the staircase. I sat on my bucket, shaking like an aspen leaf, and rueing the day I had first encountered Liz's immoral beauty.

"Rue, rue," I moaned into the dark. If we were here for any longer than ten minutes, I'd have to turn the bucket over, the noise would alert these new intruders, and I would be discovered in a most undignified position. The thousand decibel click as Liz locked us in shortened that estimate to about thirty seconds. Through the thumping of blood in my ears, I heard the light being turned on again, footsteps shuffling along the passage, and the handle of an office door being turned.

"The Brewsters?" Liz's barely audible whisper tightened my overworked pelvic floor muscles even more.

"Who else?" I breathed back, "We're toast."

"No, I think they're leaving." As my eyes adjusted to our black hole, I could see Liz's head pressed against the edge of the door. The footsteps returned to the sitting area, where, I recalled with the heart-stopping terror of nightmares, I had left my gloves.

"Someone's forgotten their gloves," a male voice I recognised all too well boomed out. "That's funny, they look like. . ."

"Leave them," a second, female, voice instructed.

"No, let me have a look, they can't be. . . I'm going to have to sit down."

My mind caught up with my ears, and Liz moved to clutch at me, her body as trembly as mine. In the minimum of whispers, we planned our next move.

"Now!" she hissed.

Woman and woman moving in perfect balletic sequence, she unlocked and threw open the door, and out I jumped, brandishing a mop and the air freshener.

"You're nicked, my son," I hollered, spraying triumphantly to maximise the effect.

Tom and Stella's screams could have been heard inside the prison.

"What language, Pearcey. Does Pat know you're out?" It was always a pleasure to see Liz crying with laughter, and this was doubly sweet, as was the fixed image of those two faces in the far reaches of shock. I was sure I had riled Tom many times, but he had never used such Anglo-Saxon terms to me before, nor did I realise that Stella had such a colourful turn of phrase.

"I knew you were trouble the first time I clapped eyes on you. Jesus, my poor old heart." Tom slumped back on the pub settle, and pummelled at his ribs.

The four of us, Liz and I hooting, and Tom and Stella hyperventilating, had charged out of the building, belted for the nearest pub, and collapsed in the old-fashioned snug, away from the barman who must have thought we were escapees from an amateur dramatic production. I still had my overall on, and in deference to her and Tom's as yet unexplained mission, Stella was sporting a man's giant black opera cape with a scarlet lining over a silver lame sweater and her crimson trews. Now she threw off the cape, and pulled out the thin artist's paintbrush which was keeping her hair in place.

"You scumbags. You've made me strain my vocal chords."

Liz made a cross with her fingers at her, "Ok Dracula, what were you doing there anyway? How did you get in?"

"How did you get in?" Stella shook her hair, leaned forward, and pressed her thumbs to the base of her cranium.

"I asked you first, creature of the night."

She shut her eyes, "Leave me alone. I'm going to re-calibrate my energies."

Tom knocked back his whisky chaser, "Those gloves you left on the chair are Pat's," he accused me, "I should have known it was you, you pickpocket, they gave you away."

"She lent them to me. Did you think she was lurking in ambush for you?"

"It crossed my mind. It's hellish hard keeping anything from her. I think she's bugged my shop." He emptied loose change from a pocket, and began to count it, "How much is whisky these days? Looks like we've all reached the same conclusion, doesn't it? Caring Hands is the hub of a ripping off valuables scam. Stella told me she was getting bad feelings about her boss, and talked me into this. . . visit."

I took a pound from his pile, "I'll get you another. How do you know I wasn't there legitimately? Cleaning could be my new day job, and I could perform a citizen's arrest on you for breaking and entering."

"I've noticed all legitimate cleaners hide in cupboards with their no-good partners. Besides, technically speaking, we didn't break and enter. Stella's got a key. We could arrest you."

"Yah boo, we've got a key too," I said with infantile relish, "and I did the cleaning, and we found a clue, so that makes us better than you."

"What clue?" He didn't want to ask, and was unable to stop himself.

I looked at Liz, who'd been tittering into her beer. "Not telling," she said smugly, "If Stella's got a key, how come you didn't go into the offices?"

Stella opened her eyes, put the paintbrush in her mouth, and started gathering up her hair again, "Marie, who works in the office, is always leaving her keys lying around." She removed the brush from her teeth, and stabbed it expertly into the loose bun she'd created, "Being the smooth operator I am, I palmed them today, had them copied at that kiosk in the market, and slipped them back. It was a bit of a rush job, though, and the office key didn't work, more's the pity, since I know the password of the main computer system, and I could have had a look through the files."

"Really?" Liz struggled not to sound too interested.

"Really. Marie let me send an e-mail last week, and gave it to me."

The two of them eyeballed each other like gunslingers waiting for a flicker of movement. It was Liz who at last gave an infinitesimal twitch, and smiled in recognition,

"Hm. Maybe we should pool our resources."

I got to my feet, "Maybe I should go to the bar." A voice of caution and restraint would carry no weight with these two. "Same again, everyone?"

I returned in time to hear the end of Stella's exposition of how her suspicions had been aroused. Liz had relinquished our clue to Tom, who was whistling at the prices.

"A couple of the other girls were talking about Mrs Cardew, and how she'd been the ideal client, and the name rang a bell. Then when I saw that Edna Braithwaite had been a client as well, I knew something fishy was afoot. I mean, I said that home helps could be the bad guys at Tom's that Sunday, but I was joking, and now I can see that it would work, with Mrs Brewster's system that Shirley told you about. I never had anything to do with Mrs Brewster while I worked away from here, and she was only an efficient voice on the phone. Seeing her nearly every day, though, and I can tell you, she gives me the willies."

"Why?" I was curious to see if Stella's opinion of her tallied with Shirley's.

"Euch, she gives herself such airs. She sits in that office of hers like Lady Muck, handing out orders and name-dropping like nobody's business. She'd like us to believe that she's best friends with all the local nobs, you know, 'Oh, Sir Ollie is such a sweetie', and garbage like that."

"Bleah. There you go, that's just like what Shirley said," Liz said ungrammatically, "I bet she and her husband keep their loot somewhere near their house, and that's why he shot at you both."

I took another nip of vodka, "Terrific. I'm not going out there again, and I don't think you should either. You'd be no use to me full of bullet holes, and it wouldn't promote Stella's singing career."

Stella jumped, as if someone had pranged her with a hatpin, "Singing career! I can't be sitting here boozing with you. I was meant to be at Dave's five minutes ago for another music lesson." She downed the best part of a pint of stout, and rose without a wobble.

Liz made a moue of disgust, "Puh-lease. You can call a spade a bloody shovel with us."

Stella's laugh shivered the panelled timbers of the snug, "Seriously. I'm learning a lot. I'm nearly ready for my debut, he says." She donned her cape, "I'll ring you tomorrow, Liz, and we can discuss giving the offices another try. Be good, my lovies."

"Why don't you just give me the password?" Liz pleaded futilely to her retreating back.

She turned and waggled her finger, "Because mutual support and cooperation is an ideal we should aim for. See you." She was gone before Liz could seize her by her train and beat the password out of her.

"Pizza time?" I put in my tentative request.

Tom cradled his whisky, "I'll have to go home, I told Pat I was at the shop, and she might ring me there. Don't want her imagining I've got a mistress." He frowned slightly at us, "Don't think I'm being impertinent or ungrateful, but why are you two so bothered about who's behind these little thefts?"

"Because we're your friends, and whoever's doing this is harming your business," Liz said baldly. She blushed becomingly, and strove to make amends for her descent into honest emotion, "Oh Tom, it's fun. It's a mystery, it adds some sparkle to life. And I want to solve it, and hand you the answer on a plate, so you can see what a ·smart southerner I am."

"You don't have to convince me of that." He gave us both

unexpected clumsy pecks on the cheek, "Keep me posted, and don't do anything silly, you hear?"

He backed out quickly, in case any more embarrassing truths were exchanged.

While I was willing to accept Liz's explanation of her motives, particularly after she'd bought us a large take-away version of my favourite pizza, one unanswered question tugged at me with the obstinacy of an obstreperous toddler. Ignoring it was impossible, and I took the plunge as I was licking the last of the melted cheese from my fingers.

"Liz, how far do you think Brigitte's Harry is involved with the Brewsters, always assuming that they are thieves?" I thought it would be more tactful to lay the emphasis on Brigitte's business partner, rather than on her.

Liz took the pizza box, empty apart from a few scraps, away from Dainty's nose, "Overweight cats shouldn't eat pizza. I don't know, and I'm not about to phone Brigitte to find out. We'll see what Caring Hands' computers come up with, if I ever get the password from Stella."

Cravenly, I didn't kick at the door she'd closed in my face. "All right. What do you hope to find in the computers?"

She pursed her lips, "Patterns. Hidden files. Anything different in Mrs Cardew's and Edna's files to show they've been robbed. Incongruities, anomalies, strange e-mails, the list is endless. There should be something there."

I altered course, "I'm quite busy for the rest of this week, and we're off to Dorset on Saturday. I can't see when I'm going to have time to clean again."

She regarded me more kindly, "I know, honey bun. Don't worry, Stella and I can do the necessary." She moved in to disarm me, "We won't do anything that can be traced back to us, and I promise you we won't get caught. I'll let you know what we're up to, so you don't have sleepless nights at that luxury recording studio fretting over me, I'll stay out of the nick, and I'll feed Dainty. Trust me."

"As far as I can throw you." My usual response was a lie. I'd fallen prey to gullibility, and believed every word she had said.

15

In the few days left before the band went to Dorset, I continued to be peculiarly blase about whatever Liz and Stella might be cooking up between them. A major contribution to this sorry state of affairs was Liz's off the cuff remark on Wednesday night, after a rowdy evening at the Billhook.

"Stella and I've decided not to mess around in those offices again for the time being. It was fun the first time, but we can't see that it'll be that productive." She carried on with her minute search for grey hairs, aided by two mirrors and a strategically placed lamp.

I gingerly peeled off my shirt, "Aw, look, this is ruined, that beer stain will never come out. . . what?"

"We're going to lie low for a while, and see what happens. Gotcha, you little bugger." She plucked fiercely at her head.

"How many times do I have to tell you?" I dropped the shirt and concealed my relief by moaning at the condition of my jeans, "Hell and damnation, another cigarette burn. Ten grey ones will grow back for every one you pull out. You'll have to start dyeing it."

She scowled, and got heavily into bed, "This is only the start. Soon it'll be reading glasses and driving more slowly, and before you know it, it'll be hot flushes and HRT. At least your wrinkles will be worse than mine because you smoke so much."

I hopped in beside her, "Cheers. It's so nice to have a ray of sunshine by me, when I've had booze poured all over me by a drunk, and pulled every muscle in my back from dancing."

Her arms were warm creepers around me, "You see? We're not teenagers any more, we need to look after ourselves. You'll have to take it easy in Dorset without me there to make your cocoa and give you your vitamin pills."

My eyes began to close, "You don't half talk rubbish. Drinking all night and making whoopee is part of the job specification. That singer is really attractive as well. . . ow, any more of that, and I'll go into the spare room."

"Please do, I might get a decent night's sleep. Tell me again, when exactly are you coming back from Dorset?" She slipped the question in so cleverly among her butterfly kisses, that I missed its significance until later on.

"A week on Monday." I kissed her back, and thought I'd give the spare room a miss.

Naturally, I couldn't avoid the knowledge that, even if it didn't involve another nocturnal visit to Caring Hands' offices, Liz was up to something nefarious: her devoted attention to me before Saturday made sure of that. However, I didn't waste any energy on trying to discover her intentions. Instead, I practised hard for the coming recording, instructed her on Dainty's preferred feeding schedule, and joined the band's van on Saturday morning in an anticipatory mood, heightened by the presence of a large walnut and coffee cake in my luggage. The recording studio experience was everything I'd hoped it would be. The countryside was tranquil, the weather obliged us with frosty mornings and nights so clear you could snap the air, the food was magnificent, and the singer was a charming perfectionist, who drove us beyond the limits of what I'd thought I could achieve. It was all going swimmingly until disaster struck on the Friday morning. A cruel laryngitis bug attacked our singer, sent her back in tears to a throat specialist in London, and left us twiddling our thumbs and debating how to fill the weekend. I would have been quite happy to stay on in Dorset to play around in the studio, Fred and Jo suggested following the singer to London to look up old friends and pubs, Bill was easy either way, and Dave wanted to go home. I realised this from his unusual unspoken agitation when it appeared that a frivolous jaunt to London in the van was emerging as the bookies' favourite. I guessed that he was missing Stella, and would rather have his wisdom teeth extracted without an anaesthetic than admit to it. He disappeared at lunchtime, and came back wearing an expression of embarrassed determination.

"Look chaps and chapesses," he began diffidently, "if it's all the same to you, I've had the offer of a lift home tonight I might take up. I could use a free weekend to fix my kitchen."

This was such an outrageous lie, that we all accepted it with murmurs of "of course", "no problem", and "go ahead".

Emboldened by the success of his mendacity, he became generous, "There's room for you Kate, if you want to get back to Liz. You'll have to make up your mind quickly, though, because I need to phone this guy back."

I havered. The prospect of a wild time in London had been quite appealing in theory. I could get drunk and sing in the streets without running into anyone I knew, and I thought I deserved a break. The downside was that I would spend too much money, and would probably end up sleeping on someone's floor to wake up to a stiff back and monstrous hangovers. It wasn't as if I was in the market for a chance fling, either. If I was at home, I could spend all weekend lolling about, with Liz at hand to attend to my creature comforts. . .

"I'll come with you," I said quickly.

He smiled for the first time since breakfast, "Great. I'll just make this call, then you can ring Liz and give her the good news."

After I'd spoken to Liz, I knew I'd made the right choice. Even allowing for the fact that the reception on Dave's phone was lousy, the startled gulp with which she initially greeted my glad tidings travelled the miles between us like an arrow, and left me in no doubt that she had plans for the weekend which didn't include me.

"That's fantastic," she attempted an unconvincing recovery, "I'm working for most of tomorrow, so I'll see you in the afternoon sometime, if you get back after I've gone out in the morning. Customer here, got to go sweetie." She made a hasty kissing sound and rang off.

"And I'll fettle you," I said uncouthly into the receiver.

"All sorted?" Dave had crept up behind me, "Ta." He took his rotten phone off me, and gave me his customary 'I'm a lot smarter than you' look. "There's two things I didn't tell you about this lift."

"And they are?" I was just too wishy-washy to ever get him to treat me as an equal.

He stroked his beard lovingly, "It leaves at three in the morning, and it's with a gang of leccies from Glasgow who're working somewhere down here, and going home for their days off. In a minibus."

I felt myself going grey with shock, "Why three in the morning? Human beings aren't designed to do practical stuff at that hour."

He looked even more as if he'd pulled a fast one, "Well, their shift finishes at six, and they like to clean up and go for a drink and a curry before the drive home. All we've got to do is be on time at the car park in Dorchester where they meet up. Len here at the studio says I can borrow his car, and leave it in the car park for him to pick up later. Don't look a gift horse in the mouth, Katie dear, you'll be back in your little love-nest in no time."

Some gift horse, I mithered to myself, if it involves sitting in a minbus with a crowd of tanked-up electricians, and some love-nest if Liz wasn't over the moon to see me.

My inner critic was working overtime by half past two in the morning as I humped my bags through the aching cold to Len's car. I should have tried to get some sleep instead of sitting up drinking with Len, I should have gone to London with the others in the holiday-mood van, I should have quit the band ages ago, found a respectable job, and stayed at home to keep Liz on a tight rein. I wasn't greatly enthused either by the sight of the minibus and our fellow passengers. They stood around in groups of twos and threes, tough-looking men smoking vigorously and wearing only shirts and club-going trousers in the arctic night. Several of them were drinking from cans, crates of which lay at their feet, and they greeted our approach with the expected shouts.

"It's yer hippy hitchhikers, Sandy."

"Gie us wan o' yer tunes pal."

"Youse can sit on my lap, hinny, I'll keep youse warm."

"Thank you Dave," I muttered, following their rolling progress up into the bus, "I'll have a limo next time."

He pushed me into an empty seat by a window, and tried to fit his legs in beside me, "Better keep a civil tongue in your head, young lady, or I won't defend your virtue."

"Don't flatter yourself, you wouldn't stand a chance against them. I'll have to fall back on my black belt in karate if they get frisky."

That made him laugh, and I took off my jacket, bundled it up against the window as a makeshift pillow and shut my eyes. "Wake me up when he stops to drop us off. Don't leave me here."

"I wouldn't do that." His voice was surprisingly sincere, "Good night sweetheart."

Exhaustion and alcohol soon took its toll of our travelling companions, the van quietened down after several miles, and I fell into an uncomfortable draughty doze, to wander down the twisting corridors of confused dreams. The motion of the minibus translated into the rocking of a train, and I was sitting opposite Liz and Brigitte who were laughing at me.

"She hasn't a clue, Busy Lizzie," Brigitte stroked Liz's thigh, and spoke into the downy softness of her ear, "she hasn't a clue what we're like together."

Liz smiled her private smile of about to be satisfied desire, "She's a silly little girl. Forget about her, my honey-bee."

The ticket collector shook my shoulder, "Are you travelling without a ticket? Wake up, Kate."

"How do you know my name?" I began, thinking that his whiskery face was familiar.

"Wake up, Kate," Dave repeated quietly, "it's only a bad dream."

I pulled my head sharply away from my jacket, as if I had been resting on a nest of vipers, and fought for consciousness. I was in a minibus, I was going home, Liz wasn't with Brigitte. The icy sickness of betrayal still squeezed my heart, and my knees knocked together in a spasm of chilly shivering. A skein of lights drifted past the window, a nameless place in the harsh loneliness of the motorway night.

"You were crying. Use this," Dave said calmly, and handed me a clean man's handkerchief. It smelt safe and fatherly, and I clutched at it, a thread to guide me out of the labyrinth.

"Foul things, nightmares," Dave confided, "I still dream of terrible things happening to my kids, and have to stop myself phoning the ex. It kills me."

It was the most intimate thing he'd ever said to me, and I didn't know how to answer.

He gave a self-conscious smile, and bent down to extricate a bag from under the seat, "Coffee? Jammy dodger?"

I could have kissed him, the flask and the packet of biscuits he conjured out of the bag.

"Of course, this is your department," he pronounced, pouring out a steaming cup, "but I thought I'd prepare a back-up."

I salivated like one of Pavlov's best dogs, "What do you mean, my department? Give me that cup, and I'll wash your socks all the time we're in the States."

He held it to his chest, "Promises, promises. How about me, you and Liz together in one of those big motel beds?"

"You filthy bugger. Ok." He surrendered the elixir of life, and I drank like a desert nomad at an oasis. "Whoops, I've changed my mind, the deal's off. I'm not going to tread on Stella's toes."

"She won't be there." He meant to say it lightly, but it came out bursting with regret, and he swiftly went back to answering my earlier question.

"It's your department because you're the catering manager for the band. Didn't you know?" He gave me an opaque look, "You always know where to get a cup of tea, wherever we are, and you remember every late night kebab shop and 24-hour garage in every obscure town we've ever been in. Don't you realise that this is your most important function?"

I laughed with him, "Darn, and all these years I've been thinking you wanted me for my musical ability."

"That's my department. Have another biscuit." He rubbed his eyes, then looked sourly at the snoring heaps surrounding us, "I'm pooped. Can you see yourself doing this forever?"

"What?" Our voices were hushed and exclusive in this alien company.

"Bashing up and down the country at odd hours, playing with the band, never knowing if the money's going to keep coming in."

There was nothing to be gained by being flippant or economical with the truth, "I think about it sometimes, but I can't see myself in a proper job. Though if I decided to go for having children, I'd have to stop." In heaven's name, why had I let that slip out?

He didn't bat an eyelid, "Yeah. You could always go into teaching. If Fred and Jo's grand plan for a music centre at home comes off, which it might do now they're talking with the council, there'd be an opening there."

No-one in the band had spoken so explicitly of this project before. I'd always thought of Fred and Jo's dream of a music centre, with recording and teaching facilities, a library of tunes, and a performance area, as so much pie in the sky.

"I didn't realise they'd got so far with it." I filched another biscuit, "D'you think it'll get off the ground?"

"There's a good chance it might, what with all these funds they can tap into nowadays, the lottery, European money. . ." He proffered the flask again, "Ah, the lesson of impermanence, as the Buddhists say. How did you get Liz to stop rampaging round, and stick with you?"

Twenty four hours ago, I would never have imagined having such a conversation with Dave. I tried to be modest, "I must have just caught her at the right time, when she was ready for a mite of stability. Why?"

He did the man thing of weighing up what he was going to say, then found his laces fascinating, "I'd marry Stella tomorrow, if she'd have me. Is she at the stage of wanting some stability, in your opinion?"

The plastic cup from the flask clattered against my teeth, and coffee trickled becomingly down my chin. This was when I could pay him back for all his sarcastic put-downs and close to the bone comments. I could burst into raucous laughter and tell him that he hadn't a chance, that Stella never stayed long with anyone, and that he was off his head to be putting marriage and Stella in the same sentence.

I patted his forearm, "I honestly couldn't say, Dave. I would just see how it goes, and not rush anything."

"Ok." He turned eagerly to me, "Isn't she the most amazing singer? And she's so quick to learn. . ."

He was off, and I had to do little more than intersperse his monologue with 'mm' and 'yes' until the minibus swung into a service station.

After an injection of grease and tannin, the bus livened up, and we were still refusing cans of beer and being treated to a penetrating analysis of how we could improve the band's sound system, when Sandy kindly veered off the motorway and deposited us at the taxi rank outside the city station. I feigned desolation at parting from our new friends, and willed Dave to instruct the taxi-driver to drop me off first, before I threw a sleep-deprived tantrum. He must have seen that I was about to blow, because less than ten minutes later, I was coochy-cooing over a three quarters asleep Dainty, and reading her the note Liz had left me. "Dearest Darling," I said aloud to a dozy face, "two weddings today, I'm afraid, back late afternoon, don't go out, love, Liz." She had emphasised her point with exclamation marks, kisses, and a graphic cartoon. "She can't get around me this time," I promised Dainty, and in the woozy mania of fatigue, prowled the house in search of any indications of why she hadn't wanted me to come home early. I drew a comprehensive blank. The sheets were neither suspiciously clean nor infused with someone else's perfume, there were no strange undergarments under the cushions of the settee, no incriminating messages on the answerphone, no invitations to clubs with a bad reputation, and no cat burglar's balaclavas or sets of lock picks lying around ready for an assault on the Brewsters' property. Defeated, I retired to bed with Dainty, her comb and a pot of tea. Far too wiped out to cogitate the implications of my heart to heart with Dave,

I checked out that Dainty hadn't lost too much weight or hair through pining at my absence, and made us both comfortable under a defiant covering of cigarette ash and lumps of fur. I eventually caught on that my threats to tug her tail mercilessly unless she told me what Liz was scheming were the symptom of an unbalanced mind, curled myself up against the Saturday shouts of boys kicking a can along the street, and let the undercurrent tow me down to forgetfulness.

I came to with the house quiet, apart from the wet chewy sound of Dainty cleaning between her toes. My stomach rumbled, and mentioned something about toast and marmite. My legs, reluctant to venture out from under the quilt, argued pathetically back. My stomach prevailed, and my legs sulked along the passage towards the stairs, then decided to take a diversion into the spare room, so I could have another gander at Liz's office space. Her canvas briefcase was open, and my hands crept guiltily inside to shuffle through papers covered with figures and instructions in the foreign language of technicalities. They stopped at a folded sheet of a slightly different texture, and pulled it out. What I saw was as effective as a cold shower. It was a printed out photograph, similar to those Liz had concocted of me with Kristin Dale, although this was of a tweedy Mrs Brewster, leering avariciously at a case of medals. I clucked like a hen in a thunderstorm. Was this another piece of clever trickery, or had Liz been creeping round with her telephoto lens again, exposing herself to peril while trying to catch the Brewsters red-handed? Were these even Edna's medals? Where was the photograph taken? Was Liz planning to blackmail the Brewsters? Most crucial of all, how was I going to get the truth from her when she came home, without letting on that I'd been through her briefcase? I thrust the print-out back, and shot a look at her slimline clock. Four in the afternoon. I had an hour at the outside. I did a rocket-propelled leap into the shower, and ran dripping back into the bedroom, where I flung a shocked Dainty on to the floor, gave the quilts an energetic shake, and bashed ash off the sheets. I clattered downstairs with my tea things, permitted myself one piece of toast, and ratcheted around for the scented candles I knew we had somewhere. In the bedroom, I arranged them where they wouldn't set fire to the soft furnishings, lit them, drew the curtains, and dug out my one proper nightdress. I'd worn it once when Liz had joined us on tour, and she'd been very taken with the row of tiny pearly buttons down the front. I combed my hair, dotted ylang-ylang on my wrists, told myself I was irresistable, and, practising poses of sleepy abandonment, mentally ran through my foolproof plan. I had reached the nadir of game-playing, and saw no alternative other than to seduce her into honesty.

16

"Well, well, yet another beautiful woman in my bed."

I opened one eye, "So how many does that make since I left?"

"I didn't count." The mattress gave way under Liz's weight, lighting a trailing fuse through me, as she sat down, dropped her jacket to the floor, and bent over to take off her boots.

"What's with this shrine business?" Her lips and fingertips were cold at first on my face, and I smelt other people's smoke in her hair.

I opened both eyes, so I could see her expanding irises, and then the way her eyelids fell when our mouths met. There was plenty of time before I had to put my plan into practice.

"I thought it would be soothing. And I can tell you haven't kissed anyone else for a week, you tease."

She lay down on the quilt, "Is it that obvious?"

I didn't need to answer. Making small talk was a lot less interesting than tiny movements undoing buttons one by one, and the backwards and forwards conversation of eyes, skin and breath. I would wait until she had unfastened that next button, or maybe the one after, because then she would be able to touch my breasts properly. . .

"Liz?" I made my voice try.

"Shut up!" the rest of my body shouted.

"Mm?" Her hand slipped beneath the quilt, "Oh Kate."

"Oh yes," everything, including my vocal chords, chorused.

"Oh darling." Her matching response pierced the

barricades of material between us, "Hang on."

She moved to undo her jeans, and we pulled at clothes and the nightdress. There went my plan, I wanted her as much as I had done the first time we made love.

She paused excruciatingly, "Did you want to ask me something?"

"Take your socks off."

No matter that we had done this so many times, her cries still sounded surprised, and I was still carried far away from the cramped streets and the winter sky. The return journey, eased by a stream of kisses and the murmured compliments I loved to hear, was almost as good.

"You're so rewarding. . . aah, that's lovely, your hands are so sensitive, it's all that violin playing."

I tasted salt on the fine skin of her throat, and let my fingers caress their way back to hot damp hair. "What do you mean, rewarding?"

"You know."

I was drowning in the bliss of shared smiles, the rasping quickening of her breath, pulsing beneath my lips, the ringing of her mobile phone. . .

"Don't answer it!" I said from her stomach.

"Fuck. Oh no. I have to. Only be a minute, it's in my jacket."

She turned over, and I clung to her legs while she hung off the edge of the bed, batted through the heap of clothing on the floor, and spoke into the beastly invention.

"WHAT?. . . Tonight?. . . Jesus, isn't that pushing it a bit?. . . Ok, ok. . . yes, she is. . . well, what do you think I'm doing?" I ran my tongue along the fold below one buttock. "Just naff off. . . yeah, yeah, it's all set up, I'll ring you if anything happens." She switched off the phone, threw it out of the bedroom door, and lay supine again, "Where were we?"

I slid down her once more, "Who was that?" This wasn't nice of me at all.

"Not now, please. . . I can't believe you're doing this to me, it was Stella." Her head went back, "Yes, just there."

"What did she want? What are you two up to?"

Her upper lip curled, "I'll tell you later. . . God almighty, do you want to kill me?. . . We're planning to trick the Brewsters into robbing Mrs T.'s house. . . tonight. . . oh baby, don't stop."

It was getting difficult for me, but I had to know, "And the picture of Mrs Brewster with the medals?"

She squealed, and her fingers clenched in my hair, "Back up. Plan B. I made it up on the computer. I can't stand it."

"Stop talking, then," I said, and loved her in earnest.

"I didn't guess you had such a nasty side," Liz said, watching me dip a chocolate biscuit into my tea.

"I get it from you. You loved it anyway, it was a bit of variation." Very happy with myself, I smiled at her, "Now you're going to give me all the details of this trick." I hadn't believed what she had said, it had only been the principle of the thing which had spurred me on.

"Or else what?" She attempted a belligerence which didn't go with her post-coital glow.

I licked melted chocolate from the biscuit, "Do you want to jeopardise your future chances of the ecstasy you've recently experienced?"

"Bloody hell, I knew it was a mistake to tell you how good you are in bed."

All this giggling was distracting me from my quest for the truth. I stopped painting her lips with chocolate and kissing it off. "Talk, and I'll be inventive with the entire contents of the kitchen."

"You trollop. Only if you cross your heart and promise not to blow a gasket."

"I won't blow anything. Entertain me." Nothing she said could possibly pop our self-contained bubble.

"This isn't meant to be entertainment. It's totally serious. We've killed off Mrs T." She nearly ruptured herself at my reaction, "Metaphorically speaking. Or do I mean figuratively?"

I lay down again, "I'll metaphor you. Have I missed the funeral?"

"Give us a chance, she only died an hour ago. That was what Stella was ringing to say."

I ground my teeth, "Maybe you could start at the

beginning, my dove."

"Can do, my peach. You didn't realise this, but last week before you went away, Mrs T. had a bad fall. Even though she didn't break anything, it gave her a scare. Stop shooting up like that, this is part of the story."

I reminded myself that this was all a small price to pay for transcendent sex, and resolved to hear her out in immobile composure.

"So," Liz continued, "she immediately rang Caring Hands to demand domestic assistance as soon as possible, and asked particularly for that lovely woman, Stella, who comes with the highest recommendations, because she's very fussy about who she lets into her house."

"Is she? I hadn't noticed."

"She's undergone a bit of a character change. And her accent has gone up a notch or two, which is all by the by now she's dead, after only a week of Stella's services. She was rushed into the Infirmary yesterday, and expired today. Stella was informed by a pal of hers in the hospital, and rang Mrs Brewster as per instructions. Mrs Brewster was so upset, especially since she thought Mrs T. was such a lady when she went to see her for her initial interview. Stella told her not to worry about what Mrs T. owed Caring Hands, because her daughter will be here tomorrow to make all the necessary arrangements."

*And where's the corpse, may I ask?"

"At Pat and Tom's, making shortbread, the last I heard."

I gave myself some Indian head massage to stimulate my brain pan, "Correct me if I'm wrong. You, Stella and Pat and Tom. . ."

"And Pru and Dodgy."

"And Pru and Dodgy, are pretending to Mrs Brewster that Mrs T. is dead, and that her house will be empty for one night, namely tonight, in the hope that Mrs Brewster will instruct her minions to burglarise it?"

Liz looked proud, "Got it in one, my little cabbage. I would have preferred to give the Brewsters tomorrow night as well, but apparently Mrs T. doesn't want to be dead for so long. She's not convinced she'll be able to watch her programmes at Pat and Tom's."

"One more thing." This was my favourite quilt cover, and I wasn't going to spoil it by chewing it to pieces, "Is this why you didn't want me to come home this weekend?"

There wasn't a shred of guilt on her face. "I didn't want you not to come home. I only thought I wouldn't bother you with this, in case you worried about it while you were away. I was thinking of your career."

It was a short jump to my open bags, to a stack of handy missiles. Pelting someone with dirty washing had never been so fulfilling. "You're barking! You're all barking! How could you and Pat and Tom put a frail old woman in such a position? Suppose they trash Mrs T.'s house? Suppose Mrs Brewster rings the Infirmary and finds her out? What if she gets beaten up? Are you incapable of rational thought? Are you completely devoid of ethics?"

The echoes of my shouts hung in the corners of the room, and the candles trembled.

Liz rose roaring through the unlovely bombardment. "I knew this would happen! I wish you had stayed away, you make such a mountain out of everything. I've got more ethics than you, you briefcase sneaker-in."

"Sneaker-in? What kind of word is that? Give me my bag, I'm leaving."

"No you're not."

The biscuits got squashed on my quilt cover anyway, in what was one of our best fights.

Liz beamed beatifically, "That's better. That was the reaction I wanted. Wasn't it more fun like that?"

"It was exhausting. I've got chocolate all over my back."

"Delicious. Come and soak it off with me in the bath, and I'll tell you why all your fears are groundless."

"First off," Liz said from the tap end, "this was originally Mrs T.'s idea."

"I find that hard to believe."

"It was so. She popped round the Wednesday after we visited those offices, and caught me before I left to join you at the Billhook. That's why I was a bit late. Don't look at me like that, she definitely planted the seed, and was more than happy to go along with it. She came because she wanted to find out if we knew anything more about Edna's medals. You're still doing it."

"Perhaps this is my natural expression, and you've never noticed. You didn't tell her everything, did you?"

"Not the part about the offices, or you getting shot, but all the rest." She broke off and examined her thigh, "You bit me."

"It was a weeny nip. You didn't complain at the time, and I can't help it if you make me lose control."

She grinned, "Would you like me to get my nipples pierced?"

"No I would not! Nor your tongue or anything else," I added as her smile grew ruder, "I like you as you are, not clanking with ironmongery."

"Just checking. So, as you can imagine, Mrs T. was distraught at the thought of someone nicking her friend's heirlooms, and stirring up more trouble between Ray and Brian. Then she got quite aerated, and was all for me driving her straight to the Brewsters, and confronting them. I had to restrain her, and gently impress on her that we didn't have any solid evidence. That was when she said, 'Evidence, we'll get evidence,' and the idea was born. I had a chat with Stella at the Billhook while you were auditioning for the Royal Ballet, she went to see Mrs T. on Thursday morning, Mrs T. had her fall, and the wheels were set in motion. Pat and Tom think it's a gas."

I sighed and soaped my arms, "I don't suppose anyone mentioned handing it over to the police?"

"Don't swear. Mrs T. wants revenge, not justice." She turned into a social worker, "I think this is beneficial for her right now. It's giving her a new lease of life, and an outlet for her grief over Edna."

I slapped my forehead, "How ignorant of me not to have seen that. Perhaps you should set up a scheme for retired people, 'Rejuvenation through crime', instruct them in the black arts of breaking and entering, lifting wallets. . ."

She cut me off at the pass, "Don't be so snitty. You're only pissed off because we didn't include you."

I hated it when her shots hit home. "I'm going to check on Dainty." I floundered out of the bath, picking up the largest towel. Liz splashed after me, and trapped me in a stubborn embrace.

"You need supper. I'll tell you the truth. It was mainly Stella who wanted to do this while you and Dave were away. She knew he wouldn't be into it, and she couldn't face dealing with him. She thought you might tell him if you knew. I went along with her because it was easier, and because if anything did go wrong, you'd be safe."

Maybe one sad day I would be innured to her sweetness. "Oh, feed me, you wretch. What are you going to do if these burglars do call?"

Their strategy would not have given Napoleon sleepless nights. Liz had been detailed to watch Mrs T.'s house all night, and to call Stella immediately if any suspicious-looking types turned up. Stella and Dodgy would then spring into action and drive to the end of our road, ready to tail the getaway vehicle. At this point, it all became vague.

"Naturally, we're hoping they drive to the Brewsters, so we can ring Pat and Tom, and they can bring Mrs T. out for a showdown, heh heh. If that doesn't happen, we'll play it by ear."

I twirled spaghetti round on my fork, "You're staying up all night, in the vain hope these ruffians appear? Suppose they've been and gone, while we were upstairs?"

"Er, I'd have been warned." She began to blush, "Dodgy's a bit of an electronics geek. He's wired up the door from the back alley to Mrs T.'s yard, and if anyone opens it, it'll set off a buzzer in our kitchen. It's on that thing called a cooker, to which you are a stranger."

My neat bale of pasta unravelled down my chin, "So all this time since Stella rang, you've been listening out for it?"

"Not with much attention, my dear. It was only another back up, in case I fell asleep down here. But now you're back, we can take it in turns to keep watch. I've made some modifications to that sheddy bit next to our coal hole, for a look-out post."

Beyond protest, I let her lead me into the yard to our

outhouse, a poky slum that had originally housed the outside loo and a washhouse. We kept coal in the old loo, and used the other half for all those worthless articles we couldn't quite bring ourselves to take to the tip. Liz had cleared out the mouldering cardboard boxes and broken kitchen units, cleaned up the calorgas heater, and erected the rotting deck chair. The small wobbly step ladder with one broken rung stood against one wall. She climbed up it, and balancing neatly on the top, removed a couple of bricks at eye level.

"You see? Mrs T. had her outhouse knocked down years ago, so I took a crowbar to the wall, and now I can see right into her yard. I reckon that if anyone tries to rob her house, they'll bring a van up the back alley, like they did at Edna's, and come through the yard, right in front of my watchful eyes. Pretty nifty, hey?"

"You think of everything." Never mind, I told myself, I've slept today, I can suffer one more disturbed night, no-one will come, Pat and Tom will see sense, and we can go back to being like any other loving couple.

"I'm not just a pretty face." Liz jumped off the ladder and dusted her hands, "Time for a cup of tea, and to work out our spying rota."

"Statistics show," I said as I lit the fire, "that the majority of people our age, especially those in long-term relationships, spend Saturday night entertaining their friends, or going to the pub, or watching a video with a takeaway, and then making love."

"Statistics lie. Anyway, we're not so conventional. We do the making love bit first, and then have an adventure."

I wished she wasn't blessed with so much energy, and would flake out and go to sleep. If the buzzer sounded, I could pretend it wasn't working, or I could pull wires out if its sockets, and say that Dainty had done it. She was already in a huff from our cavorting in the bedroom. I suspected that she hadn't come across much of that kind of activity at Edna's, and was a bit of a prude.

Liz gave me a mug of tea and a lump of cake, "This is how I think we should do it. At midnight, we'll switch all the lights off down here, and put the bedroom lights on for a while.

I'll go out to the shed for a two-hour stint, and you can relax on the settee, then relieve me at two o'clock. I'll come out again at four, and so on until it gets light. Please, Kate, if you hear the buzzer and want to come out to see what's going on, be totally quiet. Don't turn on any lights, or slam the back door. We don't want to scare them off." She frowned at me, like my father used to do when he was ordering me to be home by twelve. "It won't be too cold in the shed with that heater on, and if they appear when you're out there, and I haven't heard the buzzer, creep in and wake me up. Ok?"

I gave her a smart salute, "Yes, captain. Permission to ask a question."

"Stop that. What?"

"Can I take a flask into the observation post, and were you honestly going to spend all night in there by yourself, if I hadn't come home early?"

"Yeah, well, it would have made a change from an empty bed. If Mrs T. was prepared to stay dead for longer, I'd have got Tom or Dodgy to help. Take a flask, as long as you don't keep popping out to pee."

I pulled at the lock of hair falling over her serious forehead. "Tadaa. You're glad I'm here, aren't you? You couldn't boss Tom or Dodgy like this, and you wouldn't have had such a nice time earlier."

She couldn't deny it, and we stretched out snugly on the hearth rug.

"How do you think Stella will have reacted when Dave turned up?" I asked after a while, "He's mad about her. He wants to marry her." There was no way I was going to keep this nugget from her.

"Phew. Heavy. I know she's enjoying herself, but I don't think matrimony figures in her plans. Maybe she told him she had to wash her hair tonight. Did he tell you that himself?"

I told her something about our bus trip, and time passed pleasantly until midnight. After that, the endurance test began. By the end of my first two hours in the shed, I was ready for a divorce. I was being gassed by a heater that made not a scrap of difference to the sub-zero temperature, and

Liz and Stella's plan was appearing more and more as the product of minds which had over-indulged in chemicals in the past. I couldn't even feel sympathetic towards Liz, when, yawning and pale, she relieved me at four in the morning. I shoved surlily past her, and lay in my boots on the settee, full of self-pity. Why did I have to go and fall in love with such a flawed person? Why couldn't I have fallen for Issy when she was available, or any one of the sane, dependable women I'd come across over the years? Why hadn't I tried harder with Chloe? She would have been a professor by now, if we hadn't split up, and she hadn't given up her job, and we would be living in a big house with a vegetable garden and a host of intellectual friends. I sniffed. Even my cat, snoring on the armchair, was ignoring me. I had a good mind to charge out to the shed, slamming every door and turning on every light, to insist that Liz come back inside, or I would go back to Pat and Tom's, and Stella could move in here. I would do just that, as soon as I had warmed up a bit more. I shut my eyes, and pictured myself in my old flat, free as a bird and tracking down a compatible woman. Two strange and dreadful noises woke me up. One was a whine like a chainsaw. The other was the rhythmic dry heaving of a cat about to be very sick indeed.

17

I fell off the settee. Dodgy's buzzer was going wild, the bad guys had arrived, and Dainty was all set to deposit her supper on the carpet. Proving that women can do more than one task at a time, I made a grab for the retching beast, tucked her under one arm, scooted through to the kitchen, tore the buzzer from its wires, noted that the cooker clock said five fifty, and, with time running short and my arm about to break, noiselessly opened the back door, and flung Dainty out.

"Heuaaagh, bleuaaagh," she said, and a splat hit the concrete.

"What the fuck was that?" A nervous voice came from Mrs T.'s yard.

"Have a look," another foreman-type voice said.

Creep, Liz had told me. I dropped to the kitchen floor, and pulled the door to. I saw a torch beam play over into our yard, and I imagined poor Dainty, caught in its spotlight in her hour of misery.

"Just a massive cat barfing," the voice reported, "let's get on."

I heard a key in a lock, and feet in Mrs T.'s kitchen. I had watched enough old POW escape movies to know what to do next. Head down and with the gait of an early version of Neanderthal man, I reached our shed without skidding in any cat sick.

"Bleuagh, bleuagh," Dainty continued behind me, helpfully disguising my footsteps.

I was so quiet, creeping into the shed, that I didn't hear a thing apart from her and my trip-tripping heartbeat. Liz heard nothing. By the light of a small candle and the red and blue gas fire, I saw her wrapped in rugs on the deck chair, fast asleep. I could have felt gloating triumph, or the bad taste from my angry thoughts, but only managed a shot of tenderness. Instead of putting my hand over her mouth and a finger on whatever pressure point is meant to wake up a sleeping sentry, I kissed her cheek.

"Darling, I think your thieves are here."

"Print it out, and I'll check," she said, her clear 'I'm at work now' tones filling the shed.

"Ssh." I covered her mouth after all, "Wake up, two men have just gone into Mrs T.'s house."

"Mmf." Her eyes struggled open, and I moved my hand. "Nuts. I must have dozed off."

"The buzzer buzzed," I whispered. Something had gone wrong with my metabolism. I was alert and focused, my mind sharp and my ears capable of hearing a mouse move a hundred yards away. "You phone Stella, I'll take a look through the hole." Panther-like, I climbed up the ladder, and stuck my head through the gap. In a city, it's never completely dark, and even with my range limited by rough brick and mortar edges, it wasn't hard to make out two figures carrying loot to the yard door. They disappeared, and there were the clunks and clangs of a van being loaded.

"One more trip with the pictures, and we'll do the grandfather clock last," the foreman voice said, and the two figures jogged back to the house.

I pulled my head back. Liz glided in through the door.

"Stella will be in position in minutes. I've got your coat, we'll nip out the front door, and go with her in her van." She could have spoken even more quietly, my super-heroine hearing would have picked it up, "Why did you let Dainty out? She's on the wall."

My super-heroine powers deserted me, "She threw up. I'll have to catch her and put her in." I was lucky I'd never wanted to be a policewoman, I didn't have the low pulse rate necessary for undercover work.

"So that's what I stepped in. Leave her. We'll leave the

kitchen window open for her."

"Don't be stupid, we might get burgled."

She started laughing, pushing her face into my shoulder. I thumped her back silently while the two strangers made their second trip to the van. I couldn't call the cat, I'd have to jump up and snatch her from the wall, why was she being such a pig, she was doing it on purpose because I'd left her for a week. . .

"Euch, get lost mangy animal," the nervous voice said, "go and be sick in your own yard."

"Don't kick it," the foreman chided, "we'll take it for me sister, when we've got the clock in. Be some company for her in that flat."

That did it. A primal growl escaped from my mouth, I did my missing link lope to our yard door, and pawed at the latch. Liz didn't have a fraction of the strength needed to stop me feeling my way past the van parked in our back alley, and entering Mrs T.'s yard. The white patches on her coat betrayed Dainty sniffing at the night air. One stride in my seven league boots, and I had her in my arms, three more strides, and she was a prisoner in our kitchen.

"Don't scratch me, you wicked scuzzbag," I said, "I've saved you from a fate worse than death. And don't start on me," I turned to defend myself from Liz who had caught up with me, "they'll take forever trying to get that grandfather clock out, they won't have seen me in the yard."

She gave me my coat, "Kate," her low slow voice stilled the crazed churning in my guts, "I really love you. Let's find Stella."

All right, a big house and a vegetable garden weren't everything.

She took my unresisting hand, and only let it go when the front door refused to open.

"It's that fucking lock." She twisted and tugged in vain, "We can't go out the back, they're bound to see us this time."

"Why didn't you oil it?"

"I can't do everything."

"Let me try. You need to give it a little lift." Professors' houses would have perfect front doors.

The door opened with a bang, and we exited smartly.

"Still love me?" I asked as we scanned the street for Stella's camper van.

"Suppose so. Could you make a bit more noise? My nerves aren't shredded enough yet."

"I'm still whispering, aren't I? There she is."

The camper van, its curtains drawn, was parked a few doors down on the other side of the road. I squatted between our car and our other next-door neighbour's tarpaulin-covered jeep. He worked in oil, and was hardly ever home, which suited us fine.

"You go first, I'll cover you," I said, "go, go, go!"

"Prat," I heard, and was dragged across the street.

Close to the van, we could see chinks of light escaping through the curtains, and a slight rocking as someone moved inside.

"I hope that's not Dave, messing around with my driver," Liz said, and knocked apprehensively on the side door.

There was a bigger rock, and the door opened an inch. Now I was hallucinating, I could smell bacon.

"That you?" Dodgy's eye appeared in the gap.

"No, the flying squad." Liz slid the door further, and climbed in, "What's this? Scout camp?"

"Mind the kettle, we're having a brew. Get in, Kate, you're letting all the heat out. Sit over there."

I shut the door behind me, and sat on the bench running along the opposite side of the van. This was my kind of surveillance operation. The brass lamp was lit, and Dodgy was tending a two-ringed camping stove on the floor. A kettle steamed on one ring, and a frying pan of bacon spat on the second. On the driver's seat, Stella was cutting bread rolls in half, and next to her, disapproval writ large all over him, Dave was peeking out through the windscreen curtains. I rubbed my cold hands.

"I couldn't get to sleep at Pat and Tom's," Dodgy explained, "so I came out and fired this up. No point in unnecessary suffering. I nearly lost it all coming round the corners though." He shifted the kettle, "He's in a hump," he mouthed, gesturing at the back of Dave's head.

Liz and I pulled horrible faces. Liz rubbed it in, "Bad timing, Stel, you could have phoned half an hour later."

Stella wasn't pandering to her lovelorn suitor, "You're an animal. Bring us up to speed on what's happening."

I tried some damage limitation, "They've got a van in the back alley, and they're on their last load. The grandfather clock, the bastards. I had to rescue the cat, they were going to take her as well. Can you see them yet, Dave?"

He grunted.

"You're the tops, Dodgy," I chirped, "that bacon looks about ready to me."

"You don't eat meat," Liz said, putting an arm ostentatiously round my waist.

"I'm going to make an exception."

"Lights," Dave grunted again.

"Camera, action." Stella drew back windscreen curtains with one hand, and flung rolls at us with the other. The engine phuttered into life.

"This is the hard part," Dodgy said. He turned off the ring under the frying pan, "Grab hold of that, Kate, and you keep the kettle steady Liz."

"They're off," Stella said.

"Follow that van," Dodgy sang, and picked up scattered rolls from the floor. The van reared and bucked, and tried to shake its interior fittings loose. I gazed in awe as Dodgy assembled bacon rolls, and made a pot of coffee, without wasting a crumb or spilling a drop of water.

He looked at me, "You can tell I was a navy chef, can't you. This is nothing. Breakfast, everyone?"

"Yum." Liz had abdicated responsibility, "Where are we going, Stella?"

"Heading north-north-west-south and east a bit to the A6, I think. Pass us a roll. Want one Dave?"

"No thanks."

"I'll save it for later, mate," Dodgy said smoothly. "Who wants a tot in their coffee?"

"Me, me, me," we all said, and the atmosphere lifted.

I peered out of the windscreen. Even at just after six o'clock on a Sunday morning in December, people were about. A milk float, a delivery truck, lights coming on in a newsagents. Happiness overwhelmed me. I wasn't going off to work, I was sitting with a bacon roll, a tin mug of coffee and rum, my lover and friends, we were on a mission and I'd saved my cat. Liz was right, life needed a little pepping up now and then. I finished my roll, and reached for my tobacco and papers.

I was still savouring my cigarette, when Stella pulled into the verge, "Are we smart, or are we smart. There they go, down the Brewsters' private road."

We watched the headlights twisting and turning round the bends.

"What now?" I asked, before Dave could put another damper on things.

Stella clapped her hands, "Follow them on foot. It's too obvious in the van. We can skulk in the shadows."

I was game, the navy must have lost its edge when it ended the free distribution of rum.

"Ready for skulking," I reported, when we'd tumbled out of the van.

"Equipment check," Stella said, zipping up her orange jacket. "Satellite radios." She and Liz waved their phones at each other. "First aid kit." Dodgy raised his hip flask. "Photographic devices." Liz showed the miniature camera in her jacket pocket. "Good. Arms and ammunition." She rattled a large aerosol.

"What's that, furniture polish?" Dodgy looked concerned, "I'd have fixed you up with something better if I'd known you were expecting violence."

"Pepper spray, it's only for self-defence," Stella warned, "I'm often a single woman camping alone."

"I thought that stuff was illegal," I whispered to Liz.

"Probably is," she whispered back, "don't startle her."

"Synchronise watches," Stella commanded, "and. . .skulk."

Our ragged column marched off. Breakfast and the exercise did their stuff, and I didn't feel the cold. The clear weather had found its way north, and the last stars of night glinted over a moonscape of stiff grey pasture and rigid trees. Orion reclined on the horizon, about to slip down and hunt in different skies. Liz and I linked arms.

"Jeez, it's beautiful," she said, "I'm glad you're here."

Fate smiled on us, the van didn't return to catch us straggling down the private lane, and we came through the bend where Stella and I had been forced off the road. Then we had another break. A light came on in the middle of the fields ahead of us, and we all heard the creak of a heavy door being pulled open.

"What the. . .?" Dodgy began.

Stella stopped, and we clustered around her. "They must be at that barn," she said, "in the field where Kate and I got shot. If we get off the road, we can hide behind the walls, and creep up to it from the back."

I was fairly satisfied with my creeping, and was the first to climb nimbly over the railings and set off through the frosted grass. The freeze had hardened the ground, and I skipped from tussock to tussock. This was good. I was re-visiting the scene of my trauma, and wasn't scared at all. There was the wall I had cowered behind, and it was an old friend, not a place of torment.

"Shit," we all breathed in unison, and fell to the earth.

Uncomfortably close, the door crashed shut, and powerful headlights challenged the kind shadows.

"To the wall," someone whispered.

The noise of our creeping woke sheep three fields away.

"Bloody baa to you to," Dave said, hunkering down next to me. "This has gone beyond a joke. Did you know about it in Dorset?"

"No, I swear."

"If I had my phone, I'd ring the police. Stella won't give me hers."

"Don't even think of asking Liz. Probably nothing will happen, and we'll be home within an hour."

"She's got pepper spray. She won't rest till she's used it."

The van started up and moved off. The headlights were masked by trees for a minute or so, then we hugged the wall as they arced back down the private road. They didn't see us, and the red tailight pin pricks faded off through the bend. There was a general cracking of joints and moaning as we stood up, and lifted our heads above the parapet. No-one was hit by a sniper.

"Easy-peasy lemon-squeezy," Stella said. "There must be a drive to the barn from the Brewsters' house. Onwards and upwards."

Ice crackled underfoot in the bog by the gate, and the bars stuck to ungloved palms.

Liz tucked her hands under her armpits, "At least I won't be leaving any fingerprints. I can still see your body outline in the mud."

With unspoken consent, we congregated at the back of the barn, by a flight of ancient worn stone steps leading up to some kind of back door, set about ten feet off the ground.

"Nice example of vernacular architecture," Dodgy said, "lovely stonework, even in this light. Look at the way they've used these rough pieces. . . ok, I'll go and have a shufti at the front door."

Dave followed him, as if determined to participate in men's work.

Liz nudged Stella, "Why did you bring him? He's no fun at all."

"God, I couldn't get rid of him. He came round and wouldn't go. He's not so bad, he only thinks he's too grown up for this."

The men came back. "Too many locks," Dodgy said, "I don't want to be fiddling there for hours, I'll have a look at this one." He tapped up the stairs, "Only a padlock. . .come on baby, open up for me. . .dum diddly dum, chastity belt, chastity belt, give me the key to your chastity belt tra la. . .do you know that one, Kate?. . .that's it, a little to the right, as the actress said to the bishop, there we go." A clean snap preceded more wittering. "I'll give this door a push, where's my torch, whoops-a-daisy, there's a step, bugger me!"

We tussled with each other to get up the stairs first. I lost, went in last through the dark aperture, and forgot about the step. I flailed in space before hitting a floor knees first. My hands went out, and only the gloves I'd found in my pocket saved me from losing my prime assets to splinters.

"Yoow!" I said.

"Classy entrance, is that how you go on stage?" Dodgy helped me up, "You all right?"

"I've broken my kneecaps."

"Not if you're able to stand," Liz stopped me walking forward with her arm. "Don't go any further, you might decide to jump off this as well. Take a look at Aladdin's cave, danger woman."

Dodgy's torch was powerful, and I saw that we were on a wooden platform, suspended above the main body of the barn. If the back door had been better positioned, I would have landed on the pile of straw bales which covered half the platform area. From the far corner, a ladder went down to the barn floor, a floor completely hidden by a mass of tea chests and objects covered in dust sheets. A wink of silver flashed in the torch beam, and I could have sworn I saw a piano against one wall.

Liz held me tighter, "Let's check if Mrs T.'s stuff is here. Careful down the ladder."

Our way lighted by Dodgy, we zig-zagged through other people's lost treasures to the double front door. It didn't take long to locate Mrs T.'s grandfather clock, or the pile of pictures I'd last seen hanging on her walls. Next to them, the lacquered box she had promised to Liz lay half out of a refuse sack of photograph albums and knick-knacks. A blistering rage overtook the pain in my hands and knees. How could they, how could they rob personal histories like this? How could they deprive Liz of this tenuous connection with her origins? If Mrs Brewster appeared in front of me now, I would set about her with that copper warming pan propped against the wall, force her fingers through that antique mangle and jab at her with that toasting fork.

"Oh my God," Dodgy sounded on the verge of tears, "hold the torch for me, Liz, I need to look at them."

He knelt down at the pile of pictures, and lifted one up. His hands were trembling. "Jesus, put the beam closer, the back man, look at the back." He turned it over, "How did these end up with her?" He glanced up at us, his face a mixture of reverence and desire, "Do you know what these are?"

I shrugged, "Dancers in floaty costumes." I'd never cared for them much.

His eyes narrowed, and for long seconds, he seemed to be battling with some unseen force.

"Dammit," he said finally, "they're the lost Kirov designs. Designs for costumes for the ballet from the end of the last century. I'm not an expert, but if these are originals, which I think they are, they're priceless. Priceless." He made his hands relax, and lowered his voice even further, "I've a wife and baby, and I love them more than anything. But if you left me here alone for five minutes, I'd have a hard job not to pick this lot up and disappear into the night." The barn interior went colder and blacker.

Liz touched his shoulder, "Yeah, it's not easy."

His eyes met hers, and they recognised each other. He smiled, and was Dodgy again, "You're not going to leave me here alone, though, are you, you're too clever. Use me to pick your locks, then discard me like a dirty floorcloth."

"Too right. What use would you be to Pru if you were on the lam? We women have to stick together."

"Don't I know it." He stood up, and brushed his hands on his jeans, "That's enough temptation, get thee behind me Satan." He addressed the platform, where Dave and Stella were hissing at each other, "Mrs T.'s things are here, shall we call in the cavalry?"

I wasn't sure how we arrived at the decision to split our forces. Stella went outside, roused Tom on her phone, and came back in with the intelligence that it would take some time for Mrs T. to rise from the dead. I was beginning to yawn, and didn't contribute a great deal to the following debate, so I couldn't complain when it transpired that Stella, Dave and Dodgy were going to wait for Tom in the camper van, using the argument that he would need a guide to the barn. Mine and Liz's lot was to stay in the barn, well away from the hope of more breakfast, and warn them of unforeseen developments.

"You've got your phone, we'll leave you the torch and the pepper spray," Stella said, "I can't think that you'll need it."

"What about the hip flask?" I asked Dodgy.

He winked, "Sorry. Don't want you tripping over again."
Three shapes climbed out of the back door, and we were left alone.

18

Liz kissed my palm, "They won't be long. Help me take some pictures, if your hands and knees are up to it, then we can make ourselves comfortable."

I held the torch for her while she snapped away at the barn interior, puzzled as to how she intended to create comfort with no kettle or means of heating in sight. The exhilaration I had felt earlier had dwindled away, leaving me hollow, tired and possibly hypothermic.

"That'll do." She stuck her camera back in her jacket pocket, "Come on, grab a few of these." She started whisking dust sheets off pieces of furniture, "Don't trip going up the ladder."

I draped a couple of sheets over my shoulder, and followed her painfully back up to the platform, where she began delving into the pile of straw, moving and stacking bales to make a little three-walled hideaway. We wrapped ourselves in sheets and burrowed inside.

"There," she said, when we had managed to get our arms round each other in our musty cocoon, "who says I don't know how to show a girl a good time?"

"You bring me to all the best haystacks," I agreed, warming my nose on her neck, "just don't expect me to take off any clothes, Farmer Giles."

"Don't worry, pretty milkmaid, your honour is safe with me. I've a confession to make."

My core body temperature was rising from gelid to tepid, and although bits of straw were working their way through my hair to prickle my scalp, I was becoming less distressed at being deprived of the comforts of the camper van.

"What's that? Have you stuffed one of those pictures up your shirt?"

She patted her chest with my hand, "I'm clean. It's Dainty. I think I know why she was sick and you had to throw her out. It was something she ate."

I lay quite still, "I'm not guessing. Tell me what you fed her."

"Er, sort of prawns in chilli sauce from the Chinese. She really liked them, she lapped them up. So I can't be too cross with you for nearly blowing our operation by chasing after her."

"Cross with me? You've got a nerve, cat poisoner."

I was too hemmed in by sheets and straw to hit her effectively, and I made do with some mild head-butts.

She pinched my arm, "Let's call it quits. You went into my briefcase, and I gave your kitty indigestion. Isn't that picture of Mrs Brewster with the medals a masterpiece?"

"I'm not going to ask how you did it."

"Ner ner, I'm going to tell you." She nattered on about snapping Mrs Brewster as she walked into her office one lunchtime, and then mixing up the best picture with some photographs of medals from the museum. Words like "scanning" and "juxtaposition" went way above my drooping head. I couldn't say that our resting place was the most luxurious I'd known, but I was certainly warm enough now to contemplate a quick nap.

"Do you know one of the things I love about you?" she asked unexpectedly, when I had tired of saying "how clever", and "it's amazing what you can do nowadays".

The bacon roll had gone straight to my eyelids, and they were far too heavy to lift, "I'm in tune with the new technology?"

"Yeah right." I could tell she was smiling, "No, it's that you're not tempted by things. You'd risk yourself for that overgrown cat, but not for valuables or money."

"I would for a Stradivarius," I remembered saying, and then my disrupted circadian rhythms rebelled and knocked me out. I would have to pursue this promising opening at a more opportune moment.

It was another dolorous awakening. A car engine, footsteps, talking and the screech of opening doors cut through walls of bales, dust sheet and hazy dreams. I could have cried. Why hadn't Mrs T. delayed her resurrection for another hour, and let me enjoy my rustic couch until I was ready to move? I flicked straw from my nostrils, groaned and sneezed. My eyes watered as Liz's knee came into contact with mine, and her hand over my mouth silenced my convulsive squeal.

"Did you hear that?" A woman's voice I didn't recognise shocked me into full consciousness. "Is anyone there?" She sounded like a South African imitating the queen.

"Must be those damn rats again. That poison's bloody useless, should've brought me gun." Overhead, fluorescent lights buzzed, flashed, dimmed and jerked into life. "Can't see anyone. Ah yes, here's what you wanted. Come in, m'dear." I knew those fruity tones right enough.

A lighter set of footsteps pattered through the door and stopped. Liz and I lay like two hastily shrouded corpses, not needing to poke each other to confirm that the Brewsters had turned up to offload some booty on a customer.

"These pictures are very nice indeed," the customer was satisfied, "I'm so glad I didn't get up at sparrowfart and drive down here for nothing. Harry's as much use as a chocolate fireguard on Sunday mornings."

I looked at Liz's face. Her even features were hard and twisted, and her body had knotted where it touched mine. I knew what she was thinking, and pressed down at her leg. I had to stop her rising out of our haven, and shouting at Brigitte to leave before our reinforcements arrived. She lifted my arm off, as if it belonged to an over-amorous stranger.

"No," I mouthed. She shut her eyes, and swore mutely.

"Anything else I might be interested in?" Brigitte wasn't in a rush, "And I'll have another look at that Rackham book if you've still got it. How long before breakfast?"

"Mrs Thing's very slow to get started. At least a quarter of an hour. The books are over here." Mrs Brewster's assumption of superiority made my skin crawl.

The footsteps came further into the barn, and I found my ears were straining for the rattle of Stella's camper van. If only they would turn up now, before I lost the wordless battle with Liz. All her muscles were bunched ready to spring, and the desolate abandonment of my dream in the minibus had come back to me.

"It's not like me to dither, but I can't make my mind up about this," Brigitte was being blithely chatty, "I mean, they're so sought after, yet the condition's truly appalling. Why do these old dears let their grubby grandchildren handle valuable books? They've no idea."

"Get out, Brigitte, get out," Liz muttered hopelessly.

"I know m'dear. It's not as if they appreciate them. Why don't you take it, and give us a little something if you manage to pass it on? We trust you, don't we Verity?"

Verity gave a non-commital humph.

"You're an officer and a gentleman, Billy. What's that fine looking weapon you have there?"

Brigitte's archness was ten times worse than Verity Brewster's snobbery. I betted that Billy was blushing.

"Cavalry sabre. Carried at Waterloo, if you want to impress the American market. Still bloody sharp."

Brigitte giggled, "You old rogue. Chuck it in with the pictures, and we can do a deal."

"Anything else?" Mrs Brewster was tart, "And what have you done with those dust-sheets, Billy? I thought I told you to keep everything covered."

"They were all here the last time I looked. Maybe the boys took some for the van. I'll have a word with them."

Mrs Brewster wasn't soothed, "They would have taken them from nearer the door. Are you sure you haven't used them for something else?" I had another bet that she was eyeing up Brigitte, the hapless Billy and the pile of straw.

He was saved, and we were lost, by Liz's phone trilling at full volume. With what I trusted had been post-modern irony, she had downloaded the William Tell overture as its ringing tone, and the synthetic gallop filled the barn.

"Fuck." She didn't bother to whisper. I rustled away from her as she dragged the happily winking machine from a pocket, and pressed the talk button. "Yeah?"

Stella's voice crackled into our den, "Tom and Pat have just left. ETA fifteen minutes, roger over and out." The phone went dead. We were done for.

Billy Brewster took the lead, "Come on out, you bastard, we know you're there." There was a sound eerily like that of an antique cavalry sabre being drawn from its scabbard.

Liz pushed at me to keep me lying down, put a finger to her lips, then knelt up, so that her head would be visible over the straw, "Well, you wouldn't exactly have to be a genius, would you? I knew I should have turned it off. Hello Brigitte darling."

"Good morning, sexy Liz. Is the straw in your hair a fashion statement?"

Nothing in her voice suggested that she was flabbergasted, stunned or even surprised.

"Who is this? Get down here and explain yourself." The sight of a lone female turned Brewster back into a stupid bully.

"I'm coming. No need to wave that sword at me." I dug my nails into my sore palms. He could jab her in the kidneys while she went down the ladder, or nick an artery with a careless swipe. He would probably do it to show off in front of Brigitte.

"Ach, she's an old friend," Brigitte seemed entertained, "come for her cut at last, I think."

I heard the thud as Liz jumped off the ladder, "Not really. I'm sorry Brigitte, I'd get out as fast as you can. That was a call to say the law are coming. The doo-dah's entered the fan, and is spraying out the other end." I guessed that this was a worn catch-phrase between them.

Brigitte wasn't angry, "You rotten turncoat. What's happened to your morals? . . .hey, watch out, Billy boy, that nearly took my ear off."

Steel squeaked against wood, and someone fell over under the platform. It must have been Liz.

"God, you nutter," she panted. Rolling and crawling scraped the ground underneath me, and I bit against dust sheet to stop myself from screaming. Should I stay hidden, or try to help? Could I drop a bale on to Brewster's head?

"Come here, you lying bitch." There was another swish and a splintering of wood.

"Mind that cabinet," Mrs Brewster yelped.

"I think I'll get my coat," Brigitte said, "dismemberment isn't my scene."

There was more scuffling and grunting, running and crashing into furniture.

"Catch her, Verity," Mr Brewster wheezed, "I want the truth from her."

"Stop it you silly old man. That's enough playing with swords . . .I said stop it!" A rising edge in her command betrayed Brigitte's panic.

Brewster was beyond rational persuasion, "Out of my way, Brigitte, I don't want to hit you. Move her, Verity."

I tore off my dust sheet. I would drop it on Brewster to blind him, or throw myself off the platform and flatten him. He wasn't going to skewer Liz while I did nothing. My hand felt warm metal. Stella's aerosol, the angel. I ripped the cap off and shook it wildly, bounding up from the straw and yelling nonsense,

"Freeze everyone, this stuff hurts and I'm not afraid to use it."

I stared straight into the astonished 'o' of Brigitte's mouth. She was shielding Liz with her body, both of them dancing backwards out of the path of Brewster's hacking sabre. His rear view was towards me, and I couldn't get a shot at his face. Verity was on the touchline, flapping like a landed trout. I saw Brigitte understand, and threw her the aerosol, my aim and trajectory inch perfect. She caught it neatly, put an arm in front of her nose, and squirted. I didn't like Brewster's cry, even though he dropped his sword immediately, and fell to his knees, clawing at his eyes. Liz darted forward, snatched up the weapon, ran to the door and threw. A distant splash registered its descent into a pond. I clambered down the ladder, and we both fell into Brigitte's arms. For a second we were all each other's favourite person.

Brigitte broke away, and brushed at the dark designer donkey jacket that had probably cost more than our car,

"End of group hug. Here's your spray. Are the law really coming?"

Liz took the can off her, "More or less. Please go. I don't want you to get caught."

"Are they coming from the main road?"

Liz nodded.

"There's a back way from the house, through the lanes. I'll take those pictures, and be on my way."

We were ignoring Mrs Brewster who was holding a handkerchief to her husband's eyes, and telling us to ring for a doctor, we had blinded him, he was having a heart attack. Her choice of words owed more to a farm in the bush than to upper class society.

"No," Liz said to Brigitte's face.

"No what?" Brigitte smiled as if indulging a child.

"No you're not taking the pictures. They're not yours."

"Welcome back to the real world, babe. You can't stop me. This is a major investment."

Liz rattled the aerosol, and took a step away, "Please don't. Just get out of here."

"You wouldn't sweetheart. I saved your life, or at least your looks and one of your limbs." She smiled more introspectively, and held out her hand, "You could come with me. We could have fun again."

The can shook in Liz's fist, her face was breaking up, and all my bad dreams were real.

Brigitte was sincere and reflective, "I've been thinking about you a lot since the party. About what I threw away because I wasn't ready. Are you sure you're happy? Is Kate what you want? The humdrum life you always laughed at. . ."

Liz's spine straightened, and the spray was pointing bang on target.

"I swear to God I'll use this. Leave with nothing, and we never saw you here. That's my best offer." She was in the cold rage that frightened even me.

The lines on Brigitte's face showed stark under the fluorescent lights, and I saw a weariness I had been lucky enough never to experience.

Brigitte paused, then bent forwards and kissed Liz on the

lips. "The parting of the ways. Look after yourself, Busy Lizzie."

Liz didn't watch her strolling empty-handed out of the barn.

"All right?" Liz asked formally.

Good manners forced me to reply. "Yes. He didn't get you, did he?"

A smile ghosted along her mouth, "I was much too quick for the old fart."

I was a failure as an action hero. "I should've got the spray to you sooner. Sorry."

The smile became less spectral, "You did fine. Any later, though, and we'd have been chops. Thank Christ he didn't have his gun." Her eyes reverted to coals, "Brigitte wasn't here, whatever they say." She nodded at the Brewsters.

"Ok." I might as well have not been there. I hid my face from her by looking at the Brewsters. Billy Brewster wasn't having a heart attack. He was sitting up, his eyes and nose streaming.

"Whad you doon' id by barn?"

Mrs Brewster pulled herself and her accent together, "Exactly. Breaking and entering and assaulting my defenceless husband. . ." She obviously wasn't sensitive to the nuclear power of Liz's anger.

"Can it, Verity." Liz's voice was unemphatic and quiet, "There's shitloads of stolen property here. We know you're a common thief."

Verity laughed, setting my teeth on edge. I was reminded of a deposed dictator's wife, who had no grasp of the concept that she could be brought to justice.

"My dear, you're deranged. We rent this building out. I've no idea whose property this is."

"Yes you do. Some of it belongs to me." A lone diminutive figure, dressed in her best coat and hat and high-heeled shoes, walked ramrod-straight into the barn and pointed a Grim Reaper finger at Mrs Brewster, "Repent, worthless sinner. I've come back to claim what's mine."

_19_

I was glad I was there. It was like watching a face-lift in
reverse. Verity Brewster's jowls descended, her lips took on
an odd blue-ish tinge, and flesh wobbled on her neck. My
one attempt to bake a sponge cake had produced something
similar.

"They said you were dead." I had never seen anyone
clutch their bosom for real.

Mrs T. was having a ball, "Maybe I am. Maybe I'm a
figment of your guilty imaginings, the first of a long line of
those you have wronged, returned to seek revenge."

Verity settled on her beam ends, joining Billy on the floor.

"The veil between the living and the dead has parted,"
Stella intoned from behind the door. "What you reap, you
shall sow."

"Hubble, bubble, toil and trouble. Call the cops at the
double." The blackness had left Liz's eyes, and she was
laughing again, "You look smart, Mrs T. Dressed up for St
Peter?"

"I wanted to look good at the Pearly Gates. Now I've
forgotten my next line. Never mind, what did Mrs High and
Mighty here manage to take from my house?"

Verity was unwise enough to open her mouth, "I haven't
a clue. . ."

"Bog off, punk." Mrs T. had watched too many unsuitable
programmes, "Is that my clock?"

I answered for Liz who seemed to be choking, "Yes. I
hope they didn't damage it, you'll have to bill them for
repairs. And they took a box of bits and your ballet pictures.

Over here."

"I knew she'd fall for them. I pointed them out specially."

"You're too tricksy for me."

"Poker, my dear, you should play it more yourself. It's a great preparation for life." She put her fingers to her mouth, and whistled like a small boy, "Come on in, gang. Let's load up the waggons and roll."

Any residual hope that they would not be outnumbered drained from the Brewsters' faces, as Tom, Pat, Stella, Dave and Dodgy filed through the door and stood in a semi-circle behind Mrs T. Stella saw Mr Brewster's puckered eyes.

"What's wrong with him? Liz, you didn't, he's a pensioner. I didn't mean for you to use it."

Liz thrust out her lower lip, "It was self-defence. He came at me with a bloody great sword. Tell them, Kate."

"He did. He went crazy, it was horrible."

Stella took the aerosol off Liz, "More complications. I'd take him to casualty, Verity, you shouldn't have to wait longer than a couple of hours on a Sunday morning."

In extremis, Verity still disapproved of Stella's familiarity. "I'm not sure that I care for your attitude, Stella. I'm very disappointed in you. Caring Hands has no place for employees who can't maintain workplace discipline."

Pat stirred impatiently. She wouldn't want to hang around in a draughty barn, losing her righteous momentum.

"Are you totally thick or what? Get your head round this. You've been caught. Do you want it in words of one syllable? We-will-take-Mrs-Tweddle's-stuff-and-call-the-police.   Are you perhaps intending to run your filthy business from a prison cell?"

Spitting feathers, Verity remounted her high horse. "Don't you know who I am? Nobody speaks to me like that. . ."

Billy silenced her with a clumsy push. Decades of feminism clearly cut no ice with him. Striving to override his discomfort, he braced himself to take charge, and find out what those who mattered, namely the men, had really come for. He stood up, using Verity as a prop, and selected Tom as a likely candidate for man to man negotiation.

"Shuddup, fishwibes. Cub on, whad's the deal here?

Whaddo you wandt? Money?"

We all oohed at his aspersions on our public-spiritedness. Tom chewed on an imaginary toothpick.

"There's no deal, loser, not now you've insulted my wife. Yo, Stella, ring the police now."

Stella held her phone in front of Billy's face, and started pushing digits with cruel deliberation. Verity whimpered, and Mrs T. halted Stella's hand as it hovered over the third nine.

"There's one thing," she said.

Billy and Verity looked at her with pitiable expectation. Verity gabbled.

"You can take your things, and anything else you want, and compensation for your trouble. It's all been a silly mistake."

Mrs T. was dry, "I doubt it. Here's the deal. I want the medals you stole from Edna Braithwaite. Produce them by midday, and we might not tip off the bizzies. Otherwise," she drew her finger across her throat, "you're going dahn." Her accent was a puree from all the different soaps she followed.

"We didn't take any medals." Lying must have been ingrained in Verity.

Liz unfolded a familiar-looking piece of paper. "Excuse me, this says you did." She allowed the unhappy couple a quick glimpse of her doctored photograph, "You're wasting time. It's after nine o'clock already. Where are they?"

Verity pleaded, and a queasy compassion squirmed through me, "We can't get them back. We moved them on. How do we know where they are now?"

Liz was inflexible, "Get on the phone, then. Ring Mrs Tweddle by midday with good news, or it's curtains.

That ended the negotiations. None of us took much more notice of the Brewsters as we retrieved Mrs T.'s possessions, and tried to fit them into the camper van, which stood outside the barn next to Pat's superannuated wreck of a car. The heat of the moment had passed, everyone was feeling the cold, and neither Billy nor Verity made any move to stop us. They waited, like the unwilling hosts of a failed party, for us to get off their premises and hit the road. Stella explained

Mrs T.'s silent arrival while Dave was arguing with Tom and Dodgy over the best way to transport the grandfather clock.

"We went to the house first, and a downtrodden woman said her employers were probably at the barn. It's downhill from the house, so we coasted along with the engines off to add to the surprise. I'd say it's all gone like clockwork."

"Clockwork up your bum." Liz's derision made Stella smile, "Your stupid phone call gave us away. We were tucked up in the straw. There'd have been no squirting if you'd kept quiet. What if I'm charged? Assault with an illegal weapon, it's not a joke."

"It's a minor hitch. There'll be no evidence." She gave us a pointed look, "A car passed us and came down here a while ago. I couldn't make out the driver. Was anyone else here?"

"No," Liz and I said loudly together.

"Have it your own way. There, they've finished. You two will have to go back in Pat's car. I'm not having you sitting on that grandfather clock and breaking it after all this effort."

We didn't argue. I much preferred squashing in the back seat between Liz and Pat to travelling in the van with Dave and Dodgy who, by now, weren't speaking to each other. Enthroned in the front next to Tom, her hat still clamped majestically to her head, Mrs T. handed round a bag of glacier mints.

"Payment for services rendered," she said. "We can have a warm and some breakfast at my house."

We sucked wordlessly until we turned off on to the main road.

Mrs T. took off the hat, and whooped, "Praise the Lord and pass the ammunition. I was expecting an ambush. Drive like hell, Thomas, in case they send a posse."

Tom gripped the steering wheel so that his knuckles went white. "Maximum acceleration. There's too much weight in the back seat, jump out Kate, and save the rest of us."

Liz's arm was over my knee, "No, no, push Pat out instead." I didn't care if she didn't mean it, at least she was acting normally.

Pat pulled at the hairs on the back of Tom's neck, "This is

no occupation for a grown woman. We aren't being followed, and if we were, it would be your fault for not remembering to put anti-freeze in your car so it could actually start on cold mornings."

I'd wondered why they'd come in such an unsuitable vehicle; we could barely keep up with Stella's camper van.

Tom understood her reasoning if no-one else did. "How can I remember things when you keep moving them? I had that can all ready to use, and you. . ."

Mrs T. stopped their well-reheared quarrel, "Now, dears, it's a Sunday, let's not get nowty with each other again." She peeked round at Liz, "Are you sure you're all right? Did that Billy Brewster really come after you with a sword?"

Liz gave a brave smile, "Sure did. It was six feet long, and sharp as a razor. See how much shorter my eyebrows are now?"

Since everyone appeared determined to keep it light, I added my exaggerations, and we crossed the bridge into town over the muddy tidal river in high spirits, increased by the sight of an aerosol being flung from the passenger window of the camper van over the parapet and disappearing in the cocoa-coloured water.

"There goes the assault weapon," I said. "Good old Stella."

"Is it just me, or is there a teensy weensy bit of tension between her and Dave this morning?" Pat mused.

"Hur, hur," Liz and I replied, and Tom had to put up with our psychological analyses for the rest of the way back to our street.

He still wouldn't let Mrs T. out of the car until he had had a quick unobtrusive word with Stella, who was supervising the unloading of the camper van. I saw Stella nod, and he rushed back to give the car door the exact combination of tugs and kicks it needed to open.

"There's no mess in your house, but would you like to wait in Liz and Kate's 'till we've put everything back?"

I beat myself up for not noticing the strain under Mrs T.'s jaunty ensemble. How would I feel if burglars had been in our house, pawing over my instruments and Liz's equipment?

"Yes do," I tried to be casual, "I left the heating on, so it'll be warm, and I have to check on Dainty.

"There's cake," Liz encouraged.

Fussing over Mrs T. in our place for half an hour was a welcome distraction from glooming over Liz and Brigitte, and so was the following victory breakfast in Mrs T.'s crowded front room. Dodgy contributed the remains of the bacon together with the contents of his hip flask, and amongst the toasts and fried egg sandwiches, none of us saw precisely when Dave slipped away. At half past eleven, Pat picked up on Mrs T.'s yawns.

"We should leave you to get some peace. Would you like anyone to stay with you?" She tactfully didn't add, "In case the Brewsters come to get you."

Flushed with rum and over-excitement, Mrs T. gave a slavic puh, "The girls are next door, and I'll slide all my bolts across. If that dreadful couple ring about the medals, I'll let you know."

Stella stopped, one arm in her orange jacket, "If you're going to call the police, we'll have to get our stories straight."

It took another round of tea and coffee, and a combined racking of brains to come up with an account that no sober policeperson would believe. Taking advantage of Mrs T.'s absence, while she stayed with Pat and Tom for reasons which remained obscure, I had hosted an all-night jam session featuring Dave, Stella and Dodgy on spoons. We had heard suspicious noises in the early hours of the morning, and had decided to tail the van, rather than dial 999, because we didn't want to waste police time if the van was on an innocent errand. We had delayed calling Mrs T. to check that she hadn't sent her clock to a furniture restorer, (a detail I thought was entirely convincing), until a more reasonable hour, and then events had unfolded more or less according to the truth, although there had been no sabre from Waterloo or pepper spray. All that remained was for Stella to find Dave and drum this tissue of lies into him, and we would be home and dry.

Mrs T. saw us to the door, "Anyway, I haven't made my mind up about the police. I think I'll sleep on it, and decide later."

That meant I had only Liz's state of mind to concern me. The few yards between Mrs T.'s front door and ours harboured a warp in the space-time continuum, which pushed Liz right back into her shell.

"I've had it. I'm going to lie down," she said, heading straight for the stairs.

A furious lassitude at having to deal with her moods overcame me. I wanted to do something routine for myself, like buying a paper, lighting the fire, and having a catnap on the settee with Dainty and attractive pictures of food in the restaurant review pages. I looked in the hall mirror for any wisps of straw still in my hair.

"Go ahead. I think I'll pop round to the shop for a paper before they run out." She didn't reply, and I went out, slamming the door behind me.

By two o'clock, I had kidded myself that I was maturely detached from her problems, and had come through the night with no after effects except for bruising on my palms and knees. Dainty, having forgotten the indignities of her illness and capture, was washing her face endearingly in front of the roaring flames, and I was engrossed in the repressed interior of a designer's house in Clapham. Could anyone genuinely live in such a preciously artful space? Did people really pay thousands of pounds for such ugly chairs? I felt that I was reading about another species, and quoted random phrases to Dainty. "Design is at the heart of this home, where the distinction between 'work' and 'play' is deliberately blurred . . . for example, a computer terminal on the kitchen worktop lets me check my e-mails or download a tricky recipe while I am cooking for my friends . . . instead of being conventionally tucked away, cables are exposed, their ordered flow complementing the flow of ideas around my table, whose top is ingeniously welded from old circuit boards under a conserving seal of perspex. . ." It made me want to find a stray rabbit, and set it loose among those contemporary exposed cables. I turned the page, and salivated over a photograph of fish stew. "The true bouillabaise," I continued for Dainty's sake, thinking that this was more up her street, "as opposed to the thick over-stuffed concoction of any left-over pieces of fish, including, God help us, giant prawns, which is far too common even in supposedly reputable establishments over here, is a dish of precisely ordained ingredients. . ."

"Kate? Kate. . ."

I never found out what these ordained ingredients were. The folorn, frightened cry from upstairs had me on my feet and running.

"What?" I said, winded at the bedroom door, an irrational part of me expecting to see Billy Brewster in there, his sword at Liz's throat.

Liz turned muddled eyes to me from where she lay alone. "I thought you'd gone."

She had sweated through the tee shirt she was wearing, and it was damp under my touch.

"I did. I went to get a paper."

Clammy fingers searched my face. "No. I mean gone."

"Well, I haven't." It was simpler to lie down next to her, and reassure her with my material presence, than to delve into verbal explanations.

She wasn't easy in my arms, "Brigitte didn't really want me to go with her. She only wanted those pictures. I wouldn't leave you for her." She turned again, and muffled her voice in the pillow, "The law might catch up with her anyway, but I still can't be the one who gives her away."

I had heard all I needed, and victory over my rival washed away the rest of my mature detachment. "It's a bugger, having friends on opposite sides. Do you wish you'd never got involved with Tom's thieves?"

"Perhaps." The tee shirt had wrinkled up with her twisting, and my hand was on accommodating skin, "But he and Mrs T. are my friends as well, so I have to help them too."

I risked a kiss, "Concern for your friends is one of your most attractive virtues, believe it or not. I don't mind perjuring myself for Brigitte as long as it's me you want to be with."

She was ready to kiss me back, "Even though I'm a moody bag?"

"Even though you're a moody bag with divided loyalties."

Soon, perhaps, she would think about putting a hand up my cumbersome sweater.

She paused. "I'm going to ask you a question, and you have to think very carefully before you answer."

I played at the tee shirt's hem, "I will, I promise."

She gazed lovingly into my eyes, "Will you make me a cup of tea before you take all these clothes off?"

My vows to leave nearly eclipsed the knocking at our door. I escaped to the window.

"Could be Mrs T.," I said, opening it a few inches. I was dreadfully wrong. I didn't know the attractive, if annoyed, woman who was standing with an overcoated man on our doorstep. It was too late to pretend we were out.

"Ms Halton or Ms Sharpe?" she asked, tilting her head back, and flipping open some sort of wallet, "Detective-Sergeant Simpson, CID. May we come in, and have a word with you?"

20

"I'm sorry, I don't quite follow your version of events."
Detective Sergeant Simpson didn't look the remotest bit
sorry. She looked like a woman hell-bent on making
someone pay for her ruined Sunday and messed-up
investigation, and about to home in on the easy target Liz
and I presented. "Tell me again, how was it that my officers
found your electricity bill during their search of premises
belonging to Mr and Mrs Brewster?"

"I told you, it must have fallen out of Liz's pocket when
we were in that straw," I said, not very kindly. True, it hadn't
been my fault that Liz had had the incriminating item stuffed
in her jacket, although I could have shouldered my share of
the responsibility, and implied that either of us could have
dropped it. It was a typically sneaky twist of fate too, that
apparently it was only this unpaid bill, rather than someone
ratting on us, that had led DS Simpson and her silent
colleague, DC Brough, to our door. I had gathered this from
the way she had brandished it, already sealed in a clear
plastic bag like exhibit A in a murder trial, and demanded an
explanation of how it had turned up in the course of an
ongoing case. At the mention of straw again, she raised her
neatly plucked eyebrows, and I repeated our potty story. Liz,
clammed up as a barnacle, and Dainty, sniffing enthusi-
astically at DS Simpson's shoes, were no help at all. Maybe
it would have been better if they had reversed roles, Liz
switching on her sultry charm, and Dainty not trying to jump
on the policewoman's lap and drool all over her. It was also
a significant drawback that I didn't know Dodgy's real name,

and, forced back on my wits, added the lie that I thought his nickname came from a Dodge van he had once owned. I pulled Dainty away as I finished,

"Ignore her, she's a trifle indiscriminate in her affections."

DS Simpson gave no sign that she possessed a soft, animal-loving side. "So, none of you called the police this morning?" she accused, exchanging a glance with Mr Voiceless.

"Not as far as I know," I said, lifting an antagonistic Dainty on to my knee, "Mrs Tweddle said she might ring later."

"And Mr and Mrs Brewster were there when you were at their barn?"

"Yes." She was good with her eyebrows, and I swam out unprompted into more dangerous waters, "Look, they probably weren't very happy that we turned up and took Mrs Tweddle's things, but what could they do? They said it was all a mistake."

"And you believed them?"

I attempted a shrug, "It doesn't matter what I believed, does it? We got our neighbour's bits and pieces back, and it's up to her if she wants to press charges. It's none of our business really." I went too far, "How did the Brewsters explain it to you when you went out there?"

God knows what hole we were digging ourselves into, if they had worked out a convincing tale of attack by spray-happy maniacs.

Her temper overcame her professionalism, "They weren't there," she snapped viciously, "I don't know how you two are involved with them, but my guess is, you tipped them off. We've been building up this case for months and. . ." She swallowed and I could tell she was counting to ten, "Either deliberately or not, you've interfered with, and hindered, police work. Don't think I'm going to let it rest. We'll interview you all, at the station if necessary, till we get to the bottom of this. Now, which house is Mrs Tweddle's?" She closed her notebook, picked up our bill and stood up. It sank in that we might not have been the only people clever enough to work out that the Brewsters were not the cleanest towels in the pile.

Liz lowered herself to speak, "You're not going to question her on her own. She's old, she's had a tough morning, and she gets confused. I'm going to phone our solicitor, and ask for advice."

Eleanor would be delighted, and so would Mrs T. when she heard that she wasn't to be trusted with lying to the police. I wondered if DC Brough had a truncheon concealed in his overcoat, and if I was going to find out the truth behind the rumours of police brutality towards minorities. One tap from a stick, and I would sing like a bird, blowing the gaff on Brigitte's involvement in a trice. DS Simpson's ice-blue eyes rested thoughtfully on Liz's bellicose features, a muscle wriggled along her taut jaw, and she sat down again.

"All right. Jim," she turned to her escort, "why don't you and Ms Halton go and make some tea? Ms Sharpe and I can discuss whether we want to make this little talk more formal."

"Super. Poor Ms Halton must be parched. Lead the way, maestro." I jumped a mile at vowel sounds rarely heard in our street. He had more plums in his mouth than a greengrocer's, and if he did have a truncheon, it would be a bespoke ebony model with a silver handle from a gentlemen's outfitters in the West End. He stood chivalrously to one side as I floundered towards the kitchen, and then compensated for his earlier reticence by keeping up a relentless barrage of meaningless conversation, effectively preventing me from catching more than frustrating snippets of talk from the front room.

"I say, you have a cosy house here. So much nicer when these original dividing walls aren't knocked down completely, don't you think? Does your cat have a smidgin of Persian in her? Lovely-natured isn't she, not like my scraggy mouser. You wouldn't have a spot of the old darjeeling, would you? The boss is terribly partial to it, might make her a tad less. . .exercised, shall we say."

"Ok, Liz, I admit having met you socially makes this awkward for us both. . ."

". . .The champagne of teas, I believe they call it, not that I can tell the difference. Brown tea's my tipple, though I'm more of a coffee man, to be honest. Sounds frightfully boastful, but I'm as good with coffee beans as your old wine tasters are with grapes."

I had to fill the kettle, which drowned out most of Liz's rejoinder. Where had this policewoman met her socially? I'd never seen her before, and they had given no indication that they recognised each other once Liz had thrown on some more clothes and come downstairs.

". . .Haven't actually done anything illegal, have we?" Liz's tone was more factual and friendly than combative.

Damn them both to hell and back, they were having fun playing mindgames, while I was stuck with motormouth, who was boring on about roasting coffee beans. I decided to make the most of my perplexed innocence.

"What's going on here?" I concealed my bad actor's face by ransacking the back of a cupboard for a packet of darjeeling I knew had lingered there for months, "We've told you what happened. It turns out we've done a good deed for our neighbour, and, yes, I know we should have rung you, instead of charging in by ourselves, but nothing awful went on. I mean, let's be honest, if we'd left it, and Mrs Tweddle had come home and found she'd been burgled, what chance would she have had of getting her stuff back? No disrespect to you, of course, but not that many minor burglaries are cleared up, are they?"

"Minor burglaries, no, you're sadly right, but major antiques rings are a different kettle of fish. . .what's that?" He stopped being indiscreet, and picked up Dodgy's box of tricks from the cooker.

I slapped the darjeeling on the work surface, and turned away to swill out the teapot.

"Don't ask me," I said loudly above the running tap, "some technical toy of Liz's." Let her get out of that one. "What did you say about an antiques ring?"

He put the box down, "Me and my big mouth. I'm not at liberty to say. I'll just mention inter-force cooperation, countrywide investigations and inconvenient amateurs. Kettle's boiling, ooh biscuits, jolly good show. Here, I'll carry that tray."

"Did you go to Eton or something?" My impertinent question might mask the work my brain was doing to calculate the significance of his remarks. It was starting to appear that we might have unintentionally scuppered one part of a larger police operation, and were about to suffer the consequences.

He smiled, "Not quite. I'm following in the family trade, starting at the bottom and all that."

I blocked his way out of the kitchen, "You're not related to Edward Brough, are you?" Red Ed, as the tabloids dubbed the most liberal Chief Constable in the country, who regularly hit the headlines with his support for the legalisation of drugs, and his unfashionable opinion that locking up an ever-larger proportion of the poor and mentally ill would not do a great deal to reduce crime.

He made a face, "My old man. I have a lot to live up to."

I tried not to make a face. If Jim was half as bright as his father, he would have seen through our story as easily as Dainty saw spiders in the dusk.

Back in the sitting room, Liz and DS Simpson were gracefully fencing.

"Hypothetically speaking," Liz feinted, "if someone had a vague suspicion that an offence might be committed, and succeeded in defusing the situation, that would be a good thing, wouldn't it?"

DS Simpson recognised the manouevre, and flicked her foil threateningly towards Liz, "If someone knowingly let a crime be committed for their own dubious ends, then we would be very concerned."

Liz skittered out of reach, "Well, I can assure you that Kate and I have no connection with the Brewsters. They were at a Chamber of Trade function we attended, and that's that."

Her opponent swiftly advanced from another angle, Do you know a Brigitte Dargue?"

"Of course, we went to college together. We were at her place for a party last month. What's she got to do with this?"

DS Simpson probed for a breach in Liz's defence, "When did you last see or speak to her?"

"At the party. To tell you the truth, we've not got much in

common nowadays." She smiled effortlessly at Jim Brough, me and the tea tray, "Shall I be mother?"

We bought time by stringing out the business of establishing the law's milk and sugar requirements, and then pulled the lemon move.

"Oh darling," I became vague, "I forgot your lemon." I wandered back to the kitchen, banged a few cupboard doors, and fumbled in the vegetable rack.

Liz raised her voice, "It's in the fridge. The fridge! Jesus." Before she could be stopped, she strode in to join me.

Heads together at the point when we usually snatched a quick snog if we wanted a break from entertaining respectable people in the front room, we held an urgent conference. Liz was on the verge of cracking.

"I can't keep this up. I'll have to give them a version of the truth, they could go on all night."

I shook at the thought of this Mad Hatter's tea party extending until dawn.

"Go for it. How d'you know her?" Our hands met over a lemon.

"Toni's party. Keep mum and back me up. I didn't know she was a cop, dammit."

"She was the one who chatted you up?"

"She told me she was a civil servant."

I scowled, "If she tries to arrest us, I'll say it's out of spite because she can't have you."

"Don't go down that road."

We returned with the lemon, and Liz gave every impression of conceding the duel.

"We'll come clean. It was something of a set-up. . ." To their official faces, she spun a tidy cobweb of half-truths, admitting that she had persuaded Mrs T. to go away for the night, in the hope of flushing out mysterious thieves, rumours of whom were making our neighbour paranoid.

"I didn't totally a hundred percent expect anyone to turn up," she finished disingenuously. "We were quite surprised when they did, and we followed them because we thought that if we rang 999, they'd be long gone by the time your lot arrived."

DS Simpson told us off. We sat, heads bowed and faces contrite, while she gave us the equivalent of ten detentions and a letter to take home to our parents, warning of possible suspension.

"Is that it?" Liz muttered, when the storm seemed to have passed. It didn't escape me that she would already be praising herself for avoiding any more questions about Brigitte.

The detective sighed, and picked up her trappings again, "We'll call it a day. I'll ring Mrs Tweddle to make an appointment, and you can be there if you like. I'll be in touch with the Pearces, and the rest of your friends as well." She hesitated, and a flush decorated her comely cheekbones, "I'm not going to ask how you obtained them, but you haven't got any more photos of Kristin Dale, have you?"

"Villainous reprobate." I jumped on Liz where she lay laughing on the settee, having sent DS Simpson on her way with the second best photo of Kristin, "Now you'd better ring everyone and tell them the story's changed. I hope you can remember what you said."

"There's no mad rush." She spent five minutes convincing me that I was much more desirable than the policewoman, and then paused distracted, "Do you think they'll mind that I've grassed us up?"

I kissed the worried wrinkles on the bridge of her nose, "Just be willing to take the blame, and keep telling the police it was all your idea. I suppose it's better to keep somewhere in the vicinity of the truth." I bit the bullet, "No-one knows Brigitte was there, apart from us and the Brewsters, and if the Brewsters have disappeared, she should be safe."

She wanted to keep the lid on this Pandora's box, "Someone must have rung the police today. Otherwise, why would they have gone out there on a Sunday and found our bill?"

I got off her, and made a malicious guess, "Could've been Dave. He was having conniptions all this morning."

She began laughing again, "The little tell-tale. Pass us the phone, and I'll start persuading the others to get on message."

I listened while she worked the phone, cajoling first Stella and then Tom to go along with her new story, larding her blandishments with apologies for crumbling under pressure.

"I'm sorry, they kept on at me, and I couldn't take it any more. . ." She made DS Simpson sound like Torquemada.

I drained darjeeling dregs, and marshalled my intellect. The Brewsters' barn had been remarkably full, and Brigitte couldn't have become so prosperous on the back of a few thefts from local pensioners. What had I read in the Sunday paper some weeks ago, about a book fair robbery? Thieves had broken in overnight at a hall in Manchester where a prestigious two day book fair was being held, and had made off with hundreds of collectable volumes. Had the article hinted that police thought there might be a connection between this break-in and a spate of similar robberies at northern antique fairs? Perhaps the Brewsters and Brigitte were part of a much wider network, and Mrs Brewster's dying clients were merely a sideline. No wonder DS Simpson had been so cross at our vigilante efforts. I could take a dive into the recyling bin in the kitchen, and see if the paper was still there.

"Dave's disappeared," Liz interrupted my train of thought, "Stella spoke to him earlier, but now he's not in his house and his mobile's switched off. We need to find him to coach him in our latest version, and to see if he's the grass."

I took another guess. "He'll be in that grotty pub he goes to when he's in a sulk. The one with no carpets and a hundred year-old pickled eggs."

Liz made to reward me for my braininess, "Top banana. Let's go."

I unwillingly moved her hands from my shoulders, "No, I'll take the car and speak to him alone. You nip next door, and work your magic on Mrs T., if she's awake."

Tact and guile would be needed here, and I couldn't depend on Liz after the day's upheavals.

Foiled, she let me go, and a drive through the darkening city took me to Dave's unreconstructed local. He was there, among the old men nursing pints in smeary glasses, concentrating on a snowy television screen propped on a shelf by a wonky dartboard. I sat down next to him.

"You don't like football."

He didn't move his head, "I do now."

I checked the strip of the winning team, "Well, you certainly don't like Manchester United."

"I do now."

I watched an obscenely expensive striker miss-hit a perfectly weighted cross and bobble the ball out for a goal kick. "What a waste of money. I could have popped that in myself."

His ears twitched with some change of facial expression, "And the rest. Mine's a pint if you're stopping."

I brought back his pint, and a soft drink for me. Getting done for drunk driving would not be a perfect end to the day. The final whistle blew, and I lit up.

"You don't have to lie to the police if they come calling, and it doesn't matter if you were the one who rang them. They were round at ours earlier, and Liz told them we'd been lying in wait for burglars." I pressed on, not looking directly at him, giving him the salient details of our afternoon with the Inquisition, as if I was telling him what he needed to know about a gig. He heard me out, pretended interest in the illegible league table jumping up and down on the screen, and turned his attention to his beer glass, seeking the meaning of life or an errant pickled egg in its foamy depths.

I flicked ash into a rust-pitted ashtray. "Crisps?" I suggested. "Pork scratchings?"

He rolled his eyes, "Not from here. The landlord thinks sell-by dates are a communist plot. I'm not down enough yet to embrace food poisoning. We should have gone to London with the others."

"What, and missed all the thrills. Would you really have preferred living it up in Soho to lying in a frosty field with the sheep?"

He scratched his beard, "Bloody hell, Kate, it isn't my idea of a good time. All I want is to play my music and have a bit of luck with women. I'm not into that kind of nonsense, and if Stella is, it's too bad."

Perhaps it was our talk in the minibus that had turned me

into his relationship counsellor. "Come on, you can still make it up with her. You don't have to be the same as each other to make it work."

He knocked back beer, "What's the point? The band's going to the States, she'll probably want to move on in a bit, it's not going to last. . ."

I yowled at him in a way I'd never done before, "What's the point in anything? The band might split up after the States, Fred and Jo might leave to do their music centre, you could get hit by a bus, a meteorite could be headed for earth to finish us off like the dinosaurs. If you like her and you're having a good time, make the most of it."

He had a gazing at his laces moment. "It's so hard," he mumbled.

I tore a beer mat in half, "Of course it's hard. Is the band always easy? Do you know the number of times I've nearly walked out on Liz because she's difficult and always doing stupid stuff like this morning? Do you ever wonder why I've aged so much in the past year?"

His niceness, usually so well-disguised, was surfacing. "Why do you stay then?"

"Jesus, Dave, I'm not going to give you the details here."

He came closer, "Go on, you can whisper in my ear."

"Pig." I should retrain as a psychotherapist, "Some things have to remain sacred."

He carried on smiling, "Am I too drunk to go round and see Stella now?"

"Absolutely not. I'm off home, this place is the pits."

He picked up his jacket, "It's how a pub should be. No jukebox, no hygiene, no damn women. Get away, then, you've achieved your mission."

He held the door open for me, and walked me to the car, thumping on the roof as I drove off. One awkward customer satisfactorily dealt with. It only remained for me to manage whatever mood had taken Liz over now, and to pray that the law hadn't found out about Brigitte and arrested everyone, and I might possibly be in line for a full night's sleep.

21

Liz's pensive smile as I came in told me she had fallen into thoughtful calm. She made room for me on the settee, and I rested my head on her thighs.

"You hungry? Shall I ring for a pizza?" she asked, dropping a handful of snapshots on to my chest.

"Might as well. We should make the most of our time as free women. What are these?"

"Old pictures of me and Brigitte. I was going to chuck them on the fire."

"Whatever for? Oh my God, is that you?"

There were no two ways about it, she looked a fright. Skinnier, with a shaven head sprouting a defiant crest of maroon hair, a torn vest and a pair of jeans that were mostly rips and seams, she stared at the camera with the dead-pan expression of a career criminal. She was leaning against a graffiti spattered wall, next to a fatter, giggling Brigitte.

"Don't fancy me like that, then?"

She had never shown me anything like this in all the time we'd been together. I held one picture up, and examined it more carefully. Not even her frightening cool could hide her beautiful body, or harden the soft curve of her neck flowing into her shoulder.

"I don't know. Snazzy hairstyle, though."

She scoffed quietly, "Embarrassing, isn't it? You'd have run a mile if you'd met me in those days."

"I sometimes think I should run a mile now." I let the photograph go, and checked that her neck was still the same.

"I don't notice you jogging yet," she said a little later.

"Shall we forget the pizza?" I didn't want another interruption to her hand's progress.

Her fingers slowed. "Yeah. Take me to bed, Kate, I need to feel you're with me."

"Kate? Are you asleep?"

I kept my eyes shut, "I was trying."

Her body cuddled closer into mine, "I want a huge favour from you."

"Darling, I'll love you till the end of time, but I couldn't possibly do that again now."

Being the great lover had its drawbacks, I yearned for sleep like an addict for her next hit.

"Oddly enough, it's not that."

"And I haven't the strength to go downstairs and put the kettle on."

"It's not that either." She carressed my stomach, "Little dormouse," she added beguilingly.

"What is it then?" I held the mobile bones in her wrist, "And no hanky panky. I'll die if I can't get some sleep."

"Medically, that would be very unusual. I rang my ma while you were out."

"So?" I had met Liz's mother briefly when the band had played in Bath on our tour. She was half Liz's height and twice her width, and I had found it hard to believe that this comfortable woman had produced such a daughter. I imagined that she felt the same sometimes.

"Don't say no right away. She's asked us down for Christmas."

"Oh. I see." Now I had an uncomfortable choice to compound my fatigue. Every Christmas Eve since I'd left Chloe, I'd joined the band in improvised carols in the main bar of the Billhook until closing time, and every Christmas Day, we'd all piled into Pat and Tom's for an afternoon of eating, washed down with rivers of booze. Last Christmas, Liz had seemed quite content to participate in our ritualistic games of Racing Demon and telling ghost stories. It would be weird to think they could carry on as usual without me.

Liz's hand sidled out of my grasp. "We needn't stay too

long. We can go to the Billhook on Christmas Eve, and I won't drink much, then I'll drive us down first thing on Christmas morning. You can snooze all the way. You know my step-father's an ace cook, and my half-sisters aren't too bad when they've had a drop."

She didn't use all the arguments she could have employed. She had moved, dropped her old friends, given up her freedom, and tried to change in order to please me, and all she was asking from me was to forego one tiny part of my life, and to enter hers.

I laced my fingers with hers, "Sounds all right. Will I be able to drink?"

"As long as you don't do the dance of the seven veils. You don't mind?"

"I'll say yes to anything to stop you talking. Your mum won't give us separate rooms, will she?"

She snuffled, "Are you crazy? She's so pleased I've found someone nice, she'll probably go out and buy us a four-poster bed."

"Goody, goody. Can I go back to sleep?" I tucked my feet between her calves, exceptionally gladdened that her mother approved of me.

"Mm." I waited. "Did you know," I wasn't going to reach dreamland until she'd finished, "Mrs T.'s still friends with people she went to school with before the war. I think I envy her, somehow."

"Why?" I couldn't see where she was heading.

"Oh, having roots, a place where you belong, knowing who you are and all that."

I realised what was upsetting her, "Don't burn those pictures of you and Brigitte. She's a part of who you are. Who knows, in twenty years time, you might be friends again." I was being too magnanimous, so I gently dug a toe into soft flesh, "Besides, I might need to blackmail you with that hairdo some day."

"That's another good reason for setting them alight." She yawned to disguise the importance of her next remark, "If I get the chance, I might ask ma what she knows about my father's family. Some of them might still be around. I could try and make contact with them."

How like her, to drop such a bombshell. If I expressed my shocked approval, and gave an emotional speech, she would go right off the idea. I stroked her back instead.

"Good thinking. Promise me one thing."

"What?"

"If you find relatives in Siberia, don't make me spend next Christmas with them, with Mrs T. as chaperone."

Liz was late for work the next morning, and I slept again after she'd left, waking up to the realisation that the police were still on our case, and would probably not take our happiness with each other into account as a mitigating factor. Then nothing happened for two nail-biting days. No repeat visit from DS Simpson, no phone-call making an appointment to interview Mrs T., and no reports from the others of any contact with the local CID office. On Tuesday evening, worn by discomfort to shadows of our former selves, we went out to the Anglers, our women-friendly pub, to meet up with our friends, Toni, Issy and Eleanor, and discuss which festive parties I would be free to attend. By the third round, they were still making hay over our plan to spend Christmas at Liz's mother's house.

"Next thing you know," Toni opined, "they'll be telling us they're getting married. Where will you have the reception? The Grand or a marquee in your backyard?"

"But who'll take the pictures? Liz can't photograph herself, and who else can live up to the Wedding Photographer of the Year?" Eleanor asked between crisps.

Liz had been right, there was plenty of mileage left in her accomplishment.

I couldn't beat them, so I joined them, pointing at Eleanor and Issy, "Why don't we have a joint ceremony with you two? We could hire the park, and have the party of the century."

We were compiling an imaginary guest list, consisting mostly of everyone's ex-es, when a cordial voice came from behind me.

"Hey Toni, everybody. Can I interest you in these?" I spun

round to see an off-duty DS Simpson proferring a handful of flyers. "We're having a New Year's Day Hangover Cabaret in aid of the Women's Refuge. Upstairs here."

"Free bloody Mary included in the ticket price," said a curvaceous red-head over the detective's shoulder. "It's going to be good. No terrible poetry and some proper acts."

I limply accepted a flyer. "Great, I'll come if I can," I stuttered.

DS Simpson grinned at Liz and me, and touched her friend's arm, "I just want to steal these two for a private chat. Be back with you in five minutes."

She jerked her thumb towards an empty table, and we followed her meekly, leaving three intrigued faces primed for speculation.

"Drink?" she asked sociably as we passed the bar. We shook our heads, and I looked for the outline of handcuffs in her sexy rear pocket. I had been dragged out of bars before, but never under police escort. My parents would disown me.

Her grin stayed in place once we were sitting opposite her. "For heaven's sake, I'm not going to read you the Riot Act again. I'm only giving you an informal update." She relished in our obvious relief, "It's all out of my hands now. The police in Manchester arrested the Brewsters yesterday at a house belonging to known associates of theirs." She drummed the table with her fingers. "Apparently, they had their suitcases packed, passports ready, and tickets to Spain. Which they won't be using for a while. The Manchester police want them for a series of crimes committed in their area, they've got solid evidence and a water-tight case, so your pals might as well go down for that, as for anything they've dabbled in up here."

I tried out my theory, "Was it anything to do with antiques fairs?"

She pushed her eyebrows up in mock astonishment, "Clever you. Of course I'm not pleased that it wasn't us who nailed them, but it makes the job worthwhile to see greedy people who should know better get caught. Much better than operating the revolving door for people who go on the rob to fund their drug habits."

"How come the Manchester police are so sure?" Liz asked. Maybe she wanted cast-iron confirmation that we would be left alone, and not dragged into some court case.

"I'm not meant to say. But in practice, most people like that are put away because of informers, disgruntled minor criminals who've done jobs for them, and then turn Queen's evidence." She looked Liz straight in the eye, "Has Brigitte Dargue been in touch since the weekend?"

Liz told the truth, "No."

She gave Liz a card, "Ring me if she does, would you?" She waved at a bevy of women who had just come in, and were crowding round the bar, "This isn't really the place, but please pause the next time you're tempted to take the law into your own hands. We're quite approachable, you know." She slipped out from behind the table. "Lecture over, see you on New Year's Day perhaps." On her way off to the other side of the pub, she tapped Liz's shoulder, "From the angle of your photo of Kristin Dale, I'd say you were in the grounds of Brockhurst House. Don't give me an excuse to have you up for trespassing."

We made sure she was safely back with her friend before saying anything.

"She'll have her eye on me for ever, now," Liz grumbled. "What's the betting I'm in her little black book of troublemakers? I won't be able to do anything exciting for as long as we're both in the same town."

"If you sow the storm, you'll reap the whirlwind, or something," I replied, "that's what comes of chatting up strange women at parties. Do you think that was a threat?"

"Definitely. She's got a handle on me and she knows it. Buy me a double, sweetheart, I have to see off my criminal past in style."

I guessed that the slow workings of the justice system meant that the Brewsters would not come up for trial until the Spring, and that our luck had changed for the better. The few weeks left before Christmas proved me right, and we had no more trouble from a force too tied up with seasonal misdemeanours to spend time on a confused investigation into the affairs of two thieves who were securely banged up elsewhere. Mrs T., still sore over Edna's medals, threatened to muddy the waters by marching down to the nearest nick and telling all, and we had to buy her off with pledges that we would pester the police in Manchester as soon as the case came to court and was in the public domain. I would have liked to have engineered a fairy-tale reconciliation between Brian and Ray by producing the medals, but clearly that was beyond my super-heroine powers. I'd had more success with Dave and Stella. They arrived arm in arm at the Billhook the day after our encounter with DS Simpson, and disrupted my digestive system with their turtle-dove murmurs, and their insistence that we should publicise Stella's debut with Mac's band at a rival venue the following evening. Stella did break away to give me the low-down on how their boss's sad disappearance had affected staff morale at Caring Hands.

"We had a champagne party this lunchtime. The firm's solicitors told us she wouldn't be back, and we're exploring the possibilities of turning the agency into a workers' co-op. We can't abandon our clients, and we might all make some decent dosh." She gave me a coy smile, "I'm giving up the Constellation map for the time being. I'm not saying I'm stopping here for good, but I'll stick around for a time at least. And don't read too much into it, Cupid, this is a fun city, and I like the flat. I'm not letting you keep it as a bolt-hole any more."

"As if I needed it," I jeered, "some of us know how to commit in a relationship."

"I can see you've crossed your fingers. If you and Liz survive Christmas without a massive row, I'll buy you a bottle of vodka."

"Get your purse out now, honey, we never row these days."

"Why should I sign a card to your cow of an ex-lover?" I bawled at Liz a week later.

"Don't then, I'll just write your name for you." She scribbled, and I grabbed the card from her.

"You haven't even done joined up writing. I'm not letting you send this." I made to scrunch up the gaudy picture of a robin from our bargain box.

"Remember the vodka," she warned, before things got nasty.

"Damn." I straightened the card, "This is putting me under a terrible strain."

"I can make it worse," she said hard-heartedly, "this came today." She skimmed a postcard in my direction.

It was a standard view of the Costa del Sol: blue sea, white sand, green foliage and balconied apartments. I turned it over.

"Dear Liz and Kate," it said, "having a lovely time. Thanks. Love, B."

"Brigitte?" It fluttered to the floor.

"Must be. Looks like she's fled the country to be a gangster's moll in the sun." She put the smudged post-mark right up to her eye, "I bet if I scanned this into the computer and played around with it, I could find out where she is." She drew another Christmas card from the box, "Now, sign this one to the woman I had a little fling with the Christmas before last. Any nonsense, and I'll be on the next flight to Spain."

I snatched at Brigitte's missive, "Yeah, and I'm taking this round to DS Simpson. The police computers will be better than yours."

Dainty bolted from the hearthrug at the din, and goggled from behind the settee at my Thai kick-boxing technique. My ankle in Liz's relentless grip, I tried to hop backwards to the door, holding the card behind me.

"Help me, useless cat. Spring on her neck and dig your claws in."

Liz let go, caught me as I fell, whipped the card from me, and flung it into the fire, where it flared up in a turquoise flame and crumbled to a blackened whisp.

"That's solved it," she said.

I rubbed my aching hip, "But you won't know where she is now."

She went for the rugby tackle option, and sat on me,

pinning my arms to the floor.

"Get this into your noddle. I don't care where she is. She's history, gone, over and done with. If the police can't find her, that's fine, but I'm not wasting any more of my limited span worrying about her. From now on in, I'm going to be a model of probity. Ok?"

I looked at her dishevelled hair and pink ears, "Anything else?"

"Hm." She glanced around at the boxes of cards, envelopes, pens, address books and lists. "I'm bored with cards. How about a little Christmas present in advance?"